She rais
shutting

"Gabby." Chip's voice was a grumble. "Is this what you want? Because I've wanted this. I've wanted you."

She opened her eyes and was met with a mirror of her emotions, his expression almost lost in a mist of attraction. Of need.

There were thoughts about the repercussions of crossing this line... Yes, she was having them, but they were muted, smothered by the swirl of emotions that had been surfacing in small bits in the last few weeks.

So, she went with the most prominent thought and that was..."Yes, I want this."

Uncoiling herself from him, she pressed her hands against his front, his heart pounding against her left palm. It raced, like hers. Still, she could not tear her eyes off his face, his eyes, his lips, which were parted. All of him was too far away, so Gabby pulled him down by his neckline.

Planner Gabby surrendered.

Dear Reader,

Welcome back to Peak, VA, this time for Gabby Espiritu's chance at love—with her best friend, Chip! These two are truly the sweetest, ever. <3 Both are such good people, each a version of a golden retriever who deserves only the best. It makes perfect sense that they are the best of friends, and that they fall in love.

But the thing about best-friends-to-lovers stories is that they're complicated, aren't they? It's never easy to make that leap. The stakes are high, even if this story is lighthearted and a slow burn. When two people are conscientious, and in some ways people pleasers, putting oneself out there is tough. When your heart is open to love of all forms, discerning romantic love can be confusing. But it comes through, I promise you that! These two deserve it.

Thank you for taking this special path through Gabby and Chip's story in the Shenandoah Valley! See you on the other side with heart eyes and confetti!

xo,

Tif

THE FOREVER
WEDDING DATE

TIF MARCELO

SPECIAL EDITION

Harlequin®
SPECIAL
EDITION™

Recycling programs
for this product may
not exist in your area.

ISBN-13: 978-1-335-18001-8

The Forever Wedding Date

Copyright © 2025 by Tiffany Johnson

 Harlequin Enterprises ULC
22 Adelaide St. West, 41st Floor
Toronto, Ontario M5H 4E3, Canada
www.Harlequin.com

Printed in Lithuania

MIX
Paper | Supporting
responsible forestry
FSC® C021394

Tif Marcelo is a veteran US Army nurse and holds a BS in nursing and a master's in public administration. She believes and writes about the strength of families, the endurance of friendship and heartfelt romances, and is inspired daily by her own military hero husband and four children. She hosts the *Stories to Love* podcast and is the *USA TODAY* bestselling author of adult and young adult novels. Learn more about her at www.tifmarcelo.com.

Books by Tif Marcelo

Harlequin Special Edition

Spirit of the Shenandoah

It Started with a Secret
Love Letters from the Trail
The Forever Wedding Date

Visit the Author Profile page at Harlequin.com.

To our sweet Boxer-doggo Sugar,
who we will love forever and ever

Chapter One

Twenty-two days until the wedding

"Top of the world, my behind."

Chip Lowry inwardly winced at his father's judgment on what would have been celebrated by any other person.

"You don't like it?" Chip gestured at the plans taped on a wall at the Top of the World Senior Center and then to the ongoing construction in front of them. Beyond were his contractor and some workers demolishing a wall with sledgehammers, pry bars, and saws. "You'll have a much bigger multipurpose room with a stage. And a working kitchen. Just think how much better the holiday party will be with so much more space. They'll be able to fit a DJ and everything."

But in his classic George Lowry way, his father snorted. "*When* it gets done. I could be six feet under by then."

Chip choked on nothing but shock. "Dad. You're barely seventy. Don't say stuff like that. And, anyway, it should all be done in three months."

"That's a lifetime for a person my age. And until then, we have to live with *this*. I thought this was just going to be a paint job."

Chip shrugged. Top of the World was the place his father called his second home, a bustling community center where he congregated with his friends, and thankfully stayed out of trouble. Built in the early 2000s, barely a day had gone by without the building being full of members or volunteers, but it had fallen into major disrepair.

The center members had been intent on improving it. Multiple fundraisers had been held, some more successful than others, but they'd only earned enough to address small renovations.

To keep his father and his buddies from climbing the ladders themselves, Chip had decided to donate to the senior center by having the entire building painted, inside and out. And, well, one project turned into two. With additional investment from his best friend, Nathan, the concept expanded to encompass the new multipurpose room.

"You know how renovations work, Dad. It evolves. But I promise, it will be worth it." At the silence, he said, "What, you don't trust me? How many houses have I flipped to become short-term rentals? Three."

"That's not it." George shook his head. "I trust you. But you're going overboard. Again. Just like your mother." Except when he mentioned Mom, his face softened.

Just a smidgen, though.

"I'm going to take that as a compliment." Chip gave his dad his award-winning smile, literally, since it had won him "Best Smile" in his high school senior superlatives. He never minded being compared to Fern Lowry, may she rest in peace. She had been beloved by everyone in Peak, and very much by his father, who was her complete opposite.

Since George had moved in with him five years ago, after retiring from the water plant, Chip could now empathize what his mother had had to deal with. From George's epic nightly snore fests, to how picky he was in loading the dishwasher, Chip at times had asked himself if it had been a good idea to combine their households. It was a decision that turned his life upside down, having such a curmudgeon living under his roof.

Though, to be honest, it would worry Chip more if his father *didn't* live with him. George was a busybody despite his grumpy nature, and Chip could only sleep when his dad was safe and sound at home. With energy that hadn't waned despite his age, George could get into trouble if left to his own devices. Once, Chip caught George up on a ladder, trimming the roofline with Christmas lights. Another time, his father was standing on his flatbed truck cutting the branches back of his big oak tree.

Chip wasn't sure how he felt about the tables being turned, but there was no choice but to live with it.

"And you've spent too much on it already," George went on, now exiting the construction zone through a door and moving down a hallway blocked with plastic sheeting.

Chip waved away his father's complaint. Though, yes, the project was costing him a pretty penny, he considered it an investment. With the money his mom had left him with her distinct words in her will to "be the change you want to see", Chip was intent on sharing it with those she had loved, and that was their community.

His father, indirectly.

And what was money for, but to reinvest in things that could grow, so that one could live the way they wanted to? Thanks once more to his mother's insistence on teaching him how to invest before she passed a decade ago, he'd taken a risk with certain tech stocks and came out of it profitable.

These days, he had a lot of flexibility.

"You should be saving that money for yourself, son."

"And do what with it? I'm stuck here watching you."

"Yeah, yeah," he grumbled. "You could take a vacation.

Go away with those friends of yours. Have fun. Get out of my hair."

"Sorry to tell you, but there's not…much to get out of."

George pulled another door open and shot him an annoyed expression. In truth, his dad still had a full head of white hair, but it had thinned out as of late.

Voices and music spilled out of a room. "Do you hear that?" George said. "That's the sound of people having fun. You might want to take a lesson."

They walked into the foyer and then down to the right, into the current multipurpose room, where people milled about. Groups sat around square tables, playing cards and board games. Conversations buzzed around them; Chip loved the energy. "I don't know. You all might be too risqué for me."

And though it was a slight rib, as Chip watched his dad's friends greet George, he felt a yearning to be the life of the party, to be expected and celebrated. The fact that his dad, considered unlikable—though Chip thought it was all a facade—could walk into a room and be noticed made Chip wonder what he was missing in himself.

It wasn't the friends part of it all—Chip had friends. He knew that he was well-liked. But to break out of that wall-flower mold, to be exciting and to be paid attention to, would be nice once in a while.

His phone buzzed in his pocket; it was Gabby Espiritu. His spirits lifted, face warming as her image came to the forefront: Filipino-American with golden-brown skin, dark brown eyes, and shoulder-length, highlighted brown hair, with a smile that routinely knocked the wind out of him.

Gabby was one of his best friends; *the* best, as of lately. She also was her usual, punctual self, as if she'd intuited that he needed a little pick-me-up.

Gabby asked, Coming to Mountain Rush soon?

I've got a shift in twenty minutes.

Hurry. Bailey and Willa are coming, too. See you soon.

Huh. While Gabby was on the go a hundred percent of the time, it was usually planned. She was like him—she had her hands in everything. Another reason why they got along so well. Their schedules were as sacred as the church on the town square.

It must be important.

Then again, even if it had been nothing, he'd do his best to be there, anyway.

"Who has got you blushing, dear?" Daria Rojas, the matriarch of the Rojas family, strolled over. A widow, she was in her late sixties, though had the energy of someone in their thirties. She was Mexican American and her silver hair was brushed straight into a bob. Her dark eyes gleamed at him through her red-framed glasses.

Her kids had gone to high school with Chip, and she'd known his parents in their younger years, too.

"You know who it is," shouted his father from across the room.

"Dad." Chip rolled his eyes.

"Ah, it must be our Gabriella." Daria linked an arm with Chip's and boldly looked down at his phone screen. And as stunned as Chip was—and also a little worried about coming off as disrespectful—he didn't snatch it away. "'Coming to Mountain Rush soon.' Is this a date?"

"No, it's not a date. It would never be a date."

"But why not?"

"We're just friends," he interrupted, and said louder, "We've never been more than that."

Daria patted his arm. "Well, don't worry. Your secret's safe with me." She seemed to think twice. "I mean, with all of us."

His face burned with embarrassment as he took in who was looking their way, and more importantly, listening. Mrs. Bolen, Mr. Davis and others who had watched him grow up.

No doubt that if Chip wasn't careful, his true feelings would no longer be a secret.

It wasn't that he'd meant for his feelings to be buried down deep. It was just circumstance, and how friend circles intersected. Love needed to be managed carefully in the town of Peak. With a population of less than ten thousand, one was bound to step on toes if one wasn't careful.

Not that he was in love. *Just saying.*

Here was the real travesty: what had happened to his life that his fathers' friends knew about his relationship status? Because, yes, Chip had always had a crush on Gabby, but who wouldn't?

"You're thinking of her again, aren't you?" Daria's soft voice broke through his thoughts.

"Yes." He caved, because there was no point in pretending. "But nothing can come out of it. I'm not really her type."

She frowned. "What's her type? Someone who's *not* thoughtful, and funny, and helpful?"

"That's nice of you to say, Mrs. Rojas, but I'm in what's called the 'friend zone.'" He used air quotes with the term. "Also, she's dating someone, sort of. Some guy named William Jones."

"That's…interesting."

"It is." It was an extra paper cut to his pride that William, a guy from the internet who lived clear across the country, had been noticed well before Chip.

Not like you asked her out, bro, his conscience reminded him.

Not like I can, bro.

"That William Jones has not set one foot in town so it doesn't count. And the zone you're in doesn't sound so bad. You just need to—" she gestured with a hand "—push that zone out a little."

"I wish it were that easy."

"It is…except that you have to believe it." She tapped him gently on the chest.

"Yes, ma'am." He smiled, though he refrained from explaining that things didn't work that way. Not when it came to love and attraction, and especially with Gabby.

Chip was so deep in the friend zone that he couldn't discern where the end of it was. The line was smudged and unrecognizable. The Espiritus had moved into town over a decade ago, but he'd only gotten to know her through her on-again-and-hopefully-never-again relationship with Nathan that had spanned a couple of years.

Which, by all best-friend rules, had rendered Gabby off-limits.

Chip and Gabby's friendship fully blossomed a year ago, when she'd started frequenting Mountain Rush, a bar where Chip worked part-time. He attributed their bonding to his bartender role, which automatically qualified him to be a therapist, with everyone telling him their business.

Bartenders and kindergarten teachers—they knew everything.

"I'd better go, though," Chip reminded Daria and pointed to the screen of his phone, grateful for an excuse to exit. Daria was lovely; the reminder that he was single, on the other hand, was not. "I've got a shift."

"You don't even *need* a job," George grumbled from across the room.

"I like working, Dad." He heaved a breath. "And *that's* my cue to go." Bending down, he pressed his cheek against

Daria's and somehow pried himself from her without another well-meaning piece of advice. "I'll see you soon?"

"I hope so." She patted him on the cheek, a gesture that made his heart ache. Not out of sadness, but gratitude.

Even if he was in the friend zone, perpetually in the single zone and always in the background, he wasn't quite alone.

Once outside, Chip was greeted by the cool spring air, and his optimism rose. Winter had been mild this year, and he loved the chill against his skin. It was just enough to wake him up, and allowed him to switch his thoughts to the next activity at hand.

Even if Gabby wasn't into him, she was still waiting for him at Mountain Rush, for a reason he would soon find out.

Right now, that was more than enough.

Gabriella Espiritu paced the back wall of Mountain Rush while keeping an eye on the front entrance, waiting for reinforcements to walk in.

But they were taking forever.

"This must be a really important email for you to want to open it up here," Liza Wilcox called from the bar, gesturing to the laptop sitting on one of the high-top round tables. She was the bar's newest supervisor, and was drying glasses while multitasking and serving the sleepy, late-lunch crowd.

"It is. I took my first CPA test last week and—" she swallowed as the jitters crept up her throat "—the results are up. I got a notification on the way home from a client's house and thought, why not stop in?"

"And you always carry your laptop with you?"

"Absolutely. It's a wedding planner's best friend. Anyway, celebrating here feels right." This karaoke bar had become a place of respite; she could get lost in the chatter and in the music. Plus, her best friend and favorite bartender, Chip, worked here. Truth be told, as soon as she was notified that her test results were up, she all but sped to Mountain Rush. To share the news with her friends, yes, but especially with Chip, who'd been with her at every step of her journey to achieve her CPA degree.

Liza frowned. "So you're more than a wedding planner?"

"Yep. I just finished school." In saying it aloud, she felt a surge of pride. When she'd decided to pursue her accounting certificate in order to help manage the books at the Spirit of the Shenandoah B & B, the Espiritu family-owned business, she'd thought, why not go all the way and get her CPA license?

It could only help. And with the way so many of her college friends had sailed through grad school with a million letters behind their names, she might as well, too.

She'd buckled down and invested the hours studying, in between planning her half-brother Jared's wedding, in less than a month, among her other duties at the B & B.

The test had been hard, but she was confident that she passed.

"So after this you'll…what?" Liza asked. She slung the drying rag over her shoulder and nodded at a new customer who'd taken a seat at the bar.

"There are actually four tests, so I have three more to take."

Her eyebrows rose. "Dang."

"No biggie." She shrugged away the thrill in her chest.

Challenges—Gabby loved them. There was adventure in multitasking, in having a deadline. She sought to push her own limits; she wanted to see how much more productive or creative she could be.

"Better you than me." Liza looked over her shoulder to the front door creaking open.

Light spilled over the dim threshold, and her three best friends walked in.

Game on.

Bailey Jenkins was the first to reach her. Of Irish descent, he was blond with fair skin, though currently sported dark half moons under his eyes. A radiology tech who worked third shift, and who was certified in preparing patients for ultrasounds, MRIs, and any other test one could think of, he rarely saw the midday sun.

"This better be good." His voice was a croak, though he greeted her with their customary elaborate fist bump that they'd practiced over the course of two whole days. At the end of it, they were both laughing.

"It is. My exam results are in," Gabby said.

Willa Johnson bowled her over with a hug. A striking Black woman, she exuded a bohemian vibe and wore long braids. She was an herbalist and entrepreneur that specialized in natural skin care. "It's going to be fine," she whispered in Gabby's ear.

"Oh, I know it is." She stepped back with a grin, though her body tingled with nerves.

"That's what I like to hear."

Over Willa's shoulder came the standard high five of Chip, who was not only a bartender, but also a serial entrepreneur and a whiz with investments. Besides owning several short-term rentals, he was renovating the senior center, and contributed widely to local fundraisers to revitalize Peak. His floppy light brown hair and relaxed smile, however, gave a different impression. At first glance, one could underestimate his ambition. But Chip had an inner motor, driven by this idea that he could make things better.

Around him, Gabby felt light as a feather because he was so capable and solid.

"Let's get this over with so that we can celebrate," he said.

She nodded. Yep, Gabby was surrounded by excellence, and passing this test would get her one step closer to it.

She woke her laptop to display her inbox. Next to her, Bailey whistled. "That's a lot of emails from Jared and Matilda."

"*T* minus twenty-two days to the biggest wedding of the year." She smiled, then clicked on the email from the licensing board.

If she had advice for anyone who wanted to be a wedding planner, it was this: don't plan weddings for any of your siblings. Just say no, even if wedding planning was one's passion.

The selfish fact of the matter was that the planner would not be able to enjoy their siblings' wedding, not in a way that they wanted to.

For example: Gabby hadn't been able to savor the dress fitting experience with her future sister-in-law, Matilda, because she'd been dealing with a florist emergency for another event.

Gabby clicked the link in her email and it sent her to a login page. As she entered her password, her tummy swirled. "I'm nervous."

"We're here," Willa said.

Bailey pulled at the neckline of his shirt. "This is stressful. I remember doing this for my boards, though I was alone. I almost passed out because I held my breath."

After she pressed Enter, the licensing office dashboard loaded onto the screen. In the middle of the page, in bold blue, was the name of the test. Next to it was another button named Results.

Struck by a sudden jolt of trepidation, Gabby recoiled and stepped back from the laptop. "Wait. I can't."

"C'mon, Gabby." Chip grabbed her attention with the flirtatious tone of his voice. He shook out his body like he was getting ready for a fight. "Let it go."

Heat rushed to her cheeks. Chip was mimicking a relaxation technique taught to them by one of her mother's friends at Christmastime, when Eva Espiritu had been in the middle of a heartbreak.

At the time, it had been helpful, even if half of them had laughed.

Which may have been the point.

But in front of strangers? "What? No."

"This whole bar, we're your family. Are we not, Mountain Rush?" he asked, raising his voice, and snagging the attention of others nearby. Some faces looked up and cheered belatedly. "See? You know you'll feel better. Shut your eyes. Shake it out. You know you want to."

Gabby fought a giggle. Chip was…cheesy, but also quite convincing in his own way, and she found herself wiggling a little. To her relief, Willa and Bailey were participating in this silly ritual.

"You've worked hard, Gabby. Studied all year," Chip said, with his eyes shut.

"Two years," she corrected.

"Two years. And you earned this."

"I feel like I'm in church," Bailey whispered.

"Or some séance," Willa added.

"Hush!" Chip demanded, then opened one eye. "All those nights poring over your notes. Eating all the dessert." He kept shaking. "We've got your back."

Gabby inhaled, and exhaled. She found solace in Chip's conviction. "Minimum seventy-five percent."

"Seventy-five percent." Willa shook a hand in the air.

"Seventy-five percent." Bailey took Gabby by the shoulders and led her to the computer.

"Go on. We believe in you." Chip rested his hand on her lower back, to urge her to click.

Something inside her stirred. It was fleeting, and for a beat, sent her heart rocketing to her throat.

She turned to Chip and stared at his familiar gray eyes. He stood half a foot taller than her, and was solid, and strong.

That silliness? It drained out of her and she was left with... She couldn't tell what.

Heat. Tingles. Giddiness. A combination of all three? Though none could fully encapsulate the topsy-turvy feeling of that moment. Except that it held excitement and promise and friendship and attraction.

But.

Chip was her best friend. He was also the best friend of the only man she'd once loved. Changing her platonic relationship with Chip—just *thinking* about it—wasn't even a consideration, despite these continued surges of attraction.

Besides, there was William. Her far-away beau whom she'd soon see in person.

"She's frozen," Bailey commented.

"Gab," Chip said, waking her from her thoughts.

"Right. Seventy-five percent." She reoriented herself— obviously, her stress was getting to her.

"Wait!" Willa halted Gabby, then clumsily set up her phone in front of them. She pressed the red button to record. "For posterity."

"Good idea. This is why I love you." Her socials had been lacking these days, and a video of her test reveal would make for a great reentry from her hiatus.

Heaving a breath, Gabby set her fingers on the track pad and hovered the arrow over the Results button.

She clicked.

Hours. It felt like hours before the screen loaded, probably due to the horrible Wi-Fi access in the bar. And when the page fully appeared, it still took too long for her to scan the screen for the score. It wasn't a number that jumped off the page. Nor was it in red. It was a number in the same black font as the rest of the text.

A number that said sixty-five percent.

Sixty-five.

"No." Gabby's voice was a whisper.

"It's fine." It was Chip's voice, except it sounded far away.

To become a licensed CPA, Gabby would have to pass four tests in eighteen months. It had been suggested by her instructors that a test per quarter was ideal, to give her time for proper study.

Gabby had taken one quarter to study after earning her certificate, and now, technically, she would be behind a quarter.

"This can't be right." She looked up at her friends, bewildered.

Gabby was a doer. And she did things well. Like, straight A's since forever, summa cum laude, always on the ball. It was how she could be a wedding planner in addition to school, and be able to manage everyone's emotions, including hers, while in the depths of boyfriend drama.

And she'd studied. Late-night study sessions with Chip, skipping out on fun, gallons of coffee, and pounds of dessert...

"Don't worry, honey, you're going to get it next time," Liza called from the bar.

Next time, as in three months?

"Thanks." Gabby nodded at Liza, then noted the faces of other patrons turned her way. At the moment, she couldn't recognize them, even if they were locals—their expressions were fuzzy in her brain.

Her eyes darted to her friends and their stricken expressions.

At the propped-up phone recording her every move.

She pressed the red button so hard that the phone clattered to the ground.

"Well, I've got to go." She shook herself out of the moment, with only one thing on her mind, and it was to get far from here. To process, to plan for the next quarter. Something.

"But, Gabby…" Bailey began.

"No." She pushed out a grin and gave each of her friends the eyes that said, *Let me go and freak out, okay?*

Was she open about her feelings? Yes. Did she live a transparent life? Also, yes.

But when it came to what she was good at, what she was trying to accomplish, she couldn't fail. And that included people watching her fail.

"Love y'all. I'll text, okay?" She grabbed her laptop and walked swiftly, with her chin held high, out of the bar. She resisted showing any sign of distress, steeling her expression. Though, as she exited Mountain Rush and was hit by a gust of wind, a full-body shiver overcame her, threatening to loosen her tears.

She lengthened her strides.

"Gabriella!"

She knew who it was before she even turned around. Only one person would be brave enough to come after her when she was in such a state. He was the same person who'd seen her at her drunken worst when she'd found out that her father'd had a child out of wedlock—her half-brother Jared. The same person who'd supported her while recovering from her break up with Nathan.

But she was too upset to turn and face him.

A gentle tug against her elbow coaxed her to slow, and then to stop. Her eyes went straight to the ground.

"I was just thinking." Chip's voice was light, as if he hadn't just chased her across the parking lot. "I have a Costco-size box of Rice Krispies. And enough marshmallows for at least a couple of pans of Rice Krispies Treats."

"Those things are addicting." She struggled to keep her voice from breaking. Rice Krispies Treats were her favorite. Anything sweet was, in truth, but her late father used to make them as bribes for a quiet afternoon.

God, what was her dad thinking, looking down from above? Louis Espiritu had gone to war; he'd died there. And she couldn't pass a CPA test.

"You should come by and do your next round of studying at my place," Chip said, "because I can't eat them all myself. Sometime this week? I can help you make flashcards again. You'll be double prepped for the next test."

She bit her lip to halt her tears and allowed gratitude to flow instead. This was Chip. Never faltering, always present.

Her eyes fluttered up to meet his, brimming with his sincerity. She found zero judgement in his expression, nor was there pity. It allowed for her to release some of the tension in her shoulders, so much that she could think of the next step. "You're really going to help me study again?"

"Yeah. I mean, what else do I have to do?"

She laughed. "You're so bored and all."

"I know, right? So keep me company."

Her nerves calmed further at the idea of them spending more time. He was the ultimate hype-man. With him, she could start again, try again.

Gabby *would* rally. She would come back from this. There was no other choice.

Chip walked her the rest of the way to her car. Then he opened the car door. "Soon?"

She nodded, despite the dread sitting solidly in her belly. Her mental calendar came to the forefront. "How about the day after tomorrow?"

He looked up in the sky for a moment. "Yep, I'm free. I'll get those treats ready."

"Okay. Thank you. Love you."

"Love you." He shut her car door.

As she pulled out of the parking spot and drove away, she caught sight of Chip walking back into Mountain Rush.

And instead of tears, she found herself smiling.

Chapter Two

Gabby should have taken the rest of the day off, should have pocketed the small bit of hope Chip had bestowed upon her and tried again tomorrow.

Because the day was going from bad to worse, but for an entirely different reason.

"Sorry I'm not here to take your call, but you know what to do." William's outgoing message cooed in Gabby's ear, followed by a beep. She was lying on her couch, nestled among its large cushions.

"Hey, Will, it's me. Call me back, um, I hope you're okay," Gabby said, then hung up.

Staring at her phone, she couldn't shake a sense of foreboding. She'd left several messages since this morning; all of her texts had been left unread.

Technically, it hadn't been twenty-four hours since the last time they spoke. Will had a real job, he had a life. Stuff happened.

But if she was being honest, their conversations had begun to wane. What had been hours of texting and nightly video chats, that had only ended when one of them fell asleep, had eased into shorter phone calls and check-in texts.

Though, he *had* agreed to come to Jared and Matilda's wedding to be her plus-one. It had felt like a sign, that they were taking it to the next level. That they were a *thing*.

She thumbed to their texts from the last day; over a dozen from her, all unanswered. The first unanswered text, sent yesterday: Don't forget to buy your plane tickets to the wedding!

William Jones lived in Tucson; they'd met online. A couple of months ago, she'd swiped right simply because of his profile, where he'd described himself as someone "who took joy in the small things."

After back-and-forth relationship with her ex, Nathan, where Gabby at times had forgotten what it meant to feel joy, this had been a homing call. To her delight, the face on his profile had been the very one she'd seen on the screen when they finally met through video chat.

Will was real.

Though, at the moment, he was absent.

Her fingers hovered over the phone. She typed, You okay?

Seconds later, she was answered by her phone calendar with a reminder that the scheduled family video chat would begin in five minutes.

She sighed, and threw herself off her couch. She went into the bathroom to fix her hair and touch up her makeup. Then, to the kitchen, where she warmed up the Keurig, and attempted to ignore her study notes and books on her kitchen bar top.

Damn test.

It will be fine, right? All I need is to study harder.

She busied herself making her coffee and grabbed a handful of chocolate chips from her pantry. But when she propped her laptop on her lap, several items on her to-do list chimed in. A notice from the photographer for Matilda and Jared's wedding, wanting to talk through contingencies in case it rained, which she forwarded to the couple. An inquiry for a wedding in the fall that she'd forgotten to respond to, which she did now, with one of her standard prewritten responses.

By the time Gabby was let into the video chat, she was late. The screen had no less than a dozen faces—aunties from both the Espiritu (her father's) and Perez (her mother's) families near and far, along with her mother Eva and older sister, Frankie. Eva and Frankie were in their own cottages on the Spirit of the Shenandoah B & B property.

The greeting was much like any Filipino gathering—everyone squealed.

Gabby jumped in to squelch the chaos. "Sorry, Titas. I had to tie up a couple of things. I'll go on mute. No worries about me. I'll catch up." With a group of aunties with big personalities, Gabby was perfectly happy to be told what to do, especially since what they would be discussing did not fall under her supervision.

The point of this family chat was to decide on Jared and Matilda's wedding present. One hundred percent of the families involved had felt that a standard wedding present wouldn't be enough to show Jared how much he was welcomed into the family. Today, they would vote between funding their honeymoon or a car.

While Gabby and Frankie had immediately embraced Jared as their half-brother when he'd arrived in Peak under the guise of being the B & B's newest chef, not everyone had an easy time with it. It had been a challenge for their mother to accept Jared at first. She'd gone through a transition that, while it led her to her fiancé, Cruz, had threatened to cause a rift within the family. Similarly, some family members had been in shock, with a few not coming around until the wedding invitations went out.

It seemed that now, though, everyone was on board. Both for the gift, as well as the idea that they might as well plan a sister's reunion alongside the wedding, with the aunties set to arrive a week before. Hailing from all over the country, from Southern California, to Seattle, rural Oregon, and Chicagoland, this would be the first time all the aunties would be together in years, since Louis Espiritu's funeral twenty years ago.

Gabby sipped on her coffee and listened to the hens on the screen, eyes darting every few seconds to the notifications popping in.

Though none were from William.

"Wait. What happened to Nathan?" Tita Leanne asked on video chat, snagging Gabby's attention. She stilled, the coffee halfway to her lips.

How had the conversation turned in her direction?

"Nathan was from long ago, remember? She's bringing someone else to the wedding," Eva answered, with a gritted smile on her face.

"Who is it?"

Privacy, where art thou?

And yet, the other aunties were waiting for her answer in silence. Gabby unmuted herself. "Just someone."

"Oo-o-oh, she's being secretive," Tita Baby said. Baby was a nickname because she, too, was the youngest in her family, though it didn't quite help Gabby in the loyalty department. Tita Baby was a romantic at heart. "We can't wait to meet him."

"Not secretive. Just busy. Too busy, actually, blazing her own path to become a CPA," Eva said.

The aunties hummed their approvals.

"Thanks, Mom," she said, though wished her mother had just remained silent, because in three, two...

"CPA? Gabby, congratulations," Auntie Percy said.

"Well, technically not yet…" Gabby pointed out, but was drowned out with the talk of careers and who got what job.

Pressure and expectations—that was the neverending rhythm of her life, as a wedding planner, as an Espiritu. She couldn't get away from it.

"We're proud of you iha. And I can't wait to meet this *someone*," Tita Leanne said. "So happy that you're finding your own loves. Even Frankie has a date."

Frankie, located at the bottom of the screen, gasped. Her older sister's jaw slackened. "What is that supposed to mean, Tita?"

"Well, you know, because you're sassy," she said with a laugh. "It's not something to be ashamed of, iha. But you can sometimes scare people away."

"I'm not scary! I'm straightforward."

Gabby giggled, for the relief of having the spotlight diverted away from herself, and because she agreed, ever so slightly, with Tita Leanne's assessment.

Still, the conversation was going rogue.

Finally, their mother took the group's attention, laying out their activities for the week that the majority of the Espiritus would be in town.

Things were being planned—things that, thank goodness, Gabby didn't have a hand in, like tours and wine-tasting trips, hiking and a jaunt to the beach, though it was still freezing most mornings.

As she listened, however, unease filled her. She was twenty-seven years old. She was pretty, and dammit, she was successful, despite her failed test.

What was she missing in her life? How was it that even sassy Frankie, according to her aunt, could land a date, but Gabby had a sneaky suspicion that she was being ghosted?

It was like she had something written on her forehead,

glowing with an effervescent message that she was utterly incapable of being committed to.

At the thought, her brain took the mental slide to the image of Nathan, along with the myriad promises he'd broken. A groan escaped her lips.

"You don't like that idea?" Frankie asked.

Gabby shook herself to the present. "No, sorry. I was… thinking about something else. Wedding brain."

"Iha." The request came from Tita Darlene, the eldest of the Espiritu siblings. "I know someone who can be a distraction. A dentist here in Seattle. He's rich and—"

"Mom!" Her cousin, Kaitlin, objected. Thank goodness. "He's also almost fifty."

"Okay, okay." Darlene raised her hands in surrender. "I'm just trying to help. Just in case your, ahem, *someone* doesn't pan out. Who's going to sit next to you when the tables seat six?"

They once more circled round to Gabby's inability to land a man. She gritted her teeth into a smile. Time to shift the attention. "Now, what were you saying, Ate Frankie?"

To her relief, her sister jumped in to save her, probably sensing Gabby's panic clear across the screen. On her desk, her phone lit up with a text from Kaitlin: Sorry about my mom. She can't help herself.

Gabby responded, It's fine.

No need to lie to me.

Gabby smiled. Kaitlin, a landscape and real-estate photographer, was six months younger than her, and of the eight first cousins on their side of the family, they were the closest.

The pressure is a lot sometimes, Gabby texted back.

I feel that. We go from being sheltered to "stay focused

on your studies" in college to "when am I going to have a grandchild?" after graduation.

Gabby snorted, though silently, then replied:

My mom's not so much that, but she's got high expectations.

Growing up with a mother who was everything, who did everything, and who started a successful business from scratch made no room for Gabby to relax, or to admit when things weren't going well. Though Eva never yelled, she had this look of disappointment that Gabby never wanted to have leveled at her. The last time she'd witnessed it was when Eva had realized that Jared was her late husband's child with another woman.

So, no, Gabby hadn't told Eva that she'd failed her test.

Kaitlin texted again: We can commiserate when I'm there. Finally. It's been too long.

Laughing on the video chat took her attention—someone had shared their screen. It was the reunion schedule, broken down into hourly blocks and color coded by activities.

The information was so overwhelming that Gabby shut her eyes for a beat. Inhaled, exhaled.

Her life the last few months had been similarly, meticulously planned and it was all she could handle.

And now you have a test to retake.

The phone lit up once more.

I can't wait to meet your someone! Kaitlin texted.

<3

Gabby's heart fell. She couldn't, either.

Twenty-one days before the wedding

I think William ghosted me.

Chip gawked at the five words that popped up on his phone, and he halted.

"What the—" Nathan Paul II crashed into him from behind, grunting. He nudged Chip forward, catching himself before he hit the ground. "Bro!"

"Dammit." Chip's phone slipped out of his hand, landing face down on the dirt. He snatched the phone up, then slid it into his pocket, turning it off before his best friend could catch sight of the message.

They were steps from the halfway marker of Spirit Trail, a one-and-a-half-mile stretch that connected downtown Peak to the Appalachian Trail. Nathan had finally gotten into hiking, and with Chip being a volunteer trail guide with Cross Trails Hiking, thought it would be a good time to catch up after Nathan had returned from a series of work trips. Their goal had been to go out and back for a total of six miles, a good workout for a guy like Nathan, who was active and strong.

The sky was a burnt orange, and was its way down behind the Blue Ridge Mountains. But under the canopy of trees, it was almost pitch-dark, except for the glow from their headlamps.

"Sorry," Chip said sheepishly.

"What was that text about?"

"Nothing much." He eased his voice so as to sound nonchalant, not wanting to call attention to the text any more than he should. Namely, because it came from Gabby.

Nathan's ex.

Yes, Chip was in that sticky in between.

Even in the dark, he saw Nathan's right eyebrow rise. "That was Gab, wasn't it?"

Chip's stomach roiled. Gab was actually Chip's nickname for her, but sometime when she and Nathan were dating, he had co-opted it.

For a beat, Chip considered denying it. Nathan and Gabby have been broken up for about a year, and he didn't want there to be any awkwardness.

And yet, that wasn't how Chip worked.

"Yep." Chip readjusted his pack and gestured for them to keep going, and they both stepped out. A momentary silence settled between them, filled only by the sound of their shuffling boots.

"I heard about her not passing her test."

"Yeah? Who said?"

"Tim from the orchard was at Mountain Rush for lunch and saw the whole thing. You were there, right?"

"I was," Chip simply said, though he inwardly rolled his eyes with how quickly news flew. Cloud Orchards was the Paul family business, which encompassed a Christmas tree farm and a pumpkin patch. The orchards employed a slew of folks—of course, an employee had been at the bar that day.

"You didn't think to mention it?"

He gave his friend the side-eye and snickered. As if this guy forgot their deal. "Nate, are you for real right now?"

"What?"

"Don't play. We talked about this."

Chip had had to set boundaries with him and Gabby after a brief period of time when the two used Chip as their go-between. Then, after a situation in which Chip realized that he was spending all his emotional space comforting each of them, he'd declared that he would no longer broker their relationship. That neither one of them should put him in the middle. That he shouldn't and wouldn't choose.

It was painful enough that he'd always found Gabby cute as hell, and he didn't have the patience for Nathan's fear of commitment.

Nathan sighed. "You're right. Sorry. But…she's alright?"

"Yeah, she is." At least, when it came to her test. Though, now with the ghosting…

Damn William.

Chip had had his opinions when Gabby started talking to William. *Talking* was the term she'd used, though he would define it as *fell for*. Not in a love kind of way, but in a romantic, put-on-a-pedestal way that wasn't quite real.

A couple of months they'd been talking, and not once had the guy traveled to see her. In this day and age, it shouldn't be an issue. It was like that movie: *if he's not that into you…*

Heat clamored up his chest at the thought of Gabby's heart breaking, along with the knowledge that it had been Chip, steady at her side, for everything. Not a week had gone by without them spending time together. She'd pop by the bar. During his hikes on Spirit Trail, which ran right up to Spirit of the Shenandoah B & B, he'd swung by to say hello. Not to mention their ongoing text messages and meme sharing. Their study sessions.

Did he want to be there for her when she had issues with other men? Yes. At times, though, he wished she would realize that there was also him, right in front of her.

"I miss her." Nathan brought Chip's thoughts back to the present. "I know I messed up. A lot."

Chip picked up his pace, and that heat turned into annoyance. "You've said that before."

"It's different now. We've been split up a year, and I've

been working on myself. I tried dating other people, but no one compares to Gabby."

Chip tightened the straps of his pack, inhaling deeply to keep himself from replying that perhaps it shouldn't have taken Nathan this long to figure that fact out. Chip had known it from the very beginning, when Nathan and Gabby started dating years ago, that she was special. That Nathan had too many big dreams that involved individual success for him to finally partner with someone. Nathan was lucky that she'd given him second and third chances.

All Chip had wanted was a first, and that itself would be impossible.

"But it didn't work between the both of you the other times you got together. Because of you, I might add." Chip kept his tone nonchalant, but he felt each word down to his bones. Yes, it took two to make a relationship work, but Nathan had always had the upper hand in theirs. "If I remember correctly, other things came first."

Nathan groaned. "Believe me, I kick myself whenever I think about it. But I was a different person then. I was trying to build Cloud Orchards. Do you know how much effort it took to transition from law to business?"

Chip had heard it all before. Nathan was a workaholic, even more than Chip was. What came with it was this insatiable ambition that put everyone last. When they were together, Gabby had only wanted one thing: for Nathan to be a little more focused on their relationship.

"I'm ready for it now," Nathan said.

"Ready for what?"

"For the real thing."

A cackle threatened to burst out of Chip as he heard the familiarity in Nathan's words. Instead, a snort escaped him.

"What was that for?"

"You've said this before. But as soon as you get back together, it's the same behaviors. The drive for the next deal, the travel for work, the money making. You know me—I respect all of that, but not while dating a woman who you know needs more and deserves what she wants. And I don't know, it gets a little old, my man."

Once more, silence took over, and as the seconds passed, Chip's guilt threatened to overflow. Admittedly, his tone was a little harsh, but he could only take so much. He'd heard all of this before, this same impassioned conviction that things could be different.

"So damn protective. What are you, her dad or something?"

"No. I'm her friend. Just like you're my friend, and someone who's been around you throughout your on-and-off relationship. I've seen too much. Can you blame me for hoping that there's no repeat? Because guess who takes the brunt? Me, from both sides." He could feel it now, in the middle of his chest. "I don't like seeing either one of you hurt... because you get hurt too. The last time you both broke up, you left town for a couple of weeks. And she, well..." He inhaled to pause, because he was feeling it again, the emotional investment rising up. "I just think that you shouldn't explore this road unless you're willing to stick through with it. All the way."

Silence stretched between them as they came upon the junction where Spirit Trail met with the trail leading toward the white blazes of the Appalachian Trail to the left, and to the right, a minor trail that skirted past the B & B. The building itself was in view, with its windows lit brightly from the inside. Instrumental music and voices sounded from afar.

Gabby was on the property somewhere. Probably speed walking from one place to another, chatting with guests, as energetic as she was. She was never one to sit still, and while he wished he could stop in, with Nathan with him, he hesitated.

Chip hadn't expected this conversation, and if their paths crossed with hers, he wouldn't know how to manage their interaction.

"Do you want to turn around and track back? Not sure how tired you are," Chip said.

"I'm still good. Let's take a right."

His stomach sank. "Alright then."

They took a right turn and hiked up the hill. Laughter from the B & B's back porch echoed in their direction.

One voice was distinct, sending his heart rate to double speed. It was a visceral, uncontrolled reaction by his nervous system. Gabby.

To his right, Nathan didn't seem to notice, as he seemed to make a focused effort to put one foot in front of the other on the unsteady ground. For good measure, Chip spoke up. "The senior center renovation is going well. Still expect to be finished right on time. The permits were all approved."

"Awesome. That's great to know. The renovation is all Mom talks about."

Nathan's mother, Audrey, was a regular, too.

"She suggested a patio if the budget allows. A place they can sit outside."

"Great idea. I'll run it by the contractor and do the numbers." He thought about it. "Maybe string up some lights, and a couple of heat lamps."

"Rocking chairs."

"And a firepit."

Then, together they said, "Ye-e-aa-h."

Chip cracked up; Nathan snorted. All at once, the tension between them eased.

This was what brought the two of them together. Banter, laughter, and a lifetime of ending each other's sentences. In thirty years, it would be them in the senior center, because that was how it went with their families.

Minutes later, they came to the road and turned right onto a large path adjacent to the asphalt.

"You know, I *was* hurt the last time Gab and I broke up," Nathan said.

And just like that, the mood switched.

"I had to regroup," Nathan continued. "Look, I'm not here trying to disrupt her life by wanting to see her. But Gabby has all the qualities of a woman I want to be with in the long term. We were good together when things were working. So I'm not talking about rushing into something huge, but a date or two to see if the spark's still there. There's Jared's wedding in three weeks. I could ask her to that and see how that goes."

Said this way, Chip's empathy for his friend rose. Nathan had been the type to handle all of his fear and pain and vulnerability on his own.

But all he could do was nod.

"Do you know if she's going with someone?" Nathan asked.

"I think so." He ducked under a hanging branch. "This part of the trail's tricky. Focus, okay."

"Got it." After a second, Nathan asked, "Is it that guy from Arizona?"

"How do you know about that?"

"C'mon. It's Peak. People talk. But are they going together?"

"Honestly, I'm not sure."

"Well, maybe I'll feel her out. You wouldn't mind putting in a good word for me, would you?"

"I would mind. I'd rather not." The answer was out with his next heartbeat.

"What?" Nathan snorted, in *his* way. It was a challenge, a dare. It was the same tone he'd given to the bullies that picked on Chip in the second grade. The same entitlement he'd used when, as young men in their teens, he'd demanded a fair wage for their start-up landscaping business, the first of many projects they'd jumped into together.

It had every bit of the bravado Chip didn't have at times like this, when he was pulled between loyalties. Self or others?

Nathan or Gabby?

Friendship or love?

No, it wasn't love that he felt for Gabby, right? It was admiration, it was friendship, and yes, a deep crush. Protectiveness, no doubt.

It was the combination of the little things she did every day, from the way she was hyperfocused, to her optimism.

People thought *Chip* was optimistic and friendly. Gabby had twice his energy.

Chip sorted through the thoughts that were jumbled in his head, though his focus wasn't helped by the darkness and the crunching of the leaves. "I'm staying out of your business. I have a hard enough time getting my own dates than worrying about other people. Are you sure this is what you want to do, anyway? You haven't talked to her lately, have you?"

"No, but it doesn't mean I can't drop her a text. Catch up."

"I'd like to see you try that."

"You don't think she'll want to talk to me?"

"I think you're underestimating her feelings about this. Look," he said, softening his tone. "Try to see this situation from her point of view."

"Yeah. I guess you're right. But… I'm getting a vibe from you about this. I can't tell what it is."

Chip half laughed to lighten the moment, to ease his own nerves. "The only vibe you're getting from me is the message for you to pay attention while you hike."

As if the universe had his back, Nathan tripped on a branch.

They both exploded in laughter.

"See?" Chip said.

"Yeah, okay. I'll focus."

"Good." And Chip hoped that that was enough to table this whole conversation.

Chapter Three

Twenty days until the wedding

"**Y**ou can't fool me. I see you checking your phone," Chip called to Gabby from the kitchen counter, where he sliced thick squares of Rice Krispies Treats. It was still slightly warm, just made an hour ago.

And it looked damn near perfect, if he said so himself. Pretty impressive for someone who still burned his grilled-cheese sandwiches.

"Ugh. Fine." Gabby set her phone face down on the dining-room table, now littered with piles of notes. She buried her hands in her hair.

He brought the plate of treats to the table. "You keep saying that you're okay, but are you really?"

"Yeah, I'm fine." A look of defeat flashed on her face. "Actually, no. I think it's still settling in. Two days, and William hasn't called, or texted, or anything. What did I do?"

"The guy's an asshole. You didn't do anything. And even if you did, the right thing is to actually *talk* to you about it." Chip attempted to keep his anger at bay by leaning against the peninsula.

"With everything going on, the test, the wedding, and then there's this pressure with my aunts about being single... Besides being mad about William, I don't know what his status is for the wedding. Is he coming? Will he just show up? What do I say if he doesn't?"

Chip bit the inside of his cheek. This was a conversation he'd thought they squashed late last night over texts. "You have nothing to prove to anyone, much less your aunties."

"Right. But they just won't stop. And honestly—" her face skewed into a frown "—I'll just feel better if I have a date. I don't want to be standing around by myself. It's such a cliché for the wedding planner to be single and dateless. I'm done with people feeling sorry for me. Even my widowed mother found a boyfriend." She winced. "That sounds horrible, doesn't it?"

"Pretty freaking uncouth if you ask me," he said with a smile.

Her mother Eva and her fiancée Cruz had met on Spirit Trail and did not get along at first, only to find out later that they were each other's trail notebook pen pal. Their romance had been like a small town rom com; then again, her mother deserved a healing kind of love after years of being a widow.

She sighed. "Always the wedding planner, never the bride. It's like being picked last on the team, you know? Everyone will find partners during a slow song, and I'll be there, pretending to be busy."

A vision of him holding her on the dance floor, and how she would feel in his arms, flooded his senses, along with the one thought he'd resisted since last night. Under his breath, he said, "How about me?"

"What?"

"I can take you. I'm already invited."

She threw her head back in a laugh, and the sight of it thumped him in the chest. He laughed along with her to quell the discomfort.

"Thanks, Chip. But it wouldn't fool anyone. Everyone

knows we're just friends. They're all expecting a plus-one, not an evergreen."

Just friends.

By God, he was getting tired of that phrase. Tired of saying it, and tired of hearing it. "Yeah, you're right. You suck at the Wobble, anyway."

She gasped and tossed her pencil at him like a dart. He stepped aside with a cackle, and the pencil clattered on the ground. "I do not suck at the Wobble."

"At the Wobble, the Electric Slide, any dance that involves actual finesse. You forget, I've seen you dance."

"Not true. I can cha-cha. *The* most important wedding dance. And I'm lightyears better than you, who doesn't dance. At all." She leaned forward and grabbed a treat from the platter. Pointing it at him, she said, "So I definitely won't ask you to be my date." Biting into the square, she shut her eyes and moaned. "This is damn good. It almost makes me feel better about being rejected. Again."

Chip looked away to distract himself from her lustful reaction, eyes darting to the window that overlooked his backyard. His gaze landed on his father, skulking about by the back fence, and the sight of him was about as effective as doing an ice plunge. "I hate that you feel this way."

"I do, too."

He looked over his shoulder at her and took in her sad expression. He wanted to wipe it away. "Do you want to see something?"

"Sure."

He gestured for her to join him at the window. "There he goes again."

Gabby took his side and followed his gaze. "What's up?"

His father's telltale three-note whistle echoed through the

backyard; despite his age, it was as loud as his bark. "He's still trying to trap that stray dog."

"The pregnant one?"

"Yep. It keeps coming around but refuses to get caught." George might have been the grumpy sort, but when it came to animals, he was as soft as a marshmallow. "I don't know how it survived last winter, with that week of biting cold. But Dad's out there every day with some food, hoping it'll come close."

"That's sweet." She crunched into the dessert.

"Yes…and no. I can't do pets. You know that." He glanced at the wind chimes hanging under their covered porch, at the engraved paw hanging from one of its tassels.

"Aw, Chip. It's been so long, and your Dad's really pining for one."

"It's still a no from me." He crossed his arms in front of him, at the memory of saying goodbye to his mother and his dog within a year of one another. Goose was a loyal dog; Chip imagined that he was still trailing after his mom, but it still hurt.

He couldn't bring another dog into his house.

"What kind of dog is it?" she asked.

"A boxer. We think she ran away from one of the puppy mills up the road. Like, I'm glad it ran away because those mills are criminal, but it sucks that it's all by itself. Dad called animal control and let them know she was hanging around, and they put it out on their socials, but no one's come to claim the dog, not even the puppy mill."

"Boxers make the best family dogs." Shrugging, she turned to sit back at her computer.

"Not for this family," he grumbled. He'd had enough loss for a lifetime. He would rather build and create and do things that had some kind of permanence.

Noting that Gabby had sat back down, he said, "Anyhow, where are you at with the study guide?" If she didn't want to talk about William anymore, he couldn't force her.

What he'd noticed from these Espiritu women, because he'd been around them enough, was that for as much as they appeared to be transparent, they held so much inside. Their stoicism made it so that they were tough nuts to crack. They only talked when they wanted to. They chose the timing.

So he took the chair next to her, the legs squeaking as he slid closer.

She gestured at her notes, written in her neat penmanship. "I figured I would start from the very beginning, because I'm not totally sure how I bombed it so badly. I felt confident leaving the test."

"Look at it this way, now that you have an idea of how the test will go, you can focus on the concepts. Were there questions when you had to choose between a couple of close answers?"

"Yes, quite a few."

"Let's work on those concepts first."

"Okay." She turned to him. "But what if I bomb it again?"

He smiled. "You won't."

"How do you know?"

"I just do. You're you, which means you'll handle it like you do work. One thing at a time, and with a clear head."

"Thank you. You always know what to say." Her expression softened, her pink lips spreading into a smile. And the effect on him… It was like being surrounded by warm sunlight. He wanted to soak her up and bask in her presence always.

Everyone knows we're just friends.

His senses woke. "I think I have a book that can help you out…" He stood, grateful for the excuse, and headed to his bookshelves in the living room. He scanned various titles, found an accounting book that distilled complicated concepts simply, and pulled it out from the shelves.

"Here you go," he said as he returned to her side.

"Oh, great, another thing to read," she said wryly. "But why do you have this? You're not an accountant."

"I needed it for business school. Listen, it might help."

She fanned the pages. "Ugh. Fine."

He laughed. "You're welcome."

"Thank you." She grinned up at him.

"I'll set the timer. Twenty minutes, alright?" He turned on the timer on his phone.

As she took notes, Chip looked through his own schedule. He had a lot of irons in the fire, from being a volunteer guide, to his shifts at Mountain Rush, and managing the senior-center project and his vacation rental properties. He swallowed against the slight overwhelm of it all, despite the way each project excited him.

But he was intent on changing none of it. It was a privilege to be in a place where he can help people—even as a bartender, he took part in people's celebrations and hard times.

In his periphery, he spied his dad going out the back gate, presumably to look for the dog.

Chip sighed.

He would not, however, be adding another iron to the fire in the name of a stray dog.

Even if Chip had agreed to adopt another dog, when would he have the time to walk it, to play with it? George had a similarly hectic schedule, with all the activities he participated in.

Bad idea. Chip shouldn't even be thinking about it.

"Guess what?" Gabby asked, plowing through his thoughts.

"We still have ten minutes left."

"I have to tell you something."

He stilled, his intuition screaming. "What's up?"

"Nathan texted me."

"Oh, yeah?" Though he feigned a casual tone, he stood to put some distance between them. He turned on the faucet and took his time to perfectly adjust the temperature of the water to wash his hands.

Damn, Nathan was fast.

Breath, Chip. Relax. He needed to regulate the volume of his voice, when all he wanted was to stop her from saying anything else.

"What happened to *never again*?" he asked.

Gabby had promised everyone that there would be no going back to Nathan. That she'd had enough his of waxing and waning interest in a serious relationship. That she would make sure that the next person she dated would put her as number one on his priority list.

"He seems…changed."

"You got that from one text message?"

"Well, it wasn't exactly just one message. It was a bit of a back-and-forth. He seems a little more serious. He asked me a lot of questions. He was interested in what I was doing."

"This was all on text?" He loaded the last dish into the dishwasher, holding his breath.

"Um, he called me, too." A pause. "So in this auditing question, it asks what is the role of…"

She went on to recount a question and listed off the multiple-choice options, as if she hadn't just earthquaked their serene study session.

Nathan had indeed lobbed his shot, and he'd been right with his prediction that Gabby would respond. Again.

"I think it should be *A*," she said now. "What do you think?"

"Hmm?" He wiped his hands with the kitchen towel, his

mind still on his conversation with Nathan the night before. Chip had hoped that Nathan would have thought twice. Then again, his best friend was one of the most confident people he knew.

"The role of the auditor?" She pressed her lips together. "You're mad. I knew you would be mad. You have that thing going on with your face, when your jaw ticks."

He unclenched said jaw.

"I knew that if I told you that Nathan called that you would be upset."

He didn't know what was worse, Gabby telling him about Nathan, or not telling him at all. Shaking his head, he gathered his thoughts. "I'm not upset. Just…you were pretty clear about your feelings for him."

"I'm still very clear. I'm not here hoping that he's finally going to ask me to marry him. I feel completely different about him, actually. It's hard to explain."

"And yet, seconds ago you said how much he changed. With heart eyes."

"Not heart eyes. His call just caught me off guard, and it was good to hear his voice."

"What if he wants to get back together?"

As soon as the words came out of his mouth, Chip regretted them. He'd asked it out of curiosity, and maybe a little bit of a dare. He wanted to see where her head was at.

But with the way her face lit up, the strategy came back and slapped him in the face.

"D-did he say something?" she stuttered.

Inside, he withered. "Nothing…specific."

"What did he say?" She exhaled.

Pain. That was pain coursing through him.

Of course, she would consider it. She had been in love with Nathan, after all.

She maybe still was.

The next second, her expression changed. "No. It would take a lot for me to get back together with him, and that includes me being able to forget everything that happened between us. Which is a tall order." Her face screwed into a frown and she turned back to her computer, and clicked on her trackpad. "Yes! It was *A*."

"Great." Though it was a response to her answer to the test prep, it was also for her conviction that she wouldn't fall for Nathan's antics.

And yet, something she'd said continued to linger: *it would take a lot for me to get back together.*

There was still a window of a chance.

Eighteen days until the wedding

"Let's sit away from the windows. It's chilly today." Gabby led her half-brother, Jared Sotheby, and his fiancée, Spirit of the Shenandoah B & B manager Matilda Matthews, toward the rear of Letty's Café, to a booth in the back corner that was almost always empty. The café was a popular place, serving American fare in large helpings, so no one ever left hungry, and currently it bustled with locals.

"Don't remind me. I'm worried the weather won't turn in time." Gabby sat, and Matilda slipped into the leather bench seat across from her. She'd grown out her dark hair for the wedding, and it was well past her shoulders. And though worry had taken over her expression, she was positively glowing, cheeks pink against her fair skin.

Jared joined her. "It'll turn." He took Matilda's hand, and for a beat, the couple looked into each other's eyes.

The vibe in the booth settled; Matilda's shoulders eased downward.

Reason 6,254 that the two were perfect for one another: with one look, they knew each other's thoughts and comforted each other's worries.

It was hard to imagine that they'd only known each other a year. That within 365 days, they both were convinced that they were the one. Their relationship didn't exactly have a smooth start. Jared and Matilda had had a secret relationship; only Matilda knew that Jared, who had come to the B & B as its new chef, was actually an Espiritu son, though with another woman.

But now, it felt like Gabby couldn't remember a time when Jared hadn't been in their lives, and even in those memories where he had been absent, his spirit, she realized, had lingered all along.

This made their nuptials the most important in Gabby's career thus far. More than the most extravagant and lavish ceremony she'd planned. And it was because of this—this love between them.

Gabby wanted to gift her brother with the best celebration she could muster, even if, at the moment, she was pissed at William Jones.

Another day had passed without a word from him.

"The worst-case scenario is that we add more tents to the itinerary, right? That won't be bad," Matilda said, waking her from her thoughts.

Gabby pulled her iPad from her bucket bag and woke the screen. "No, it won't be bad. The reception will be beautiful no matter what. We're also a full two and half weeks away, and the weather on that date the last three years has been a perfect sixty-eight degrees, without a cloud in the sky. I have faith." She smiled, thumbing to the seating-chart app, and brought up a visual depiction of round tables with names assigned to each. "So full steam ahead."

"Right." Matilda heaved a breath. From her phone, she pulled up her notes. "I received more RSVPs, some last-minute regrets, and additions."

"I have more names to add, too," Jared said.

Gabby measured her next question. "For these folks that RSVP'd, were they initially invited, or…"

They both shook their heads.

"You sent out more invites?"

They looked at one another, a sure sign of a couple gone rogue.

"You verbally invited them." Gabby inwardly winced.

With matching gritted teeth, they nodded.

"You two." Gabby sipped in a breath. One. Two. Three seconds. A fourth to keep all her thoughts from jumbling together. The seating, the catering, the decor—all the secondary and tertiary things that would need to be updated. "How many more guests?"

"Four from me," Matilda said.

"Um…" Jared cleared his throat. "Ten."

"Ten!" Gabby pressed her hand against her chest. She lowered her voice. "Ten? That's fourteen guests total. That's two and a third more tables than we gave the B and B."

"It's not my fault. I couldn't say no," Jared said.

"It *is* your fault." She raised her eyebrows.

The server arrived, interrupting what would have been a lecture. He took their drink and food orders, and Gabby caved in and ordered a slice of Letty's famous chocolate caramel mousse cake.

It was going to be that kind of meeting.

Gabby had to relax. She couldn't talk to a groom this way, even if it was her brother.

When the server left, she said. "I'm sorry for my…outburst. The number was just a surprise."

"Will it really be a problem?" Jared said.

"No, ultimately, it's fine. It helps that you have an in with the B-and-B owner." She offered him a smile, even if a part of her wished that there were things such as prewedding classes. Where critical skills were taught, such as sticking to RSVPs and notifying the wedding planner of any changes. Because there are budgets and space challenges.

On the app, Gabby added three more tables, noting that chairs were sure to back into one another if guests stood up at the same time, and began the arduous process of adding one name at a time, starting with Matilda's list of four additional guests, adjusting groups as needed.

"Kuya Jared, your turn," Gabby prompted.

"Nathan Paul the Second."

Her finger hovered above the iPad screen. Was his attendance what had prompted Nathan to call her? "So he's coming?"

Jared's eyes rounded in concern. "Yes. But I can disinvite. You just say so."

"Oh, my gosh, no, it's fine. I told you I was okay with it and I am." This was their wedding, after all, though Gabby had been appreciative that Jared had broached her on the subject months ago. Cloud Orchards and the B & B had worked together on a couple of events, and Nathan and Jared had become friends.

Still, she noted the mix of discomfort and excitement stirring inside her. With Nathan, at times, she didn't know the difference. Gabby added, "Things are chill between him and me. We actually talked the other day."

Matilda raised an eyebrow. "Really."

"Yeah. We caught up a little."

"Whew. That makes me feel better," Jared said.

Gabby shrugged. "And honestly, it's hard to get away from exes around here."

"Don't I know it," Matilda said under her breath. She was referring to her ex-husband, who had gotten married at the B & B last year. "Then again, that weekend was when we got engaged. It all worked out."

"It did." Jared leaned in to kiss her on the cheek.

Yearning replaced her wayward emotions, going from the pit of her belly and traveling all the way to her heart.

Oh, she wished.

She wished she had that.

Not someone to marry, necessarily. If she ever married— with her track record, was it in the cards?—she would elope. A destination wedding followed by a big casual party would suit her taste.

She, of all people, understood how the many details of wedding planning could hamper the real mission of the event, for two people to publicly declare their commitment. It was hard enough to find someone to consider a partnership with. God knows, she had continued to try—no one could accuse Gabby of giving up the search.

What Gabby wanted was the connection. The understanding.

The intimacy.

You have that already.

Chip came to mind, and in all the ways he made her feel. The little bursts of adrenaline whenever he came near. How her heart grew twenty times bigger when he offered her that plate full of Rice Krispies Treats. How he'd suggested to be her date at the wedding.

She'd wanted to say yes. For a beat she'd imagined them together, on the dance floor. She would have been able to take off to attend to her planner duties and he wouldn't have minded. They would have laughed, a lot. He would have been the most perfect date.

But she didn't want to be a pity date. Nor did she want to set the town alight with rumor, since he and Nathan were good friends.

Dammit, William, where are you?

William was supposed to solve this big wedding date issue.

It wasn't as if she'd considered her relationship with William serious, or that he had checked all the boxes. But he was someone. Someone who she had great conversation with. Someone who was handsome, too. Most of all, someone who didn't know all of her faults and entire tenuous history with love.

Were there feelings for William? Sure. Deep feelings, though? Not really. And their physical attraction had yet to be determined.

It was why it had taken Gabby aback when Nathan called. One thing she couldn't deny was their physical connection.

Could she blame herself for wanting to feel that familiar intimacy?

The server arrived with their drinks and Jared and Matilda were still midkiss.

Gabby was grateful for the interruption, especially for her thoughts. "Alright, you two, either get focused or get a room." She rolled her eyes.

As the server set down their drinks, Matilda thanked him, then her gaze landed on Gabby. "I see that your plus-one is taken. Is William coming?"

Gabby cleared her throat. "That's the plan."

"Can't wait to meet this guy." Jared raised an eyebrow. "When did you get so protective?"

"You're kidding, right? You're my baby sister."

As he said it, Gabby's face warmed. She definitely didn't

hate having a big brother. It was a whole other dynamic that she hadn't thought she'd needed, especially with having lost her dad. Sometimes, looking at Jared tugged at her inner young self, because he and her father looked so much alike.

"In fact." He sipped his drink. "Is there a way Chip and I can meet Will before the wedding?"

Gabby rolled her eyes. "With Chip, really?"

"Yeah. He's got a good read on folks. Plus, I would trust him in a fight."

Gabby busted out a cackle. "A fight? I don't think that's necessary."

"Still, he's a guy who's got your six, your know?"

"What does that even mean?" Matilda asked.

"He's loyal."

Matilda nodded eagerly. "Yeah, I agree with that."

"But the question is, why is everyone in my present business?"

They both put their hands up in surrender. If it wasn't so annoying, it would have been adorable.

She sighed, taking a sip of her ice water. "I'm sorry." She shook her head. "Let's get back to the other guests."

The vibe settled back into a steady clip of tasks, finishing up the table seating, and going through the event schedule. In between, their food arrived, and they ate.

"How do you want to handle the first dance?" Gabby asked.

"For sure we want to do the money dance." Jared beamed.

The money dance entailed guests lining up for a short dance with the bride and groom, but not before pinning money to their outfits.

"Not the first dance, though. The first should be me and my dad, then you and your mom," Matilda said, taking a bite of her burger.

"Should I dance with Eva, too?" Jared looked to Gabby, with worry on his face. "How would that work? And do you think she would be down for it?"

"Oh... Oh, wow." A surge of emotion rushed through Gabby. Six months ago, her mother and Jared weren't in the greatest of situations. Eva had had a hard time accepting Jared at first, seeing that he was a child of another woman.

Since then, though, Eva had turned a corner. "She would love it. I think you suggesting it will make her cry."

Matilda pressed her napkin against her lower lids, eyes blinking rapidly. "Sorry. I've just been a mess lately."

"No. Not a mess," Gabby said. "You're feeling all the emotions, and that's good."

It was certainly better than some brides she'd dealt with—those who got lost in the details, forgetting that the important part was the marriage.

Not that Gabby knew anything about that. She couldn't even get a guy she was talking with to call her back.

She deflated at the thought. For a wedding planner, she had to be the woman with the least real-life experience. It was pathetic.

Gabby cleared her throat. "Do you have any specific songs you'd like to feature? We want to make sure the DJ is ready."

"The Wobble, definitely," Jared said.

"The Electric Slide." Matilda nodded.

Gabby grinned as she thought of Chip claiming that she didn't know how to wobble. She was going to show him.

"Oh, almost forgot." Jared raised a finger. "Emma wants to sing a couple of her songs. She'll come prepared with background music and all, but she'll need the mic."

"That's an amazing idea." Emma Sotheby was a bona fide rock star, and Jared's half-sister. "Hmm. I wonder if we should fit her in before the first dance." Gabby bit her lip and thumbed on the iPad. She scrolled through the timeline. "So that everyone will be paying attention to the performance."

The sound of raucous laughter brought Gabby's gaze to the front of the café, where two men walked in with backpacks, one she could recognize even while eyes closed.

Her insides lightened all at once, and her hand shot up. "Chip!"

He turned toward her voice, and when he met her eyes, his lips spread into a wide grin. Gesturing to the unfamiliar guy next to him, they unloaded their packs at the front and meandered toward the booth.

They were both in hiking gear. Chip looked like he'd stepped right out of a Patagonia ad, his gray eyes a contrast to his sun-kissed skin and touch of scruff, with his shades hanging off the front of his shirt.

His clear delight in seeing her felt like a double shot of espresso.

Chip ruffled her hair, and she giggled. "Hey, short stuff. Hey, Jared, Mat. This is Morgan. He's from Lynchburg." He gestured toward the stranger, who had light brown skin and close-cropped hair. A handsome grin peeked out from slightly unkempt facial hair. He was shorter than Chip, and fit.

After a round of hellos, Gabby had to address the elephant in the room. "Smells like the two of you have been busy."

"We just got back from a couple of nights on the trail." Chip grinned. "Got at least fifteen miles each day."

"Yeah…that still doesn't sound enticing to me," Jared said, making them all laugh.

"My brother's not an outdoorsy type," Gabby said by means of explaining.

"Are you?" Morgan asked.

Chip blew out a laugh. "Only if it's an outdoor wedding."

"Or an outdoor bridal shower." Matilda raised a finger.

"Sunsets, too." Gabby shrugged. "On a nice cement patio."

"Lowry!" called a server in the front.

"That's our to-go order." Chip pointed in the other direction. "See y'all later."

"Love you. And nice to meet you, Morgan," Gabby said, before turning back to Matilda and Jared for the next thing on the to-do list.

"You know, If William falls through, I'm sure Chip would drop everything in a heartbeat to be your plus one."

Gabby looked over at Chip at the bar; he was leaning forward casually, in conversation. He couldn't go anywhere without being stopped. It was his mannerisms, his emotions. The joy he exuded. He was the least intimidating person she knew, and yet was one of the most accomplished. All these things combined made for a person that was so fun to be around. He didn't take himself too seriously, but was a hundred percent sincere in his interactions.

He also spoke to you as if you were the only person in the room. At times, like their study session a couple of days ago, Gabby felt as if there was something more between them.

As if hearing her thoughts, Chip met her gaze for one, then two seconds. He tipped his chin up for a hello, and she did the same, in very much a friendly way.

Friends. And they would remain so.

What Matilda had said about Chip might be true, but Gabby hoped that her suspicions about William ghosting her were wrong. Because that wouldn't simply mean that she would be without a date.

It would mean that maybe, there was a part of her that was unlovable enough to be ghosted.

Chapter Four

Seventeen days until the wedding

Gabby uncovered the pink crystal from its paper wrapping and inspected its sparkling rough edges.

"It's beautiful, don't you think?" Willa passed her from behind while carrying a basket of organic towels that were rolled and tied with twine.

"It's gorgeous." Gabby laid the crystal upon a lace doily on a glass shelf, where she'd been unpacking inventory for Willa's shop, Light. Surrounded by soothing ambient music, lush greenery, and subtle scents, the shop was lit bright by soft white lightbulbs and the sun beaming through the large windows.

Outside, however, was another story. From where Gabby stood, she spied a line of shoppers waiting for the doors to open for Willa's annual spring sale.

"What's this crystal for anyway?" Gabby turned the rock just so, and the diffused rays cast a pretty glow.

"Healing." Willa met her eyes. "Emotional healing."

"Ugh. I think I need twelve of these in my bedroom alone."

Willa laughed, took her place behind the counter, and began to tidy. Her outfit of the day was an ecru, long-sleeved lace top over an ankle-length skirt. Her braids were loose and long, and her face was bare of makeup. "Wanna talk about it?"

Gabby sighed. "There's nothing to talk about. Except for how this place is going to be empty by the end of today, and how gorg you look."

"Thank you, but you're changing the topic. That was a pretty loaded no." She glanced at the clock on the wall. "We've got three minutes before I have to open those doors."

"Which means three minutes to get all this stuff out." Gabby gestured at the box at her feet, which still had a dozen things to unwrap.

Willa bent down to grab another package. "I can't tell you how grateful I am that you're helping me out this morning. Ugh, it's the third time this week that Arwen called in sick." She shook her head.

"Is it not working out?"

"If she was any other person, she would have been out on her butt months ago. But how do you fire your stepsister?"

"Sounds like drama."

"Exactly. I'm just glad my mom's coming in to help with the register. So please keep my mind off it and tell me why you've been so quiet all morning."

Gabby took two wrapped packages this time and worked to loosen the paper. "I'm not quiet. I've been busy."

"You do understand that I'm an empath. I can intuit. You're full of misspent energy."

"I'm not the only one. Save it for your customers." Gabby rolled her eyes with a grin against the discomfort that had lodged in her chest.

Willa's face softened, though still exhibited disbelief. "Uh-huh. Sure."

Three days now, three days with no contact from William.

Had she imagined this whole relationship?

Had she assumed that there was more to them than just friendship?

She'd been grateful that Willa had called with an SOS this morning. Gabby couldn't stay in her house another minute. If her professional life hadn't depended on the use of her smartphone, which reminded her by the minute that her love life was in shambles, she would have chucked it in the garbage.

"Done!" Gabby unwrapped the last of the crystals. "You fix it the way you want, and I'll take this box to the back."

"All righty. Thank you."

Gabby meandered to the other side of the shop, passing stacks of homemade soap of varying colors and scents. She breathed in the momentary solitude before tossing the empty box in the recycling bin outside.

Upon reentry, she heard giggling through the front windows. There was one shopper unabashedly peering in, hands cupped around their eyes.

"Are you sure that you're only selling natural-wellness items? Even for a spring sale, this turnout is a little excessive," Gabby asked.

Willa grinned. "I'm also selling magic."

"No, really."

"Really." Willa winked and placed a silver dollar-sized circle tin on the counter. "I advertised free product for everyone that comes in this weekend. While supplies last."

The round craft label read: Magic Body Butter.

"Oooo." Gabby unscrewed the container, and the sweet smell of lavender wafted out. She scooped a glob onto her fingernail and rubbed it against the back of her hand, and it melted exactly like its namesake. "Ah, it's luxurious."

"Glad you think so. It has magnesium for stress relief, and for sleep. I have a couple more tweaks to make. I think the scent is a little too strong, so I'll need to work on that, but I'll be able to mass-produce it soon. Thanks to Chip."

"Chip? Should I be offended that you didn't say anything to me about it?"

"Aw, honey, I'm sorry I haven't mentioned it sooner. I wanted to keep it under wraps until I was sure that it would be my next step. Chip offered to invest in Light, for me to expand. He's the only one who's not trying to charge me an arm and a leg in interest. If the body butter is received well, I may take him up on it." She shut the container and placed it into Gabby's palm. "Rub it into your calves and feet before you go to bed and let me know what you think. I want feedback of all sorts. Good, bad, and ugly. So…now will you say what's wrong with you?"

"It's not important. Here you are, doing your thing with Chip as a benefactor. It makes me sound like a brat."

A knock sounded from the front door. The time was exactly 9:00 a.m.

"Ignore them." Willa hadn't taken her eyes off Gabby. "Keep going."

She swallowed her pride. "William hasn't texted in three days."

Willa's jaw slackened. "Three days."

Gabby nodded. "I don't know what to think."

"*I* know what to think. That guy? Lower than scum." Her expression hardened. "Have you kicked his ass to the curb?"

"I can't do that if he doesn't respond."

"That's not true. What you need to do is simply end it. You take control of this situation. You can force the closure." Voice shaking, she added, "It's the worst kind of disrespect, and no one deserves it. I'm so sorry this is happening." She leaned in to hug her. "Are you okay? Why didn't you tell me sooner?"

"I was hoping he would call with some legit reason." Gabby looked away. "And I'm okay, I think. Mostly, I'm a little jealous. It seems like everyone has their person."

"What are you talking about? Bailey and Chip are single."

"Yes, but they have their passions, their *things*."

"And wedding planning isn't your passion? The way you work hard for your clients—it's inspiring. Where do you think I get my oomph when I feel like I can't keep all of it up? I look at you, I look at Bailey. At Chip. You have your work."

She shrugged. "I don't know. I'm feeling...stuck." Love. Career. It all seemed to be slowing down.

And yet, Gabby had no right to complain. Her resources were innumerable, and friends and family were all around her. If one took a snapshot of her life, they would say that Gabby had everything a person could ask for.

Then again, she knew from her work around couples, in running the social media for the B & B, that not everything people saw was the full truth.

"It's alright to feel stuck sometimes." Willa squeezed Gabby's wrist. "I think I know where this is coming from. Your test. Then this thing with William. It's a lot. But you're a total person, you know? And not all parts of you have to be planned out and perfect."

"Easy to say, when it's what I do for a living."

"And yet, weddings are not real life."

Willa was right, and Gabby nodded despite not feeling much better. What else was she to do at this moment but concede? Not only was she sick of her thoughts, but Light's spring sale was also a big event, and she wasn't going to mope when what Willa needed was encouragement and a boost.

Another knock sounded.

"You'd better open that door before they kick it down," Gabby said.

Willa rested her hands on her forearms. "I don't care about them. They can wait. They're getting free product. Are you good?"

"I mean, yeah."

"Yeah, like, for real?"

She looked into her friend's dark eyes. Eyes that reflected anticipation for her big day.

Gabby would not make this day about her. She smiled. "For real."

"Okay."

"Thank you for listening. But also, I'm proud of you." She hugged her friend and held her tight. "Love you."

"Love you, too." Willa stepped back and heaved a breath. "Here we go."

When Willa opened the door, a wave of shoppers pushed through, bombarding the space. Willa's eyes widened gleefully, then she jumped in to help someone with their purchase.

Gabby helped with customers until Willa's mother arrived. And when she stepped out of the shop, she bumped into a body encased in flannel—a red-and-blue flannel so familiar that she knew exactly which button was on the verge of being lost. Looking up, she met the dark eyes of Nathan.

Since they broke up a year ago, she'd been able to avoid Nathan. His kelly green BMW was easy enough to spot— Nathan had an affinity for fast cars and motorcycles—and he'd preferred to drive his BMW on his numerous business trips.   Those trips had been a sore spot in their relationship.

It hadn't been the fact that he'd been away a lot when they were dating.

Okay, yes, she'd hated that he was physically not at her side, but it was the fact that when he was gone, he was absent.

It was clear that his career came first, and the more she demanded of his time, the more he withheld it.

Aside from his recent texts and that phone call, this was the closest she'd stood next to him in a year.

She held her breath, anticipating the stab of pain. And also to prevent her from smelling his cologne, which she swore was an aphrodisiac.

"Whoa." His voice was a rumble. "Gab, hey."

"Hey." Gabby exhaled, and to her surprise, she didn't even feel a prick. She felt...okay.

His eyes crinkled at the corners.

"What are you doing here?" she asked.

He gestured toward the window, where Mrs. Paul was inspecting a crystal. "I'm here in support of Mom's favorite kind of therapy."

"Ah. You might be waiting a while. Willa's got a lot in that tiny shop," Gabby said, though despite her best efforts, she felt awkward. It was the way he was looking at her so expectantly, with a slight grin on his face. "What?"

"It's just, I don't think I've been this close to you in a long time. And after our last phone call...it's nice. I've missed this."

For a beat, and under his gaze, the gates around her heart unshackled. Nathan had been her first real love that counted. He knew parts of her that were unknown to anyone else. Likewise, she knew his inner workings, his pet peeves.

With Nathan, she didn't have to explain her motivations, her thoughts. He just *knew*.

I've missed it, too.

If Gabby allowed it, if she simply made one tiny gesture, they could be together again. It would be so easy. Just as she'd done in the past, they would be on again and their sleepovers would commence, and within a week half of her things would be in his dresser drawers at his home. Then would come the expectations...expectations he couldn't live up to.

The air between them still had that spark though; his first phone call after a year of silence was the clue that he wanted her back.

Or is it a red flag?

The message from her inner self swooped in and she shut and double padlocked the gates. The jarring image snapped Gabby from the memories of how they used to be.

Nathan was good at this—at the wooing, the charm. The distance he stood, exactly what tone to take with her. But just because they'd shared a couple of texts didn't mean that they were fully back to being friends.

"Well, I've gotta go." She donned a thin-lipped smile.

A gentle hand on her elbow stopped her. "I RSVP'd to Jared and Matilda's wedding. I was wondering if you'd consider…"

No. He was going to ask her to be his plus-one.

She slipped the phone out of her coat. "Oh, my gosh. Sorry. Someone's buzzing." Looking at the screen, which showed zero notifications, she said, "I've really gotta go. Crisis. You know how it is."

"Or we can get coffee," he told her.

"Okay, 'bye!" Gabby walked backward, the scene of the two of them at the wedding materializing in her head. Of Nathan, dashing in his slim-fit suit, with her in his arms.

They would be a sight to be behold, and the temptation was there. But there was no doubt that inside it would feel all wrong.

Chip headed into the doors of Cross Trails Hiking for his scheduled shift, irritation clambering up his neck. It had started out as a promising day. He'd checked into the senior center, and the contractors had arrived on time. The bar had canceled his shift for tonight, a welcome respite, since he was nursing a couple of blisters from his last hike.

He'd intended to check in at Light. Willa had mentioned giving away her product to be tested by her customers, and he'd wanted to be there to witness their reactions. He was keen to grow his portfolio, and the Magic Body Butter would be his first investment in wellness. His mother had been all about self-care, and if she had been alive, she would have been a patron at Light, no doubt.

When Willa had mentioned that Gabby had volunteered to help out, Chip had moved in double time to get there early.

And then, he'd seen *them*.

Or more specifically, he'd witnessed the way Nathan was looking at Gabby, with his determined, I-want-her way. And Gabby, despite not giving him too much of her time, had held the expression of someone who yearned for him.

The pain had been swift, landing solidly in his gut. And instead of interrupting them, he'd turned right around and hiked straight to work. It had been pure instinct, though part of him cursed himself for walking away.

Cross Trails Hiking's front area was a brightly lit room, and it lifted his spirits. From every free space on the wall hung backpacks and clothing. On the floor were stands of clothing and circular displays carrying maps and brochures. Everything screamed adventure, travel, and exploration. Totally different than the vibes of Mountain Rush, or the environment of the senior center.

Though, he couldn't tell which he liked the best. To have different interests meant learning something every day. It also meant not having to dwell, or to put his eggs in one basket. And if work in one place was in a slump, he could still find happiness elsewhere.

"Hi, Chip!" Sydney, one of Cross Trail's local college workers greeted him. Though a self-professed hater of the outdoors, she was the most reliable part-timer the shop employed. She was currently dusting the windowsills.

"Morning. Gonna check in with the boss before my shift."

Chip passed right on by, heading to the back office, and brushed against the waterproof coats. Cruz had sent a text that he'd wanted a quick chat with Chip.

"Um, I wouldn't if I were you…" she said.

And much too late, because Chip had already opened the office door, to find Cruz Forrester and Eva Espiritu locked in a kiss. Cruz's hands clutched the sides of her shirt, while Eva's fingers were buried in his hair.

Chip shut the door, his heart thudding. He turned and grinned at Sydney, who was shaking her head.

Since Cruz and Eva's romance had bloomed around Christmastime, it had been a nonstop PDA fest around town.

"It's weird, right?" Sydney whispered. She was absent-mindedly dusting the books.

He walked up to her, lowering his voice. "What's weird?"

"They're like, *old.*"

Chip pursed his lips to keep from laughing. The two were in their fifties. "They're not *that* old."

"They're as old as my parents."

He considered it. "That's fair. But, this is all new for them. They're in love."

"I guess." She grimaced as if she'd eaten a sour candy.

From behind them, the door opened, and the two walked out nonchalantly. Cruz's dark hair stood in spikes, his flannel misbuttoned, so that one panel hung lower than the other, and Eva's shirt was untucked and wrinkled.

"Be cool," Chip told Sydney.

"Are you kidding? I'm fully pretending that it didn't happen."

But when Eva passed by, she didn't care to hide the grin on her face. She raised a hand and wiggled a wave. "Have a nice day, Sydney."

"See you, Ms. Eva," Sydney answered.

Cruz nodded after the shop's door closed, though he still had a dreamy smile, and said, "I'm ready for you."

Chip entered the office.

Cruz cleared his throat. Looking down, he startled and rebuttoned his shirt. "Sorry about that."

"You're good, boss."

"Eva and I are going to have to be a little more discreet. It's just that sometimes…" A grin snaked onto his lips.

Love. It was definitely love.

If only it was that easy for Chip. Not that Cruz and Eva's relationship was trouble-free, by any means. Chip had had a front-row seat to how they got together. Each had their own commitment issues to overcome, but their friendship in that trail notebook was what brought them together in the end.

If it hadn't been true, Chip would have believed it was fiction.

Some days, Chip had wished that kind of luck would happen to him. Though, it wasn't for the lack of trying. Dating apps, blind dates, church groups—he was down for all of it.

Sadly, he hadn't been able to get past that elusive third date.

Sure, he'd had flings. But that wasn't what he was looking for. He wanted love, the kind he witnessed around him that had markers of forever. Friendship, attraction, respect. And fun.

There was only one person he could be that for him. Except that it was all one-sided.

And the fact that she was off-limits.

Cruz frowned. "Is everything okay?"

Chip woke from his thoughts and hung his coat. "Yep. Fine."

"You're a guy that's usually smiling a hundred percent of the time."

Chip wiggled his lips. Hadn't he been smiling?

"I mean, a real smile. Right know you've got this expression like you're in...pain, I guess."

Chip thought on it—there was no point in lying. "What do you do when people you care about continue to make the same mistakes?"

"What do you mean, like employees?"

He shook his head. "Personal. I've got a friend who does the same thing repeatedly, expecting different results. And I don't know what to do about it. It frankly pisses me off."

In fact, it was pissing Chip off doubly, because both Nathan and Gabby were doing what he'd warned them not to do.

"Because you've given them ample advice, but they continue to do the opposite?"

Chip nodded.

Cruz sat, inhaling deeply. "Well, as someone who did *all* the things I wasn't supposed to do, and who has a sibling who picked up the pieces, I'm going to bluntly say you gotta let them do their thing." His expression was stern. Despite the softness he'd showed toward Eva a few minutes ago, this version was pure business, if not stoic. Though, as one of the heirs of Forrester Watches, Cruz had had to live under pressure.

Chip hung on to his every word.

Cruz continued, "My sister was intent on guiding me. She was right to do so, because I was lost, man. But I insisted on my way, and even in the supposed maturity of midlife, when I should've known better, I avoided my sister and my mother because I couldn't bear to be under their scrutiny. When in fact, all they'd wanted was for me to be happy.

"All that to say, you can't force someone into doing what you think is the right thing for them. But *you* have the choice to pick up the pieces, to set boundaries. Attempting to control their experience will only drive a wedge between you."

Chip nodded, allowing the man's words to sink in. Cruz was asking him to do the absolute hardest thing, which was once more to sit in between his two best friends, and wait for the aftermath. "Thanks. I'll think on it."

"Great. For what it's worth, I wanted to give you some props on how you've stepped up here at Cross Trails. First, being our acting manager last winter when I was gone, and then leading all these extra hikes."

"Thank you. I enjoy it."

"You've brought in some new hiker blood, also. Nathan signed up as a volunteer for trail maintenance."

"Wow." Chip had mentioned to Nathan how much effort it took to maintain the trails around town, and in the past, Nathan had passed on the opportunity.

The fact that he changed his mind impressed Chip.

"That says a lot about what you've taught him about the Appalachian Trail. And since we're gearing up for spring hikes, I'm looking to add to our trail guide team. Would you recommend Nathan?"

"You're asking me?"

Cruz smiled. "Of course. Look. I know you could be doing other things besides working here. And still, you show up for your shifts, as though you couldn't buy out this place yourself."

Chip looked away.

"You don't have to be shy about it. I see some of myself in you. You don't do things just to do them—you try to find purpose."

Chip's sucked in a breath. It's not often he received validation for how he moved in the world. Often times, people were confuddled, and some poked fun at it.

For a beat, he hoped he was making his mother proud, wherever she was. "I do."

"It's why I trust you. So, a recommendation from you to add Nathan to the team is important."

"Okay." Chip took in the compliment, as overwhelming as it was, and said, without hesitation, "Nathan would be a great addition. He would be a good steward to the trails."

"Great, I'll ask him then. Though, if you could keep it quiet until I can chat with him myself." Cruz stood and started for the door, then hesitated. "With what you mentioned, about folks not listening to you and feeling frustrated by it? I want you to know that I see the good work you do, with just being you. The community sees it, too. Whatever thing you're wading through right now, just remember that people have their free will, and you have yours."

A knock interrupted them; the door creaked open. "Chip? Someone's here to speak to you."

Cruz beamed. "See? You're a wanted man."

Only, at the moment, Chip wished he was wanted by the right person.

But Cruz was right: everyone had a choice, and at some point, Chip needed to make his in how involved he was going to be in the relationship between Gabby and Nathan.

Chip stepped out of the office and Nathan was waiting for him at the cashier's table.

Speak of the devil.

"Chippie!" Nathan met him in the middle—he had a spring to his step.

"Hey." Resisting a full body cringe, his gaze wandered over Nathan's shoulder. Had Gabby followed him in? Were they an item now?

The thought of them as a couple brought on a wave of disappointment, followed by a swarm of guilt. Nathan was his best friend. Without him, Chip wouldn't be where he was today. When they were kids, it was Nathan who pushed him, who challenged him. Nathan was light-years smarter than Chip, faster on the track, quicker on the uptake, and wittier, and he brought Chip into whatever adventure he had been up to.

Including his love life with Gabby.

But it was friendship above all, right? Which meant Cruz was right: Chip had to make a choice.

Chip had to let his heavy feeling of jealousy go. Yes, he had a crush on Gabby, but he would never risk her friendship, nor his with Nathan.

"Bro, did you hear what I said?"

Nathan's face sharpened in front of him. Chip shook his head. "No. Sorry. Not enough coffee. Repeat?"

"I talked with Gabby. Saw her at Light."

"Oh?" His voice cracked.

"And…it was alright." His gaze rose to the ceiling and a grin graced his lips. "I have a good feeling about this. We've got a lot to work out, but she spoke to me and it's a start."

"I don't know. There's William…" Chip hedged, though he guessed the guy hadn't yet called Gabby. She would have said so.

"I'm not worried about that guy. He's not here, is he?"

Damn.

"I'm going to go slow, though. I thought about what we talked about the other day. I want to do it right this time, for the both of us."

"Well, that's good." It was a sliver of consolation, even if foreboding rushed through him. Because Gabby had fallen in love with Nathan at his best. Would she again?

Nathan's gaze was in the middle distance, no doubt envisioning their new life together. "Oh, I also need a pair of hiking poles."

The change of subject was whiplash.

"Oh, sure." Chip headed over to the wall that showcased their selection, scrambling to orient himself.

Then again, he was supposed to be good at this, at pivoting.

So he did what he did best—helped people—though inside he wished he could find a way to help himself.

Chapter Five

Sixteen days until the wedding

Chip's thoughts spiraled as he tried to decipher what was on the laptop screen in front of him. Instead, he was overcome by a nagging loop of words:

You need to make a choice.

"You're frowning." Gabby raised an eyebrow.

It was a glorious and rare seventy-degree afternoon—Chip and Gabby had decided to study outside under his covered back porch.

Chip refocused on a construction invoice for the senior center. He hadn't been able to shake the two drastic conversations he'd had yesterday at Cross Trails. "It's called working. Which is what you should be doing."

"I'm studying, see?" She fanned a fistful of index cards. "But there's something up with you."

"Are you sure that something's not up with you? I mean, you're wearing glasses."

"Shut up," she whimpered. "I took a midday nap and my eyes were so dry." She stuck out her lower lip and touched her clear white frames.

In his opinion, seeing her in this state of undress was sexy as hell.

That was superseded by what she'd said, though. She was

a diligent, from wake-up to bedtime, worker. "You took a nap? When does that happen?"

"I know. So much thinking these days. My brain hurts from it."

Had she been thinking of William, or Nathan? Then again, he didn't want to know. He shrugged. "I kind of like the disheveled look."

"Don't judge me, Chip Lowry. You take me as I am."

I do was what he wanted to say. He bit his cheek instead and kept a steady expression. "I draw the line at morning breath."

"So you'd make me brush my teeth before you kissed me in the morning?"

"Gab, you eat tons of garlic with your meals. That's a totally different story."

Lies. Chip would take Gabby, garlic breath and all.

She frowned and hovered a hand over her mouth, smelling her own breath.

He cackled.

"Brat." She picked up a jellybean from the bowl next to her and threw it at him, smiling.

"That's a waste of a perfectly delicious Very Cherry."

Her jaw dropped. "How did you know what flavor it was?"

He pointed to his nose. "Never fails me."

She peered at him, then her fingers made their way back to the keyboard, and back to studying she went.

Crisis averted. He wanted today to be a simple study session and not a conversation about a love life that didn't involve him.

"Hold up." She peered at him. "You distracted me."

Dammit. "From what?"

"From telling me what's up with you."

"Do you know what's up? You doing everything possible not to study."

Her shoulders hunched. "Ugh. I swear I'm trying."

"Were you this distracted during undergrad?"

"No, but it's because I wasn't dealing with boy drama."

Here it was again. Chip took a deep breath and refused to bite. "Now, you're dealing with me, so eyes on your notes, please."

"Scrooge."

Just then, his phone buzzed with a text from Nathan: Cruz asked me to be a trail guide.

Chip replied, Awesome.

He told me you recommended. I won't let you down.

Never had a doubt. Congrats.

Gabby tapped the back of his laptop screen. "*Now*, who isn't focused? You have invoices to pay out and quarterly taxes due."

He set down the phone. "Yeah, yeah."

They were silent for minutes except for the sound of their clacking keyboards. Chip paid off a couple of invoices, and logged into his tax-preparation software to update the numbers.

"Okay, so Nathan and I talked again yesterday. But before you freak out, I stepped away before…"

Her words tore his attention from the screen, and his heart rocketed into a sprint.

"Before what?" he asked.

"I think he was trying to ask me out for coffee, and I ran. To be honest, I was nervous. Though I don't know why."

"Because you're interested?" He held his breath.

"I don't know." She dug another jellybean from the bowl. Cotton candy, this time, from the looks of it. She popped it into her mouth. "There's William. Or…not."

He frowned. "So he hasn't gotten back to you."

"No."

"Are you…okay?" Her expression was unreadable.

"Honestly? My thoughts on William have been up and down. I go from being upset, to not even caring, to wondering what's wrong with me."

"Nothing's wrong with you."

"That's not what my aunties are going to think when I show up without a plus-one."

His phone buzzed. Nathan again: Should I pretreat my clothes before the next hike? It's getting warm. Ticks scare the hell out of me.

I would pre-treat. I can help you do it.

Then, in front of him, Gabby picked up her phone. The corner of her lips ticked up in a sort-of grin.

His gaze toggled between Gabby and his phone. Was Nathan texting her too?

She spoke. "I don't know. Is it so bad to hear him out? I can't avoid him. You're friends with him, and so is Jared, and so many other mutuals. If we can find a way to be civil acquaintances…"

Then, another text from Nathan: Speaking of helping. Help a guy out? Put in a good word for me with Gab? I want things to be different this time. I really miss her.

Chip suspected that Nathan would broach the subject once more. And each and every time he thought about it, it boiled down to what Cruz had said.

Who was Chip to be the gatekeeper? Gabby and Nathan were grown adults, and although frustration seeped through his pores, he leaned into the truth of it all.

"It's your choice," Chip said to Gabby, which was the most honest thing he could say, and then texted to Nathan: Just did.

"It is, isn't it." She bit her lip, eyes down to her phone.

"I just don't want either one of you to get hurt." Also honest. Sort of.

"No, I get that. I don't want to get hurt either," she whispered. "But you have to trust me too, that I know better this time around."

A text flew in from Nathan: TY

A second later, Gabby's phone buzzed.

As she texted, her lips wiggled into a smile. She ran her fingers through her hair, as if she was getting ready to go out.

Chip let out a sigh of resignation. As he watched Gabby toggle from texting to writing notes, he forced himself to focus back into his invoices, to utter failure. What Gabby had said weighed on his shoulders.

He didn't want to be that kind of friend who passed judgement, the kind who was simply protective because he had ulterior motives for her.

After a while he said, "I trust you."

She looked up from her screen and smile. "Good."

The back door flew open, startling the two of them. His father stood on the threshold, wearing his usual casual slacks, button-down shirt, and cardigan. He'd spent the morning at the senior center, and he never failed to look like a dapper Mr. Rogers. "I can't find her."

"Can't find who?" Chip asked.

"The dog. I haven't seen her today. She looked to be in a bad state yesterday and wouldn't come close. I feel it in my bones. She had her puppies." The worry lines on his face deepened.

"Aw, Mr. Lowry, how can I help?" Gabby asked.

"We have to find her."

"Dad. Where would we even start?" Chip had to squash this idea fast. It wasn't their responsibility to take care of this dog. What were they going to do, launch a search party for a dog that didn't want to be helped? "Why don't we call animal control again and let them know? They can do a drive-through. They're way more equipped than we are."

George peered off in the distance, not hearing. "I bet she's in the woods behind us. It's where she walks up from every time I call her."

"I'll look with you, Mr. Lowry," Gabby offered.

"I'll get my sneakers on." George reentered the house.

Chip jumped to his feet. "No, wait. I'll look for the dog with Dad. Just hang out here, Gab." This had the potential of taking up their entire afternoon, and of ending badly, with his father upset. Gabby had more important things on her to-do list.

"No way. I'm helping." She shut down her laptop and stacked her things into a pile; she did the same with his. "Wait for me here while I put this away."

The door slapped open and shut, with Gabby entering, and George stepping out.

"I hope she's okay," his father said.

Chip hadn't seen him this worried about anyone or anything since… Since his mother.

With that thought, Chip softened. "I hope so, too, Dad."

Gabby then bounded outside, with windbreakers for him and George, along with her own coat, and three water bottles. Chip wanted to hug her with how thoughtful she was.

"Thank you." His father shrugged on the jacket. Chip did the same, and they trudged through the backyard and out the gate.

Chip's house backed up to a thick wall of maple and ash trees, and mountain laurel bushes. And unlike the well-trodden trails in the area, what they faced were obstacles of underbrush and fallen trees. Looking up at the sky, at the sun that was headed down, Chip worried his lip. One should never underestimate the dark, the cold, and the way one's sense of direction could play tricks. "Don't go out too far. Everyone has their phone, right?"

"I don't have my phone," his father said.

"We can hang together Mr. Lowry." Gabby linked her arm around his. "And we won't go too far."

Chip nodded. "Okay."

"I named her Lucky," George said, though he darted his eyes away from Chip.

You're my lucky charm was what George used to say to Fern, a statement that Chip often had heard growing up.

He hadn't realized the dog meant that much to his dad. Although looking back at how hard he'd worked to gain her trust, he should have known. Chip supposed he was in denial for what was inevitable, which was giving this stray dog a home.

"Let's start walking," Chip said.

Together, George and Gabby went one way; Chip picked another way to traverse. He was grateful that cell-phone service was strong throughout the city and its outskirts. It made the nearby hiking trails much less risky than they used to be. Now, it was as easy as dropping a pin of one's GPS location for someone else to find you.

"Lucky!" Chip called out and whistled. Stepping over and sidestepping branches and rocks, he concentrated on sounding as fun as possible. "Here, Lucky! Wanna treat?"

Did the dog even know what a treat was? How had it been able to survive this long without an owner?

Or had George been caring for her all this time?

Ten, fifteen, then twenty minutes passed while Chip trudged under the thick canopy of trees. Birds sang in a confusing cadence above him; the leaves rustled incessantly, and for a beat, he wished for silence.

What if he'd already passed Lucky? And what if she'd barked for help, and he hadn't heard.

Chip texted Gabby: How are things?

Nothing yet. He's really worried.

That alone was enough for Chip to keep going, to peel his eyes for any movement. Would Lucky have ventured out this far? What if she'd headed toward the road instead?

No, he couldn't think that way, couldn't imagine what that kind of heartbreak could do to his father. George had already lost so much.

Chip had, too.

Sympathy for his father roared through him. Chip kept busy for his mother's legacy, true, but there was another secret reason. Having a hand in everything meant that he could keep life light, that when things got vulnerable, he could move on to the next project.

Was his father like him, a guy who kept busy because it was sometimes hard to dwell in what he'd lost?

And who was Chip to gatekeep George's happiness, as he'd tried with Gabby?

Chip's breath was loud in his ears. He halted and willed his heart to slow. No, he couldn't do that to George, to Gabby, and even Nathan. He would need to trust people, and would need to trust that everything would work out. That maybe, having a dog wouldn't be so bad, and that there was love out there for him.

And then he heard it, a whine. A dog's whine; then, an exhausted howl.

"Lucky?" he called out.

Another howl, this time deep and sad. Chip followed the noise until he came upon a couple of downed trees. Where they intersected, along with fallen branches, had created shelter from where the sound of mewling grew louder.

Chip approached the space slowly—it could be anything under there. "Lucky?"

A nose poked out of the leaves; then a dog's face with its teeth bared.

Chip halted in place.

In his eagerness to help his father, he'd forgotten to ask George how friendly Lucky really was.

He called Gabby.

"Hey," she said.

"I found her. I'll drop a pin."

"He found her," she said to his father. Then, to Chip, she said, "Be there soon. Love you."

"Love you." He worked quickly to drop a pin of his location, and remained still. Lucky, though silent, eyed him warily.

Then, from the underside of the dog, came the nose of a puppy, and then the body of another. The brown body of one, the white body of another. White? Then, faces peeked out. They were all boxers, with the telltale nose and square face, but none were Lucky's fawn color. Chip counted five: one white, one a reddish brown with a black spot over one eye, a reddish brown with a white face and white paws, and the last two a dark striped color. "Lucky, who the heck did you shack up with?"

Lucky barked, as if reminding him to mind his own business.

"Alright. I get it. I've got my secrets. too."

Lucky's face turned to the right a second before Chip heard footsteps.

"Is it her?" George yelled. "Lucky?"

The dog stepped out, eager but protective. The nub of her tail wiggled, and her mouth dropped into a smile.

"Looks like at least five puppies," Chip said over his shoulder, turning fully as he saw Gabby hop over rocks with a smile on her face.

"Good work, Chip!" Her cheeks were pink from the chill. "Thank goodness. You could have totally walked past them."

To his surprise, she threw her arms around him. He gently patted her on the back, though what he wanted was to pick her up fully and wrap her into his arms. "It's no big deal," he said.

"It is." Whispering into the space between them, she said, "You aren't exactly a fan of the dog."

"I didn't want my dad to freak out." Looking over her shoulder, he watched as George stroked Lucky tenderly on the nose.

"It's what I love about you—you do so much for others."

Was that a good thing, though? Sometimes Chip didn't know. At the moment, nothing seemed to be going his way, and others benefited from him but not the other way around.

Then again, was that selfish? What was the point of having, of being, if it wasn't to help others? Fern had given, volunteered, and loved others, and insisted that doing so gave one purpose.

But when did it become overkill?

Gabby did a double take, and Chip followed her gaze. George had already scooped two of the puppies into his arms. Next to him, Lucky was standing, unafraid.

The dog trusted his father.

"Are you two done yapping over there?" George said. "We'd better get these dogs back to the house."

Good ol' George.

Chip handed Gabby a puppy and tucked the final two into

his chest. With the warmth of their tiny bodies in his hands, he held them closer to his heart.

God help him. He was bringing six dogs into his house.

Early that evening, Gabby strolled the aisles of Pet Zone, buoyed by the buzz of planning out Lucky and her litter's new temporary home at Chip's. While pushing an overflowing cart, she skimmed an online article on her phone on how to prepare for a litter of puppies.

This was her specialty—multitasking while under deadline—because Lucky and her puppies were running free in Chip's open-concept living-room area and it would only be a matter of time before the mess would make its way to the rest of the house. She and Chip had to get back ASAP to contain the animals and give them a safe place to roam.

Gabby thought aloud. "I think the family room is the perfect place to set the puppies up. The floors are laminate, so it'll be easier to clean. Windows to air the room out. We can't forget the gates, though…"

She turned to confer with Chip, though found that he wasn't behind her. "Chip?"

"Right here." He came from around the corner with a stack of puppy pads, and he tossed them into the cart.

"Great idea! That wasn't on my list."

"Dad's been researching, too. He sent over an article." He shared his phone screen with her. "I can't believe we're actually doing this. I have no idea how to take care of puppies."

"Don't worry. I've got you. I even bookmarked videos in the car." Gabby thought back to the one and only time her family had had dogs in the house. It was so long ago—she had been in elementary school. But since then, their mother hadn't allowed pets. It had been enough for her to take care of Gabby and Frankie as a single mom, so a dog would have been overwhelming. "The good thing is that the puppies can only go so far for a couple of weeks, and Lucky won't stray. Plus, it's just until they can get placed. You know how much Peak folks love puppies."

"But until then." He looked askance at the puppy pads. "It's going to be a messy endeavor."

"Until then, your dad is going to be the sweetest adoptive grandfather," she reminded him, though leaned into him, anyway, and wrapped an arm around his. She squeezed it tightly while recalling Chip carrying two puppies, like a proud papa.

"What's that for?"

"Just because," she stated, attempting to properly convey what she was feeling. The closest thing she could liken it to was *nakakagigil*, which is the Tagalog word conveying "thrill" in a physical manner. She wanted to squeeze and kiss the living daylights out of Chip, who had been so against taking in Lucky, now decidedly housing Lucky *and* her puppies.

Who does that?

Chip does that.

But it wasn't a surprise to her either. What Chip did was the cherry on top of the kind of man he was:

A man she loved being around.

A man she could speak to honestly.

A man who, in his acceptance of these puppies, took on another quality, of a nurturer and protector.

"You're such a good guy," she said, words escaping her.

An eyebrow rose. "I'm glad you think so."

"I mean it." She tried again. "George was so worried, and you completely set your rules aside. I wish there were more people like you around."

"Someone is getting a little sappy."

"How can you not? You're a new dad. A fur-papa."

He winced. "Please stop. In fact, I'm going to pretend I didn't hear that. I've got gates to price."

As he walked away, Gabby laughed. Chip was also incapable of being serious, and she marveled at how he had readily accepted this sudden turn in their day. How he hadn't dragged his feet at opening his arms to this massive change.

Had Nathan had half the self-awareness Chip had when they were going out... Had William had an ounce of Chip's loyalty...

She pushed the cart to the aisle Chip was browsing in and watched him, at his focus on comparing two kinds of gates.

Had either man remained as thoughtful...

She wouldn't have dealt with so much drama and pain.

Chip lugged boxes to the cart. "These should do."

She shoved thoughts of Nathan and William away. "What else is on the list?"

"Some wet food for Lucky. Apparently kibble isn't enough because she's nursing. Doc gave a list of suggested brands."

"Then we should get it." She led with the shopping cart toward the refrigerated section. As she parked to one side and Chip examined the dog-food packages, she reached into her pocket for her phone.

Her ringer was off, and she'd missed a text from Nathan: I'd love to meet for coffee sometime this week. If you're free.

She'd forgotten that they had been in the middle of a text conversation while helping to settle Lucky in the house. It had been a kerfuffle, entailing moving furniture and creating a space for the puppies. It meant petting the puppies one at a time—Gabby couldn't resist. It also meant witnessing Chip call the vet and animal control to inform them of the situation, and accepting responsibility for the puppies for the time being, and writing up lists.

Of watching Chip at his best. Had there not been her real

life to contend with, she would have stayed in that dining room the rest of the afternoon and evening.

While Gabby had first been interested in what Nathan had to say on text, it had since dissipated from the day's commotion.

Now, this—*this* was exciting her. Finding the right dog food for Lucky. Spending time with a person she could laugh and be vulnerable with, and whom she could trust.

Gabby slipped the phone back in her pocket; she would answer Nathan later. She'd learned that she'd needed to slow her roll, anyway. Her planner personality dictated every part of her life, and she had a tendency to jump into things with gusto.

Maybe that was what she needed to change. Maybe she needed to chill out. Maybe she was too focused on making everything perfect, as Willa had said. Then again, this trait was what brought her here today, so shouldn't it be on other people to accept her as who she was?

Chip was still digging through the dog food in the refrigerator. A frown creased his forehead, a rarity; Gabby was entranced by how sexy that was.

She knocked on the other side of the door, snagging Chip's attention. She made a heart with her hands, to see what he would do.

His lips lifted into a smile.

Yeah, definitely sexy.

The next second, she caught herself.

No, don't think that way.

"I think this is it." He lifted up what looked like a tube of ground meat, his voice muted by the glass between them. "Should we pick lamb or chicken? Which is better for a lactating dog? I want to make sure she eats."

"Lemme see." She opened the door wider and joined him.

And though they stood in the full blast of the refrigerator, her temperature notched up by a degree. And then two. She had the sudden urge to wrap her arms around his torso, to feel more of his warmth against hers.

I can take you.

Chip's words from their previous study session came back to her. He had been willing to take Gabby to the wedding from the start.

She hadn't thought about that proposal since, and had chalked it up to a friend trying to make her feel better.

Had he meant it for real, though?

He looked down at her, expression turning serious for a beat. "Chicken?"

"That should be fine." Her answer came out as a breath.

"I think that's everything." Chip took the helm of the shopping cart and started out ahead of her.

Thank goodness, because she needed a moment to herself.

Chip had been part of her Peak, Virginia, history from the very beginning. As a fellow neighbor, as a fellow business owner, and as the best friend of the only man she had ever loved and had a hard time kicking out of her heart.

Chip had seen her cry over Nathan. Aside from her sister and mother, he was the only one who'd witnessed it.

Oh God, if Frankie or Eva found out that she'd given Nathan even seconds more of her time, they would be angry. When they eventually found out about William, they were sure to be disappointed.

As they would be when they discovered that she hadn't passed her test.

Sometimes her small town surprised her. Almost a week had passed and the news of her failure hadn't reached her family's ears. She just had to find the perfect time to tell them, when she was bolstered enough to endure their questioning.

As if knowing she needed a breather from her own thoughts, Chip glanced at her over his shoulder and then surreptitiously around him, and stepped onto the cart's rear chassis. Then he shot off, a foot in the air.

Gabby threw her head back in laughter, at how he was simply everything. The kind of guy any woman would be lucky to date. Ambitious but steady, funny but tender.

If only...

The thought resonated in her heart, and she stopped in her tracks.

No.

No, no, no, no.

There still existed the dreaded fact that Chip was Nathan's best friend. Gabby would never come in between their relationship; that drama belonged to the couples they watched on reality television.

Bottom line, she wouldn't allow her temperature to rise a single degree around Chip.

"Look, a treat bar." Chip stood next to an open cart, designed whimsically with a black-and-white striped awning. From far away, the treats were piled in mounds.

Chip held up a clear bag with a smile so big that the room seemed to brighten. "So many choices."

"Oh. Wow." Admittedly, the dog treats looked good enough to eat. One resembled Oreo cookies, another gingerbread. But what made her laugh was the sheer joy in her friend's eyes, especially with how much he was filling up that clear bag. "Are you planning to feed an army of dogs?"

"Lucky's eating for six! She's got to nurse those puppies. Why not give her all the good treats. You should know how important treats are." He winked at her.

A yearning grew inside of Gabby—she wanted to kiss him. Plant her lips against his, because of how well he knew her. It was just another Chip thing; he paid attention.

In her pocket, her phone buzzed, waking her from her trance.

She really needed to get it together.

"Someone's blowing up your phone," he said, tying up the bag with a twist tie. He set it into the cart.

She glanced at her phone. "It's Nathan. He asked me out for coffee."

"Oh, yeah?"

"Yep." She examined Chip's expression, and there wasn't a single trace of judgement, of hesitation, of anything remotely questionable, which had been his usual reaction to her previous mentions of Nathan.

Perhaps he was really okay with it? She didn't want to feel like she was disappointing him, too. She'd meant it when she asked him to trust her. After all, she knew better; she'd learned from her mistakes.

"Are you going to say yes?" he asked.

"I think I might."

"Okay, then." He pushed the cart toward the open cashier, then unloaded it.

With every beep of the cashier gun, Gabby's thoughts cleared. She *did* have the upper hand here with Nathan. It wouldn't be like before. "It could be good. A new chapter for him and me as people who can be together, in a good relationship."

He smiled, and dug out his wallet, though he didn't say a word.

It was good enough of a blessing.

So why did it feel like she was still settling?

Chapter Six

Fifteen days until the wedding

"I feel like you'd be settling, buying that dress."

Gabby lifted her gaze from the embroidered bodice of the Filipiniana-style dress pressed against her body, to the mirrored reflection of Frankie behind her. As usual, her big sister sported a frown.

"Why would you say that? It's gorgeous." Lavender, and sheath-cut, it was unassuming, but classic. And most importantly, the dress exhibited the best traditional feature: the butterfly sleeve.

"It's just not flashy enough."

"It's not supposed to be flashy. I'm not the bride. And for the record, you aren't, either." Gabby eyed Frankie's dress, draped over her sister's arm. It had been a fight to keep her from picking up an off-white number, and instead she'd opted for pale blue.

Talk about crisis averted.

Frankie rolled her eyes. "You can still stun at someone else's wedding. I'm not trying to get you to wear an A-line princess-cut dress like Matilda. I mean, show off those curves."

Gabby groaned under her breath and hung the dress back

up on the rod. Guess she wasn't buying it. "*You* have curves. I've got…bumps."

"Bumps that you can accentuate. Lean into the body you have, Gab. It's alright, you know."

They were at Terno, one of few Barong clothing stores in the United States. Located an hour away from Peak, it sold Filipino-inspired fashion and formal wear.

Gabby and Frankie's goals were to each find a dress that had the requisite butterfly sleeves. They had party dresses planned for the reception, but as the groom's sisters they wanted to represent their heritage for the wedding and the formal part of the reception.

With Gabby busy with wedding planning, and Frankie a working single mom, they both hadn't realized their tragic lack of wardrobe until this morning.

In true Frankie fashion, she had picked out her dress within the first half hour. But Gabby was striking out—at least, according to her sister's standards. She'd turned up her nose at everything Gabby pointed out.

Gabby was done, and hangry, and quite honestly, feeling hopeless about all of it. "What's the point, if there's no one to impress."

Frankie tsked. "We don't dress to impress others. We dress to impress ourselves."

"That's easy for you to say. You're all settled in life."

"You act like I have a foot in the grave. I'm only three years older than you."

"But you have a nine-year-old, and who knows who you have on your speed dial. Me, on the other hand…"

She raised an eyebrow. "What do you know about my speed dial?"

The fact that Frankie had latched on to that point gave Gabby pause. "Nothing, except that auntie mentioned you already have a date to the wedding, though I have no idea who it is. *And* you just gave it away. Something's up."

"I hate to bust your bubble, but there's absolutely nothing up." Her sister turned around and sifted through the dresses.

Avoidance. Interesting.

Frankie had been hush-hush about her dating life since her divorce. Scratch that—she informed her besties, but certainly not Gabby or their mother.

Gabby never pushed. Frankie had been heartbroken when she and her ex-husband, Reece, broke up. While they were amicable, with both intent on co-parenting Liam as seamlessly as possible, Frankie had changed since. She now kept her secrets locked down tight, and Gabby was comfortable giving her space.

Frankie pulled another dress from the rack, this time with a mermaid-style skirt. "How about this? The sleeves aren't quite as tall, but your booty's gonna pop."

Now, if only her sister was comfortable doing the same for her.

"I can't manage a wedding when I'm wrapped in a cocoon."

She wiggled her nose. "You're right. Hmm." Her hand shot up as she gazed in the distance. "Auntie!"

Auntie Patricia appeared from the billowing dresses. A petite Filipino woman wearing black slacks and a taupe blouse, she was the founder of Terno. And though she wasn't actually related to them, anything less than that title would have been disrespectful. The rule was simple: anyone from their parents' generation were aunties and uncles, and the generation above were treated like grandparents, or lolos and lolas.

Patricia gave the best hugs, too, which Gabby accepted wholeheartedly. "Girls! I didn't see you come in."

"What are you doing in town?" Gabby asked. Patricia

had two other Terno stores, one in California and another in New Jersey.

"My usual rounds. I just flew in from LA. So what's the occasion?"

"Our brother Jared's wedding," Frankie answered. "It's in a little over two weeks."

"Oh, my, you're running late."

"We kind of dropped the ball."

"This only means we have to make sure that we can tailor it in time." Patricia beamed. "Have you found something?"

"I have, but Gabby's trying to look like a forty-year-old. No offense."

Patricia tutted. "None taken. Besides, you have to earn this fabulousness."

Gabby giggled. She loved how confident Patricia was, how solidly she stood in her career. There was an ease to her spirit.

Gabby wanted that, too.

She lifted the dress. "Ate Frankie wants me to wear this, but you know I can't run around with it."

"Hm… I've got a better idea." She gestured for them to follow her and they crossed the wide expanse of the store, passing mannequins sporting custom wedding gowns. The smell of fabrics permeated the air.

"How about this?" Patricia pulled out a pale pink, wide-legged linen pant and held it up against a matching pink bolero with butterfly sleeves. "A little more modern, though still formal. You can wear a tank underneath. Add a comfortable pair of pointy shoes with a short heel. There'll be a little neck, a little midriff? What do you think?"

Gabby's jaw dropped with delight. She lifted the plastic cover and ran her hand against the linen. "I love it. It's perfect."

"I love it, too. It's so you." Frankie said.

"Great." Patricia grinned. "I'll grab a couple of sizes of the pink and the lilac and set you up in the dressing room."

"Auntie, I can do it," Gabby offered.

"It's my pleasure. Give me about five minutes, and the room will be ready."

"Thanks, Auntie." Frankie led Gabby to the jewelry section and inspected the myriad of sparkly earrings. "I think you're going to look really good. Hopefully it will help you feel a little better."

Gabby frowned. "I'm not feeling bad."

"And yet, not feeling good."

She sighed. If there was someone whom she couldn't keep fooling, it was her sister. "It's been busy."

"I've seen you busy. This isn't busy. This is…a blah thing."

Gabby bristled at her sister's maternal tone, which bordered on accusatory, like in an I-caught-you-sneaking-out-and-you-can't-fool-me kind of way. Then again, Frankie's tone rarely was gentle, unless she was talking to Liam. "I'm not blah."

"Okay, whatever. So not passing your test and not telling us was totally your plan. Or the fact that you haven't mentioned William as of late?"

She felt her body deflate. Damn, she was good. "How did you know?"

"So I'm right?"

"Seriously?" Gabby growled, just short of stomping her foot. "You tricked me?"

"You forget I've known you all your life. When things aren't great you clam up. So give me the short of it."

Gabby heaved a breath and told Frankie about her test and William, and as she did, she watched for any sign of disappointment. To her relief, she saw none.

"Ugh, I'm sorry." Frankie hugged Gabby tightly. "No wonder you're blah."

"I'm not that bad, am I?"

"Honestly? I started to worry. You've been a little, I don't know...robotic."

Gabby snickered. "Great."

Frankie's expression softened. "I'm just saying. Usually you're so...optimistic, from the moment you get up in the morning, and you haven't been. Have you talked to Mom?"

"I don't know if I can do it. She's going to be disappointed about me failing my test. She expected me to pass."

"I mean, I *am* surprised you didn't, with all the studying you did and all."

"See?"

"It's not wrong to have high expectations for others." She linked her arms around Gabby's and tugged gently. An olive branch. "I'm sure you have high expectations of me, too. I bet you have high expectations of Mom. The fact that you expect her to be disappointed is one."

Gabby rolled her eyes—her sister was right, of course. The fact that she loved to distill all of Gabby's thoughts down to a line-by-line examination was irritating, though.

"About William, though, I bet she'll be a little relieved."

Gabby startled. "What? Why?"

"William's not from around here. He has no mutual friends with anyone. What if he's a weirdo?"

Gabby's first instinct was to defend William, then she remembered that because they had no mutuals, she had no recourse and no way to contact him.

Frankie was still speaking. "To be honest, I am, too, and I think you should look at this wedding as an opportunity to just party. Find a date, go stag. Whatever. But just have fun."

Gabby was still stuck on the word *weirdo*. "I had no idea you both were against William."

"We weren't against him. We didn't *know* him. He's definitely not like Chip."

Gabby raised an eyebrow. Had her sister been reading her mind? "Chip?"

"What I mean is, Chip's someone we know well, who's around you often, whom we've seen around you, but William's like this imaginary friend—"

"Imaginary friend?" Gabby cackled at the descriptor. "Wow. You have a way with words, Ate."

"You know what I mean."

That was the thing, sometimes Gabby didn't know.

One thing was sure, though: everyone was in her business, even if people weren't talking about her directly.

Thank goodness, Auntie Patricia said, from behind them. "The dressing room is ready at your convenience."

"Thanks, Auntie." Gabby left her sister's side without a word, then entered the dressing room, where finally, she was alone.

She looked at her reflection in the full-length mirror.

Gabby turned her face from side to side. Was she blah? And what did that mean? If there was anyone who had the most even-keeled personality in the whole family, it was Gabby. It was her trademark, this levelheaded cheerful disposition. She was proud of it, that she could handle all kinds of personalities, that she didn't integrate others' reactions with her own.

She growled to herself; Frankie was simply giving her a hard time, which she was very good at doing.

Trying on the pink outfit pushed her morose thoughts out of the way. The shade was perfect for her skin tone, and the bolero hit about an inch above the waistband of the linen pants. The stretch of the fabric would allow her to move around easily. Gabby would only need to hem the pant legs, which would take no time at all.

She looked damn good in it.

She walked out of the dressing room, to Frankie clapping. "Love. It."

Gabby nodded. "It's an absolute yes from me, too."

"And your plus-one can wear any color—navy, camel, black. The light pink goes with everything," Patricia added.

Plus-one. Though her mood plummeted, Gabby smiled, avoiding her sister's eyes. "I agree. And I'll take it."

"Do you have shoes to go with it?"

"I need low pumps, or flats."

"I have something perfect." She looked down at Gabby's feet. "You're a seven?"

"Right again. You're so good at this, Auntie."

"It's my specialty. When I was a little girl, all I wanted was to dress people. Fancy clothes, casual clothes, shoes, and even hats. Luckily, I get to do exactly what I love."

"You've really done a great thing with your business, Auntie." Frankie said.

"Thank you. Though, it wasn't a success at the start. We faced a lot of detours, from sourcing the clothing from the Philippines, and then finding investors. So many people thought our mission was too niche."

"Your mission?" Gabby, intrigued, leaned in.

"To bring the clothing of our people *to* our people." Her cheeks pinked. "But I kept at it. And now with so many of our people really wanting to wear terno and Barong, along with more casual styles, I have faith that we'll continue to grow."

"I have no doubt, too," Gabby agreed. She soaked in Patricia's enthusiasm.

Maybe Gabby *had* been blah. Maybe she *did* have to shake things up.

"I'll be back with the shoes," Patricia said.

"Thank you."

Frankie woke her from her thoughts. "Listen, Gab. I don't want you to think that I wasn't trying to be supportive with William. I can't help but be protective, especially after those years with Nathan. You understand, right?"

Gabby sighed. "I know. I get it. I'm protective, too, but I guess in a different way. You're right, though, about what you said." After digging her phone out of her purse, she scrolled back to her last text to William.

"Oh? What are you doing."

"Something I should have done the first twenty-four hours without contact." She thumbed five simple words: You're an asshole. We're done.

Though William might not read it, or whether or not he cared, Gabby would always know that she'd made the decision to end it, in her heart, and in her mind.

Frankie leaned in to watch her send the text. "Go, girl."

Then she thumbed over to Nathan's last text. She hadn't responded with her actual availability to meet.

"What?" Frankie asked. "When did this start?"

"Recently."

"And he wants to go out."

"Yes." She swallowed against her sister's glare. "And I'm going to say yes. But I'm going in with eyes wide open."

Gabby braced herself for another tongue lashing, knowing her sister wouldn't be able to say anything that she hadn't already thought of.

Frankie broke the eye contact first. "Hey, no judgement from me. Do you know how many times me and Reece hooked up after the divorce?"

Gabby's jaw dropped. "How many times?"

Frankie held up five fingers.

"But I don't think I even want to hook up with him this time," Gabby said.

"Hook ups don't mean it has to be physical. Saying yes alone means that you're taking a risk. He's still shooting his shot." She raised her eyebrows knowingly. "Just… know I'm here for you through this."

Gabby mulled the decision for a second longer. Now with her relationship with William over, it could only go up from here.

She typed back: Free tomorrow night?

At the senior center, Chip hovered over the renovation plans with Justin Wells, the contractor. He was about Chip's age, from Wells Construction, a family business. With his father, they ran construction projects as far north as Charlottesville. His team had recently repaired and primed the walls, and the smell of paint permeated the air around them. But it was all coming together, and so far without a hitch in the timeline.

"I wish there was a way to speed this up," Chip said, noting the sound of music drifting from the other side of the wall. It was Friday, which meant dance classes, and this week's sounded like the cha-cha. "The center director said that they've gotten more inquiries for memberships, though they've capped them for the time being, during renovation."

"Now that you mention it." Justin slipped his pencil behind his ear. "I received word that one of our other projects is being held up for permits and funding. I can direct some of those folks here. But speeding things up means the financing changes, too, for materials and labor."

Chip didn't think twice. He had earmarked his financing

well before the start of demolition. Nathan should be down for it, too; with these kinds of decisions, he'd historically left it up to Chip to handle. "Let's do it."

"Great. I'll start on a contract amendment. I'll have to double-check that your permits can be approved on time, too. You may have to let the staff know that there'll be more foot traffic. We've already gotten complaints from the seniors." He raised a hand. "Let me rephrase that. I've got half of them trying to set me up with their kids, and there's a certain troublemaker with his buddies who's been relocating our equipment and giving us the side-eye."

Chip shook his head. "Relocating equipment?"

"Nothing too serious. You know, moving paintbrushes and paint cans to the other side of the room. Stealing pencils. Classic pranks."

The vision of George Lowry casually pocketing gear flashed through his head. "Ugh. One of them wouldn't be about five-seven with slicked-back white hair who wears a different Mr. Rogers sweater every day?"

Justin smiled. "I plead the Fifth."

He shook his head. "I will definitely give everyone *lots* of notice."

"In that case, we'll do our best."

They bid each other farewell, and Chip headed out. Since his father was next door at dance class, he'd hired someone to sit with the puppies, but Chip was eager to return. Who knew what kind of trouble five puppies and a mama dog could get themselves into?

And how had he ended up becoming the primary caregiver?

In the parking lot, Chip spotted Gabby's car. He looked back at the senior center, with the cha-cha music on repeat. With the tune drawing him back, he entered the double doors.

A woman's voice echoed in the foyer. "One, two, cha-cha-cha, back, two, cha-cha-cha…"

Not just any woman's voice, but Gabby's.

Lured in, Chip headed into the multipurpose room, where bodies shuffled and arms waved. Eyes scanning the crowd, he spotted Daria in the front row; next to her was his father. And the man was grinning ear to ear.

A more beautiful and graceful being weaving in between bodies snatched his attention. It was Gabby, counting out steps and moving with the beat. She wore pants cuffed at the ankles and a button-down shirt tucked in the front. Her hair was loose, her lips a bright red. Her hips swayed with the music.

Chip leaned against the doorway, enamored. This was a woman who had admitted to not being the best dancer, and yet had the bravado to teach a roomful of seniors a dance she *did* know.

He could line up a bunch of descriptors, but nothing could really encompass how she continued to take his breath away. The heart hands through the refrigerator glass at the pet store, the way she was so careful with the puppies. … Little things that made him wish that he could show her how he really felt.

Because little things added up.

Gabby danced her way to the front and faced front.

Their eyes met.

Her lips spread out into a wide smile, and with that, he was hooked into her spell once more. Nathan and William be damned, he couldn't shake the way he felt about her.

Then, she gestured for him to come forward.

Oh, hell no. He shook his head.

Gabby waved him over. As she did, some of the seniors' heads turned in his direction.

No. Please don't pay any attention.

But it was too late. Daria and her best friend, Cindy, clued in quickly to what Gabby wanted. They joined in the encouragement, and soon all of the seniors were in on it.

The next second, he was being pulled into the crowd. "Really, it's fine," he said—pleaded—to everyone, because this crowd knew he made a better wallflower than the center of attention.

He had two left feet that headed in separate directions whenever a song came on. Hence why he never did join in this activity, ever. And why, if required, he only slow-danced, because all he had to do was sway.

Even then, he wasn't confident about it.

"Just follow me." Gabby took both of his hands, and looked into his eyes. The music was loud, blaring, and it was going on and on, and yet it all fell into the background. The thing—person—at the forefront was Gabby, and Gabby alone.

That is, until she led him to an empty spot,

He was exposed now.

"I suck at this." Chip laughed. This was embarrassing. His face was hot; surely, everyone could see how much he was sweating.

Not sexy at all.

Not that he wanted to be sexy to the seniors.

"Who cares? Look around." Gabby was laughing, too, and when Chip did what she said, he realized that half of the seniors didn't know what they were doing, either.

The seniors did exactly what they wanted; they moved without insecurity. They didn't care what other people thought.

Chip allowed his muscles to relax, though when he did, he began to mess up, legs tangling. "Argh."

"You're doing great!"

With Gabby's encouragement, he regained his steps. Not perfect, by any means, but enough that he stayed with the beat.

When the music died down, the seniors clapped. Chip was out of breath, but in the best way. His cheeks hurt from smiling. And though he would never say it aloud, he was proud of himself. For a moment, he had let go.

He just *was*.

Lillian, one of the center coordinators, began speaking. "Thank you, Gabby, for filling in to teach us the cha-cha while we wait for our dance teacher. It was meant to be. We got to groove. Now, everyone, let's take a break until Natasha gets here."

The seniors mobbed Gabby, though she signaled for Chip to wait for her. He was glad to be able to sneak away.

Minutes later, she met him in the back of the room. She greeted him with a hug. "You were awesome!"

He scooped her up to her toes, and exercised restraint by setting her down well before he wanted to. "I don't know about that."

"Are you kidding? You learned fast. The aunties are going to love it. It's like cha-cha central at a Filipino wedding. Better than the stupid Wobble." She peered at him.

"Alright, alright. You made your point. But what are you doing here?"

"I was on my way back from dress shopping with Frankie, and I saw your car and figured I'd stop. Next thing you know, I'm showing them the cha-cha." She was out of breath. "I wanted to check in on you and the puppies."

"The puppies." His heart dipped in his chest. He'd hoped that it was just to see him. Period. "They're doing great. Sydney—she works at Cross Trails, too—is sitting with them, since Dad and I are both out and about. Animal control gave me a call today. No bites from owners of Lucky. I spoke to one of the local rescues and suggested we start a social media account for them, to help get them adopted out. I've already started taking pictures." Only a day had passed, but responsibilities for the puppies mounted, and while he felt inadequate in his new role, there was no choice but to try his best.

She pressed her hands together as if in prayer. "Please, can I help? What can I do?"

"With what time? Don't you have something to study for? And a wedding to plan?"

She bit her lip as if in thought, the act sending heat straight to his core. "I'll make the time. I've missed them all day."

"You have?"

"Yes. It feels like I'm part of the family, since I was there for the birth. Sort of." She inhaled. "How about I help you out with photos at our next study session? It'll only take a few minutes." She grabbed on his sleeve and tugged. "C'mon."

"Okay, fine. If you insist." He couldn't help but grin; they both began walking down the hallway to exit. "I didn't know that you were such a dog person."

"I didn't know, either. But I'm committed now, because I want them to go to good homes."

"Would you take a puppy?"

"No. There's no way I can take care of a dog with my schedule. With my luck, I'll forget to feed it. And I would feel too awful leaving it at home all day. Aren't *you* afraid that you're going to get too attached?"

They were now in the parking lot, they and stood in between their cars. She shoved her hands in the front pockets of her jeans. The *V* of her shirt was much lower than he'd first noticed and it dipped in between her breasts. It took all his effort to keep his eyes on hers, belatedly realizing what she'd asked.

"Don't get me wrong, the puppies are cute. But puppies

grow up to be dogs, and every day they need TLC. Dad's fallen for Lucky, though, and I'm not sure how we're going to deal with that."

"You'll have to keep her."

He shrugged, still torn, despite knowing how much George already loved her.

She frowned. "He's going to be sad if he has to let her go."

"I know. But this entire experience of caring for puppies has been a trial by fire, and I really question if we're both ready."

"Well, more reason for me to help with finding them homes. I'll create a social platform for them and can boost it on mine. I've got a big following."

"You shouldn't have to do all that."

"But this is my forte. Sort of like getting people to cha-cha."

"Alright then." He rested a hand against his neck, now warm from remembering that he had, in fact, danced in front of all these people.

"Good. It's going to be so much fun." She peeked at her watch. "Oh, gotta go."

"Where are you off to?"

"Headed up to the B and B. Mom wants to catch up. There's so much going on, with all the family coming, that we haven't really talked about her own wedding."

He remembered Cruz and Eva's rendezvous in the back office. "Have they decided on a date?"

"Yes, the date's been decided, but nothing else past that."

"Wow. I thought for sure that everything would be locked in. Is everything alright?"

"Yes. They themselves are rock-solid. But priorities, you know. Between you and me, though, Mom's feeling pretty impatient at not being able to celebrate their nuptials. I know they wanted to tie the knot right away. But with this superstition that there can't be two weddings in a year—"

"What superstition?"

"That members of an immediate family can't marry within the same year, so Mom is relegated to wait."

"Are we talking calendar or fiscal year?"

"Calendar. I was thinking of maybe throwing an engagement party sometime this summer, to kind of tide her over. What do you think?"

"I think that's a great idea. Except, your test…"

"Damn test. Do I even really need to take it?"

"What?" He frowned at this change of heart. This was unlike Gabby, who didn't quit a task. "Of course, you do."

"You're right. I'm just…thinking aloud." She spied her phone. "Mom's calling. I should head out."

"I have to head back, too. I want to spend some time with the puppies before I go to Cross Trails."

She shook her head. "I don't know how you keep your shifts straight."

"From someone who plans weddings."

She tapped her chin. "That's fair." Then she walked backward and, raising a hand said, "Nice dancing, Lowry. Love ya!"

He groaned. "Don't remind me. Love you."

Gabby broke out into laughter.

Chip was still grinning as he buckled his seat belt.

Then, his phone buzzed. From Nathan: I need your help. Gabby said yes to a date.

Chapter Seven

"Chip's mood had plummeted, much like the weather. Just as the blue sky had turned gray, with a definite chill in the air, he was filled with discomfort, all stemming from Nathan's text, and Chip's plan to meet him before his shift at Cross Trails to *give him some pointers*.

Was he really doing this?

A bark brought him out of his thoughts, and he looked out to see Lucky, trotting around the perimeter of the backyard fence. He'd let Sydney go for the afternoon and was waiting for his father to return.

The puppies were sound asleep inside the house.

As if hearing his thoughts, Lucky turned to look at him. Her expression was pointed—there was a message in it— but Chip couldn't quite make it out. Then she sniffed the air, turned away from him, and scratched at the fence.

"Do you want to go outside?" Lucky had lived so many months outside of this fence. It would make sense that she missed exploring.

After grabbing the leash from the picnic bench, Chip slipped it over Lucky's head. "Want to sniff around?"

But when he opened the gate, Lucky didn't step out.

"Huh." That was curious. Perhaps she needed some encouragement, so Chip stepped out and tugged at the leash.

Lucky didn't budge.

"What are you trying to tell me?" He stepped back into the backyard and closed the gate, realizing then that Lucky could have wiggled through the fence at any time, with how wide the slats were.

And if the slats were wide enough to let Lucky out, then the puppies could escape without a problem. While they didn't move very fast or far now, in a few weeks, the five would be hard to contain.

He would either need to reinforce the fence, or someone would have to be outside at all times, with eagle eyes.

Speaking of eagles… Chip looked up at the sky. He'd seen a couple since the beginning of spring. He then remembered watching a video of a large bird swooping down and scooping up a small dog.

Oh, God. Was that real?

He looked down at Lucky, protectiveness running through him. The thought alone made him nauseous. "Don't worry. I'll keep an eye out for them. You can trust me—"

He caught himself; he was talking to the dog. And for the life of him, it was as if she understood.

A memory came unbidden of Goose, his childhood dog. He had been of an unknown breed, another stray George had picked up. He'd been underfoot for many of Chip's late teen years, at the stove for any small morsel of food. His head on Fern's lap for all the moments she decided to plop down on the couch, and then at his mother's bedside when she got sick.

He was a good dog.

No one could replace him. Much like no one could ever take his mother's place.

The grumble of a motor took his attention. *Dad.* Relief coursed through him. Obviously, it was Chip who needed the break. A couple of minutes later, George popped out of the back door, arms open. "Lucky!"

Chip, surprised by his dad's enthusiasm, laughed. The normally stone-faced man was boxer-like himself, with a mean-looking face, but was, at the moment, a softie. If he had a nub for a tail, he would have been shaking it, too.

Lucky bounded toward him, and skipped around him, body wiggling like a jumping bean. The dog couldn't contain itself.

George bent down to give her pets, though Chip could see the effort in the way he grunted. With that, Chip's heart melted.

How could Chip separate them?

He cleared his throat. "I'm due at Cross Trails, but I'll be back in a few. Lucky's probably ready to head back inside." Chip passed by his father.

"Alright, son."

From behind him, Lucky nosed the back door and then bopped Chip in the back of his leg.

"Looks like she wants in now," George said.

"Maybe." For a beat, Chip hesitated, locking eyes with the dog.

"She's a good mama."

"Yeah, I think she was telling me earlier that the fence needs to be reinforced." He stomped his shoes against the doormat.

"Then I guess we have to fix it."

After finishing with his shoes, he slipped them off and lined them up by the back door, then opened it for Lucky. He entered the house; George followed behind.

From afar, the sound of mewling puppies brought a smile to his face. Lucky was already up ahead, and she pawed at the gate to let her in to see her puppies.

George took off his coat and hung it in the closet. "Any plans after work?"

"Nope. Want me to bring home dinner?"

He snickered. "Son, it's Friday."

"And?"

"And I'm not going to be home for dinner. I'm meeting up with my boys."

It was Chip's turn to snicker. "Your boys?"

"That's what you kids call them these days, right? We're going to the drive-in. Theo's driving."

Theo Wong was in his eighties and had recently failed his driving test. "Are you sure that's wise?"

"He just got a new prescription. He can see now."

"I sure hope so." Chip went to the bathroom to wash his hands.

"I got a question for you," George asked as his voice neared.

Chip turned. Something was brewing. "Okay?"

"Why is it that I go out more than you?"

"Not true. I'm out all the time. Hiking, working."

"I mean out for fun, son. You need to get out, experience new things."

"I do experience new things." He dried his hands on a hand towel and made his way down the hallway. The car— that was his destination.

Only, George was relentless. "What I mean is, you should be experiencing new things *with* people. Not just with the forest, or with buildings. Not just with projects. With people, without an agenda."

"Gotta go." He offered George his fist, which he bumped reluctantly.

Once in the car, Chip shut the door and heaved a breath. He sloughed off all of his father's nagging from his system with the click of his seat belt. He couldn't even begin to decipher what George had meant with what he said. He certainly wasn't going to try to figure it out right now, not when he was meeting up with Nathan in a few minutes.

The drive to Cross Trails was like the turn of a page, just as he liked it. He was greeted by the cobblestone steps of downtown, and he pulled into the employee parking area behind the building.

"Chippie!"

He stepped out of the car to the sound of his name, and Nathan running up to him. They shoulder bumped, with Chip feigning excitement, when all he felt was apprehension. "Hey, what's up?"

"I've got a date with Gabby tomorrow night." Nathan was all smiles and led the way toward the square. Chip had a half hour until his shift, and Nathan seemed restless, so he followed along.

"Ah, that's quick."

Anticipation flashed in his features. "I know, right?"

Chip's brain was revving on all cylinders. "So, what did you need?"

Nathan shoved his hands in his pockets. "I have no idea what to do. I don't want to screw this up."

"You're kidding."

"Not kidding. I was all confident that this would be my chance with her. But then I remembered that we didn't work out the first times and it was probably all my fault" He winced. "So I was thinking…shouldn't I bring something to the date? A present, maybe?" He pulled on the glass door of Winnebago, a garden store, and once inside they were engulfed with earthy scents. "What do you think about flowers?"

Chip scanned their surroundings, looking at the unlimited variety of flora, though surprised at Nathan's sudden insecurity. It was enough for Chip to feel sorry for the guy. "To be honest, you'd be better off picking out a really nice dessert." He looked out the clear front windows at the myriad of small businesses on the square. They were lucky that in Peak there were plenty of mom-and-pop shops to choose from. "Sweet Trip has this fudge that she loves. She has a goal this year to taste every flavor of fudge in that place."

"Fudge." His nose wiggled in disdain. "I recently gave up sugar."

"What? How come I don't know that?"

He shrugged. "It's part of my health journey. Like I said, I'm trying to be better."

"This why you started hiking?"

He nodded.

Chip was taken aback. Just when he thought he knew everything about a person…"In this case though, the fudge isn't for you but for Gab. Sugar *is* the foundation of her food pyramid."

"Then fudge it is," he answered without hesitation.

They headed across the street to Sweet Trip, a short building with a checkered pink-and-white awning. The bell chimed when Nathan opened it, and they were greeted by the smell of chocolate.

Chip gestured at the large display case of fudge of every color in the rainbow. Behind the counter was a chalkboard of the current flavors.

"I don't even know where to start." Nathan gritted out a smile. "Would *you* know what she'd like?"

Of course, he did. A part of him even wanted to rub that in. But the guy needed help; the grimace on his face was almost pathetic. "Maybe one of this…oh, and watermelon sounds exciting, and this, and the salted caramel for sure."

Nathan repeated the order to the worker, and the fudge

was packaged in a deluxe case. After Nathan paid, they exited the shop with the package in hand.

"Can I help with anything else?" Chip prompted at Nathan's sudden silence. They were walking back toward Cross Trails, and exhaustion had befallen him.

"There *is* one last thing." Beats of silence passed. "Will you...come on the date with me?"

"What?" He cackled. "Like a chaperone?"

"No, like an accidental run-in."

Nathan appeared so serious that Chip halted. "You're serious."

"Yeah, I am. I think you being there will help."

Chip breathed in the reality that his "help" had everything to do with the fact that he understood and delighted in all the things Gabby did, even the annoying little quirks she had. Like leaning over to look at his texts whenever his phone buzzed. Because she was also really nosy.

Very nosy. And sharp.

"If you're thinking I can hang out and give you pointers during your date," Chip said, "that's not going to work. She'll see right through it. And you won't exactly get into the groove if I'm there. Isn't that what all of this is about? To get to know one another again?"

They resumed their walking. "I just don't want to blow it, you know?"

"I get that, but I don't think it's a good idea."

"Don't say no. To make it easy, I can set you up with someone I know from work."

The moment was moving quickly. "Hold on a second. You really thought about this."

He ran a hand through his hair. "Yeah, I have. Having you there would make keep things easy and neutral, at least for the first date."

His dad's earlier statement came to mind. *You should be experiencing new things with people.*

Was he right?

Surely, though, his father had meant for him to have fun, not watch Gabby date someone else.

"Please, Chip. If it all works out, I feel like we'll be spending a lot more time together, anyway."

Some of the tension in Chip's body slipped away.

This was…nice. And wholesome. Different than the times before, when Nathan had preferred for them to hang out exclusively.

It seemed that Nathan was really trying. And if Nathan was who Gabby wanted anyway, who was he to stand in the way? Might as well get it over with.

Chip relented. "Okay, fine. But I'll find my own date, thank you."

"Hell yeah." Nathan clutched his chest in relief. "Thank you. You're saving me right now."

"You're welcome," Chip answered, though now he wondered if he would feel the same way after seeing the two of them together.

Fourteen days from the wedding

Gabby entered Oasis, a restaurant and bar, for her date with Nathan. Just opened last week, Gabby could tell from the front door that it was packed. They were on the outskirts of town, at a pull-off where an investor had built up a few shops, including an ice-cream shop within walking distance that might make a good second stop.

"Oh, this is nice," she said to herself, taking in the coffered ceilings and the vintage chandeliers. The vibe was both modern and cozy, and she relaxed.

Good choice, Nathan.

She'd considered canceling this date a dozen times, had thought of different excuses for a no-show. She wasn't sure what to expect from this date—this was the first time they were meeting in a more intimate way since they broke up. But she reminded herself that she would regret not exploring where this date could go.

She looked at her phone. She was a couple of minutes early. There was also a text notification from her mother: I'll bring my vision board over.

Their meeting earlier had been successful, and Eva was eager to start making some real plans for her wedding.

Gabby replied, Tomorrow sounds good!

For now, though, she had to get through this date.

Gabby slipped among bodies until she came up to the hostess stand.

And Chip.

He hadn't seen her yet, so she nudged him from behind, and said in her most flirtatious voice, "Hey, do you know CPR? Because you took my breath away"

Chip turned to her and laughed. "Oh my God, it's you. I had no idea how to respond."

She leaned in for a hug. "What are you doing here?"

"Oh, um…" He gestured to a woman walking away from them. "I'm on a date."

"A date?" Her spine straightened. She'd seen him yesterday, and not once had he hinted at it. Sure, they weren't in the habit of telling one another what their everyday plans were, but this was a shock. "I didn't realize you had, um, someone."

"I swiped right." He smiled.

He was on apps? How did she not know this?

"And you're actually going out…"

"I go out. More than you think." He almost looked hurt.

She leaned against the counter, eager to fix her faux pas. "I mean, you're so busy these days, especially since you're on daddy duty with all those puppies."

"Dad's covering for me this evening." He scanned her from toes on up. "So you're here for a date, too?"

"Yeah. With Nathan. How did you know?"

He shrugged. "Took a guess. You're wearing eye makeup."

She bit against a smile. "You noticed?"

"You've complained enough that you hate it because it makes your eyes water."

Oh, right. She wiggled her nose. "Don't remind me. I've been trying not to rub it off."

"Nervous?"

"I'm okay." It was a lie. But now…an idea dawned on her. "You know, you should join us."

"What? No."

"Yes. It'll take the edge off my nerves. Spot the red flags." She stepped closer to Chip, only then noticing that he wasn't wearing his usual plaid shirt and cargo pants. "Wait. You're wearing a sweater, and are those new jeans?"

He cleared his throat. "Yeah. Why?"

"I don't think I've ever seen you in dark denim." Dark denim was different. More formal, a little more put-together. "When did you buy them?"

He snorted. "Okay, Mom."

She rolled her eyes, though curiosity swarmed in her chest. Chip didn't care about clothes. Wouldn't she have known if he'd gone shopping? "Well, you look nice."

"Thank you. One of Regan's interests is fashion, so I thought I'd at least try to look decent. Speaking of." Chip's eyes locked on to the opposite side of the room, where a woman with long, dark wavy hair and light brown skin weaved through bodies. Gabby assumed that she was partially of Asian descent. She was wearing a plaid-skirt ensemble that looked like she stepped out of a royal family getaway. "Damn," Chip whispered.

A sliver of jealousy ran up Gabby's spine, though she immediately pushed it down. She imagined sitting on the thought with her full weight, because it was wrong to feel this way.

This was just a different dynamic she was witnessing, was all.

"Hi," the woman said, glancing questioningly at Gabby.

Chip made introductions. "Regan Ngam, this is Gabby Espiritu. Gabby, this is Regan. Gabby's a good friend."

Gabby smiled in reassurance. "I'm actually here meeting my own date. And here he is." She felt her body tense as the glass doors opened to Nathan, who was a smoke show himself in his slim-fit jeans and turtleneck. Had they not had their long history to overcome, she would have drooled on the spot.

Though Gabby noticed others turning at his entrance.

Nathan approached them with a warm smile, and introductions between Nathan and Regan commenced.

The host approached them and took information from both parties. "It's going to be a half hour wait," she said.

Chip looked over at the corner. "But there are seats available right there."

"It's for four."

"See? You should join us," Gabby said to Chip and Regan. "You don't mind do you, Nathan?" She looked up at him, a test.

In the past, he would have declined.

Nathan shrugged. "I don't mind."

Regan smiled. "The more, the merrier."

Gabby breathed a heavy sigh of relief. She loved how this

first date was turning out, except for the fact that Regan was beaming at Chip, clearly liking what she saw, too.

Gabby wanted to tell her to quit it.

Stop it. It's none of your business.

After an awkward decision as to who would sit where, they took their chairs—Gabby sat across from Chip and the other two across from one another—and a server approached them.

After ordering their drinks and appetizers, they settled into some small talk. Gabby noted that Chip couldn't take his eyes off Regan every time she spoke.

It was…interesting.

Chip had never brought anyone to meet their friend group. She knew of a couple of women he'd dated here and there, but none who'd lasted.

"Gabby."

Startled out of her thoughts, Gabby turned to Nathan; he was holding up a box. "I got you something."

"Oh, wow." She glanced at the rest of their group. It was sweet but also awkward. Nathan wasn't a "gifts" guy. Still, she smiled. "Thank you."

He placed the box into her hands. The scent of sugar wafted from it. The seal was labeled Sweet Trip. "I hope you like—"

She burst out in a laugh, her lingering thoughts about the other couple at their table dissipating. "How did you know?" She picked at the box's seal, cheeks warm with pleasure at how he had nailed this. "I am *obsessed* with Sweet Trip. It's my year's goal to taste every single fudge they make."

"That sounds like my kind of challenge," Regan said. "How many have you tried?"

"Twenty-one out of their fifty-eight flavors. Though, some flavors are limited edition, so I'm not sure if I'll actually get it all in. Oh, my gosh, this is taking so long." Finally, she opened up the box to four pieces of fudge. Her mouth watered at first sight.

She reached out and squeezed Nathan's forearm, which was warm and strong, taken aback at the thoughtfulness. "Thank you. This is just…special. I don't know how you knew."

"I'm glad you like it."

"I *love* it. We should split this."

Objections arose, but Gabby wouldn't hear of it. She stood and asked for a butter knife from a server, and split the fudge into four pieces, and they all dug in.

"So do you have a rating system for this?" Regan moaned after tasting one. "A one-to-ten scale?"

The conversation evolved to collections, obsessions, and favorite things. As their drinks and appetizers came, they talked about comfort foods and family traditions. About Nathan's Italian grandmother's Sunday dinners. About Regan's family, who ran a Vietnamese grocery in Florida. Gabby, however, noted that while Chip and Regan were relaxed, Nathan was far from it. He sat stiff at her side, a smile frozen on his face.

It was unlike him.

And on his plate were the four pieces of fudge, none of which he'd taken a bite out of.

She excused herself to head to the restroom, and to think. What was up with Nathan? And with Chip and Regan getting on so well—were they going to see each other again?

After washing her hands, she looked at herself in the mirror.

It's all good, she said to herself. *You're out and about. You're moving on.*

You're actually moving backward.

No, this is a new chapter. It was the first hour of one date. She was simply the waters, to see what was swimming in it.

She didn't have to read into anything. This was a simple outing with friends and she should simply enjoy it.

Gabby nodded to herself in the mirror. Then she swiped gloss over her lips and stepped out, turning left and running into a body.

"Oomph." Hands held her shoulders; she knew the sound of that voice well. "Chip. Sorry."

"It's alright. The dining room is actually that way." He pointed over her shoulder. "But I'm glad I caught you. Things going well on your date?"

"On our group date, you mean?"

"Yeah."

"Good. Fine." She shook head. "But do you notice how Nathan is so tense?"

He frowned. "What do you mean? We just had a ten-minute conversation about gel versus ballpoint pens. I don't even know how we got there."

She half laughed. "I mean, yeah, we did, but it's me, you, and Regan doing most of the talking while he just laughs. Which isn't a bad thing, because at least he's paying attention. But he's not acting like himself. Anyhow, blah blah… how about you? Regan seems nice."

"She is. We've got a lot in common. We both like to go with the flow. She's funny. She's a therapist and an artist on the side… Anyway, supersmart woman."

"That's…great." It *was* great. She was happy for him. Not only was Regan beautiful, but she was also obviously successful.

Gabby ignored the niggle of jealousy inside her chest. "I hope Nathan perks up a little. I feel like he's holding back a little and I don't know why. But…we should head back, right? They might think we're talking about them."

"Puh-leez, they're probably commiserating about us, too. No worries."

Only she *was* worried, for that very reason. Maybe she wasn't working out for Nathan, either. Maybe she was an awful date, or girlfriend, or partner. Her track record was evidence of it.

"Hey, where'd you go?" Chip asked, shaking her out of her thoughts.

"Ugh. I don't know. Maybe I should end the date early."

"Why would you do that?"

"It's not clicking."

"It might be because me and Regan are with you."

"No. I actually like that you're around."

"But if you're not bonding—"

"It's fine. Just ignore me. I'm in my head comparing this date to our other ones in the past. Let's head back, okay?" She didn't want to ruin his date, too.

Chip smiled. "You lead the way."

Gabby weaved around tables, and at the sight of her, Nathan smiled. It eased her insecurity. Maybe she was just looking for flaws. Maybe it was her being awkward.

Nathan stood and pulled out the chair for her, a sweet move. "Regan and I got to talking. Are you all up to going for a walk after this?"

"I love that idea," Gabby said, optimism shooting through her. "There's an ice-cream shop just up the block."

"I could go for more chocolate," Regan said, looking at Chip. "Unless you had something else planned."

"I'm down," Chip added.

Nathan and Chip split the check and they all meandered

to Cones & Curtsies. They walked in two pairs, with some distance in between.

The silence was deafening.

Gabby scoured her head for something to say, only to find that she'd used up all her small talk at the table, with everyone present.

They reached Cones and Curtsies' bright storefront; it glowed against the night sky, where a walk-up window slid open to reveal a worker wearing a crown. "How can I help you?"

Nathan leaned over and spoke into her ear. "Why are they all wearing crowns?"

"The proprietor is an Anglophile. The workers have been instructed to curtsy and speak in Britishisms."

He grinned. "Should I order my bloody ice cream?"

"Only if you're not knackered."

"Rubbish!"

Gabby giggled, and she breathed against the warmth that had ticked up between them. They were close, less than a foot apart now, and it wasn't bad at all. It was actually comfortable. Finally.

"Cold?" he asked.

"No. Just a weird shiver." She didn't know what she was feeling. What she had underestimated was how hard this was to start anew with someone she'd been with before, especially with her guard up so high. Or maybe it was because Nathan was trying hard to show her a good time?

She was a wedding planner with expert socialization skills—where was that talent now?

"I get those sometimes," he said.

"Yeah?"

"It happens when I'm a little nervous. Sort of like now."

Though they were in the dim light, Gabby noted bashfulness come across his face. He looked down and away for a beat. "You're nervous?"

"I mean, yeah. I've got a lot riding on this first date. I couldn't even eat."

"What do you mean?"

His expression opened to one of vulnerability, a rarity. "I know I'm lucky that you said yes to this date—you didn't have to. Looking back at how you and I were before, I regret the ways I acted. Anyway, I'm sorry, Gab. I'm trying now."

She nodded, taking in her words.

It harkened back to a conversation they'd had a while back, when she'd asked him to stay home from a business trip that he'd scheduled on her birthday weekend. She'd told him that if he loved her, he'd try to reschedule. And he'd said that he couldn't, that it was business—and that if she loved him, she should understand.

Did this mean that, finally, she was his priority?

Whispering took her attention to the right, and Chip and Regan were in their own huddle, looking down at her phone. Their lips were moving.

Gabby wondered what they were talking about. One thing she knew: Chip would never try, he would just *do*.

"Ready to order?" Nathan asked.

"Oh, yep." She recalibrated. "I always have room for dessert. What do you think you'll have?"

"Oh, um… I cut out sugar."

She frowned. "Really? But you bought…"

He grinned. "I got them for you, not for me."

It was a straightforward statement, and his gift had been generous, and yet… "Then you're not having ice cream?"

"No, but I'm not hungry. I'll watch you."

"Alright then." She followed Chip and Regan to order at the window.

Though at that moment, the idea of a sweet treat didn't give her the same sense of joy.

Chapter Eight

Thirteen days until the wedding

"I still can't believe that he doesn't eat sugar anymore. By choice." Gabby fluffed the white fleece blanket just so, and spread out fake greenery as a backdrop. Then she nodded at Chip. "Okay, I'm ready for the first baby. Time to show them off."

They were at Chip's, for a study session. Technically, the photoshoot *before* the study session, which Gabby had looked forward to more. That, and to debrief and discuss their first dates.

Chip brought her the first puppy. The litter was a few days old now, and though they weren't so great at moving around just yet, a hundred percent of them were adorable.

This puppy had a reddish-brown coat and black spot over one eye.

"I love you," she crooned, leaning in to snuggle it gently. She raised her eyes to Chip. "How do you do it, dealing with this cuteness every day?"

"Cleaning up after them dampens the magic a little."

"No. No way you're messy. Not ever," she said to the puppy, setting her down on the blankets. The puppy was perfectly still; this job, out of all of her tasks today, would be the easiest to accomplish. While Gabby snapped away on her DSLR, she asked, "How was the rest of your date with Regan?"

"It was fine."

"Do you like her?"

"Regan?"

"Yes, silly." *Snap.* Scanning through the photos she'd taken, she was satisfied with the lot. "Number one is complete. Next."

"Regan was nice. Smart." Chip's voice was far away.

"Super pretty, too," she said without looking at him, though every part of her was tense with curiosity.

The end of their double date had been interesting. Everyone except for Nathan had ice-cream cones, and all of them continued to be chatterboxes except for Nathan. When it was time to say goodbye, Gabby had watched Chip walk Regan to her car, while Nathan walked her to hers. She and Nathan exchanged a hug, which was perfect.

Had Chip and Regan kissed? Did they reconnect?

Chip handed Gabby the second puppy, this one with a dark brown coat and black stripes. Brindle was the name of the coloring. "*So* pretty. Kind, too. She talked about her family a lot. She loves to travel, loves food. Definitely the total package."

Total package. Gabby was glad to have an excuse to turn away as she posed the second puppy. She was wiggly, and the extra time Gabby took allowed her to breathe through her jealousy.

She knew it was wrong, and yet, there she was.

"Do you think you'll see her again?" Gabby asked.

"I think so. And you? With Nathan?"

She clicked the shutter button a second and a third time. "He already asked me out for a second date. But I don't know."

"Because he cut out sugar?"

She handed him the puppy while debating what to say.

Now wasn't the time to censor herself. "It kind of feels like a red flag."

"Dietary choices are a red flag?" An eyebrow shot up.

"I know I know," she sighed. "Of everything else that had happened between he and I that I'm focusing on that." She tried to right her thoughts on the issue, which she hadn't been able to kick since last night. After all Nathan *was* trying.

Was she jumping the gun? What if this was the blah that her sister had accused her of? Or maybe this was a sign that going out with Nathan again wasn't a good idea.

And after Chip admitted that Regan was the total package, how was Gabby supposed to feel about that?

The next puppy in her arms gave her some solace, and she hugged it. This one was white, male, with a pink nose. As if it needed reassurance, the puppy pressed its nose against her skin.

She tried to explain again. "I want me and Nathan's time together to be easy, without any kind of effort, I guess. In the past, it was always that—with some kind of strife, or argument. We were always fussing about something—"

"That is an understatement."

"Right? I don't want to go back to that. Though I think he understands the stakes now."

He nodded, and silence ensued while she snapped more photos. "Okay, but what does that have anything to do with him quitting sugar? It feels... I don't know, like you're reaching. Believe me, if he or you had been a jerk during the date that would be one thing. But sugar?"

Her cheeks warmed. "How can I explain it....I love Ho Hos and Twinkies, and cotton candy. Can that change? Yes. But I like what I like, and I don't want to feel guilty about it."

"Did you feel guilty for things when you were with Nathan in the past?" He frowned.

"In some ways. I wanted us to work. We were always on the rocks. It made me feel unsteady, I guess. I wanted to please him and make things okay. All the time."

She set the camera down and had to breathe through that last sentence. It was the first time she'd expressed her emotions in that manner.

She picked up the puppy and when she turned, Chip was ready with the last, another girl pup with a reddish-brown fur. Half of her face was white, and so where her paws.

Her thoughts about Nathan fell away. "Aw, Chip. It's like she has little shoes on."

"This is the tiniest of the bunch."

They made the exchange, and Gabby held the puppy close to her chest. She fit perfectly in her arms, and nuzzled herself into Gabby's chest.

"Sweet girl." Then what Chip had said belatedly caught up, harkening a memory.

The whole family had been apple picking; her dad was still alive. The goal had been to pick the largest and juiciest apples. But Gabby hadn't been interested in those. She'd been enamored of the tiniest apples, as tart as they were. She wanted the ones that could fit right her in palm and be gobbled up in a few bites. And she had found one, a Fuji apple she finished off in six bites. She still remembered it as the most perfect apple.

She pressed a kiss against her nose. "Six."

With humor lacing his tone, Chip asked. "Did you say Six?"

"Six. For the most perfect apple in the bunch," she repeated. "That's her name."

"Name?" The sides of his mouth lifted. The next words came out slow, one at a time. "You're naming a puppy."

"Yeah, why not?"

She set Six down and positioned her on the blanket. All the while, Six didn't object and gazed up at her with big brown eyes. Eyes that threatened to make her heart burst.

Eyes that spoke to her.

Gabby realized what Chip was implying.

No.

She wouldn't fall for it. She couldn't.

She was a responsible person and didn't do things like adopt pets and then realize that she didn't actually have time for them. Much less a puppy she would have to raise and train and take to puppy school.

But those eyes.

No.

She couldn't commit to this kind of responsibility. Her record with commitment was dismal.

What did her continued bad luck with men say about her?

From behind her, Chip cleared his throat. "Anytime now."

Sure enough, Six's eyes were shutting.

Yep, there went Gabby's heart.

Moving back a foot, Gabby adjusted Six in her viewfinder. From that vantage point, she saw Six more objectively, how the white flash on her face wasn't quite even, and how one ear was a tad longer than the other.

Would these imperfections keep someone from adopting Six? The thought was heartbreaking.

Six wasn't less sweet, less adorable, with what could be considered flaws.

Much like being awkward in a first date, or cutting out sugar.

"You're right," she whispered, before setting her camera down. She picked up Six and held her in her arms, wishing against all wishes that this puppy would find a good home.

"About what?"

Standing, she turned to him with newfound conviction. "Maybe I *am* trying to sabotage this thing with Nathan."

He stepped aside so she could bring Six to the other puppies. "I never said sabotage. That's a big word."

"What else is it, though?"

"Doubt, maybe? It's okay to doubt going out with Nathan, if giving him another chance is the right thing to do." He opened the gate for her so she could walk in. The other puppies gravitated toward her feet and she took care to step around them. "But sabotage… Sabotage just feels so deliberate and mean. And you're not any of those things."

She set Six down and let the words wash over her. "Sometimes it feels like I have a lot to do with it. The ruining."

She followed Chip into the kitchen, where her computer and notes were set up for their study session. Notes that had precise outlines, notes that she'd poured over.

She'd tackled her work and studies like she'd tackled her relationship with Nathan, or anyone really, with precise, step-by-step instructions. With tenacity, especially when things weren't going well.

Plopping down on the chair, she had the sudden urge to swipe everything off the table. Obviously, her strategy no longer worked. What was she doing wrong?

But because she always took care of her things, she instead flipped open her laptop and clicked through to her study guide.

In front of her, the chair pulled back with a squeak; then, a body set itself down. Chip. Placing his hand on hers, he tugged her back to the present. "Hey."

His hand was warm and steady, and she tore her gaze away from it, looking up into his gray eyes. "Hey."

"Are you done?"

She heaved a breath, shoving her brain forward. "Yep. I should have all the photos edited and uploaded tonight."

"That's not what I mean." He smiled. "You're not the ruiner of things. You're someone who brings people together. The weddings you plan, spur-of-the-moment dance classes. And weren't you just taking pictures to help find these homes for the puppies?"

"All different."

"Yeah? Different from what?" He pulled his hand back.

For a beat, she wished that he could have kept holding her. It was a comfort; it grounded her.

She refocused. "Different from me being in a relationship. In not being in one that lasted. How I continued to try, time and again, and yet nothing has worked. What if nothing will work?"

He pressed his lips together through a short pause. "It takes two to make a romantic relationship work, you know? And William, and Nathan, in the past that is…they hold responsibility for their part in it."

"Of course, they do. But how can I be this wedding planner—how can I be around all kinds of relationships, and not have the ability to suss my own out? I hear a lot of stories in my line of work, and if a groom had acted how Nathan acted when we were together before, I would gently push the card of a couple's counselor into her hand. If my cousins or sister told me that they were in a relationship with someone they've never met in person, I would tell them to wake up and smell the scam. But I can't seem to see it for myself. I'm so turned around about everything that I can't tell if this no sweets thing should really matter. If Nathan, who says that he's trying, really is."

"Then it sounds to me that you need more time."

"That's fair." Gabby thought on it. "Do you think Nathan is really trying?"

"He says he is."

She searched his face. If there was anyone she trusted, it was Chip. While he'd never disparaged Nathan, she knew he would be as truthful as possible.

His expression softened. "What would make you feel better about him?"

"Besides the fact that maybe he should speak up? I can't get a read on him to see how else he's changed. Nathan always prioritized his work over me, or over mine. So will he keep in touch with me when he's on the road? Will he include me in his plans? All I wanted was to be a part of his life. And if he can't do those things, I want to be able to walk away."

"You can't know any of those answers if you don't give things with him a second chance."

"Yeah." She bit her lip, mulling it over. Was she throwing an opportunity away because she was scared? Was she finding things wrong with a perfectly nice person?

"Look, don't go out with Nathan if you don't feel it's right. Or if you feel the need to work on yourself first, then you should. But the way you're talking—it makes me think that it could be anyone that walked through that door, and you would be in your head with some of the same questions."

Would she?

The moment had gotten thick, and she yearned to break the tension. "You've developed some mad counseling skills since you became a bartender."

He ran his hand through his hair, lips curling in mild amusement. "I'm trying to be supportive here."

"I wish things with him would be as easy as they are with you."

Though after she said it, she bit her lip. There was more

than a small kernel of truth there, and for reasons she would never be able to say aloud.

Inside, though, she innately knew that she and Chip could be something. To her, he was the total package. Chip flew green flags, with the occasional beige flags for reasons like he dipped his fries in mayo.

But Chip deserved a woman like Regan, where there was no extra baggage, like a friend between them.

She quickly pulled up her messages on her phone, clicking on Nathan's last text, to move the moment forward. "Maybe I will go out with him again."

"Great."

"So what are you doing tomorrow night?"

"I'm working at Mountain Rush until eight..." His voice trailed off. "Why?"

"You should come." The more she thought on it, the more it sounded perfect.

"Aw, I don't know, Gab."

"Let's do another double date. Bring Regan. We all hit it off the first time, and I would feel better with you being there. It can ease the awkwardness."

"What if he's not okay with that?"

"I don't think he'll mind. And if he does, then that'll tell me everything. I'm unwilling to go back to how he and I were in the past, completely ghosting our friends while we were dating. And Regan and I have to become friends if you two start getting serious."

"You're moving way too fast right now. No one is getting serious with anyone."

"Okay, fine, we'll go molasses-slow. Better yet...days-old puppy slow." She pressed her hands together. "Please?"

Chip pressed his fingers against the bridge of his nose. "Is this for real?"

"With cherries on top?"

After a beat, he said, "Okay, fine."

She jumped out of her chair and rushed Chip with a hug.

Twelve days until the wedding

Chip texted Nathan: You're sure it's cool we're coming?

I'm glad you're coming. You and Regan are a good buffer.

What's your ETA?

Be there in about ten, Nathan responded.

Remember what I said.

Make sure she knows that she's going to be my priority. That I won't be a workaholic.

OK, Chip replied.

Why am I tripping?

Try to relax.

"Hey there, stranger."

Chip looked up at the sound of a woman's voice.

Regan.

At the sight of her, Chip's breath left him. She was a beautiful woman, with a smile so pure and sincere. Their first date—he had indeed swiped right on an app he hadn't been on in months—had been flawless as far as first dates went. She'd been flexible in adding Gabby and Nathan to their date night, was amenable to changing their plans from watching a movie to going to get ice cream, and their goodbye hug at the end of the night was romantic, but chaste.

Flawless, except he was keenly aware that he'd swiped right not for connection, but for a purpose.

And he was doing it again.

He knew it wasn't right, but he pushed his conscience away. Standing, he greeted Regan with a gentle hug. She was comfy in a cable sweater and leather-like leggings and fuzzy boots, and she smelled like citrus. "Hey. You look great."

"Thanks." She sat down on the plastic chair next to him, eyes lingering on his face. "You look nice, too. Though I have to admit, I don't think I've had date at a bowling alley since I was thirteen." She gestured to a group of regulars in lane one with their matching shirts.

"At least you *had* a date at a bowling alley. This was my actual hangout spot from age eleven through fourteen."

She laughed. "You really hung out here?"

"Yep. See that *Pole Position* arcade game in the corner?" He pointed at the line of machines against one wall, where preteen kids congregated. "That's been there since my senior year of high school. Last one standing from the nineties."

"I haven't played an arcade game in forever."

"If we have time today, we should jump in the seat."

"Then I guess I won't tell you that when I did play those arcade games, I wasn't half-bad." Her eyes twinkled, and Chip remembered why that first date went so well. Things didn't faze her.

"Bowling and arcade games. Not quite fancy. Are you okay with it?"

"Yeah. Dates don't have to be fancy, do they?"

"No, and you don't mind doubling with Gabby and Nathan again?"

She brushed up against him. "I said I was fine and I meant it. Besides, I think our first date went well because we were all together. I admit, going on a group date isn't a typical first date for me, but it took the pressure off."

"Agreed." He felt himself relax. Sure, she didn't know the truth about their date, but she didn't have to. And what was stopping him from getting to know Regan for an actual relationship?

After all, Gabby was going to date Nathan for real.

"So why are you single? You're like…perfect," he said.

"Ha. That's very sweet. Keep in mind that we're only on our second date. You don't know about my penchant for workaholism." A wry smile graced her lips.

"You're talking to someone who has a lot of side gigs."

"Then you might understand. That when I get in the zone with clients, I'm all in. And while I'm away from work—us sitting here talking about our double date? All I can think of is my clients. Not that I miss them, but that I hope they're doing okay."

He sat back. "I don't think that's so bad."

"I like that you're giving me the benefit of the doubt despite me admitting that sometimes I don't live in the moment, which is considered a huge flaw." Her shoulders lowered. "But, yeah, my dating life also isn't helped by the fact that I'm usually exhausted after my day. But… I had the same question. I'm surprised you're still single. You're not bad yourself."

Guilt tugged at his belly—this date was, after all, manufactured—but he opted for a truthful answer. "Nice guys finish last."

"Ah, friend-zoned."

"Perpetually."

"They might finish last, but they still cross the finish line."

He grinned. "That is the nicest way of calling someone a loser I've ever heard."

Regan threw her head back and laughed. "I didn't mean…"

"Yeah, whatever. Let's go get our shoes." Chip stood and offered her a hand, and he felt the last of his tension unfurl. He could do this; he could enjoy himself tonight if he allowed himself.

"Oh, Gabby and Nathan are here." She took his hand while gazing over his shoulder. "Oh, my God. Was there a theme we weren't told about?"

He turned as the two sauntered in, wearing hideous, green-and-pink striped shirts. He groaned. "Gabby's in planner mode."

"Planner mode?"

"Yep. She's a wedding planner—"

"Yes. She mentioned."

"But beyond that, she likes to, well…go all the way. No birthday is too small, no celebration too little."

"Hey, you two." Gabby shoved shirts at Chip and Regan, then hugged them both belatedly.

"Um." Chip held up his shirt: it was baby blue and a bright yellow Hawaiian print.

"This is…oh, my God, I don't have words." Regan cackled as she held her matching shirt against her chest. "And it's huge."

"Easier to move around in," Gabby said. "You're gonna need it, because we're going to kick your booty."

"Strong words from someone who has never broken a hundred." Chip shook his head.

"I've got a secret weapon." Gabby nudged Nathan.

He flipped up his collar. "My average is a two-twenty."

"Oh, it's on." Regan held up a hand for a high five. "Right, Chip?"

Chip slapped a hand against hers, his chest swelling at this glimpse of Regan's competitive side. A definite, sexy contrast to her easygoing nature. "Hell yeah."

It was a whirlwind after that as everyone grabbed their shoes and picked their bowling balls. Regan went to change her shirt in the bathroom, and he did a quick change right there in the lanes.

All the while, Nathan chatted it up with Gabby.

Which was good.

Or was it?

Yesterday, while taking photos of the puppies, he'd experienced a rise and fall in emotions, from wanting to scream out how he felt for her, to vehemently wishing that either she or Nathan would fall out of interest with one another, then resisting the temptation to shake some sense into her when she called herself a ruiner.

Suggesting that she give Nathan another chance had been the one thing he could say to remind her that she deserved love, even if it ended up being Nathan again.

Though, currently, it made him want to kick Nathan's ass in bowling.

Chip knew he was being a primitive Neanderthal, but he didn't care.

When Regan came out of the bathroom wearing the Hawaiian shirt, Chip did a double take. She'd tied the long ends into a bow, so her midriff was on display. She strode toward them with confidence.

And she was staring right at him.

Damn. What was he doing mooning over Gabby when here was Regan, who ticked all of his boxes thus far? The best part was that she was available, and there was no best-friend drama to contend with.

"You're a miracle worker," he said, unable to help himself. "You took that shirt from repellent to catwalk-worthy."

Her cheeks pinked. "Thank you. Hopefully it'll make up for the fact that I suck at bowling. I'm a hundred percent sure I'm the worst out of everyone here."

"Aw, no worries. I was just acting competitive because Gabby loves to instigate."

"The two of you are close." She looked over at Gabby and Nathan, who were entering their names into the dashboard. Nathan hovered over Gabby in a way that made Chip want to tell him to step back.

He tore his eyes away and focused on Regan's face. "We are. We've known each other a while."

"Like siblings."

His tummy roiled at the description. "I guess some people could say so."

Her expression softened. "I'm an army brat, and I can appreciate good friends, especially ones that live in the same town."

"Yeah, I guess I am pretty lucky. Though, there are some downsides to small towns." Like not having enough space between his best friend, the woman he was drawn to, and this matchmaking scheme he was now tied up in.

What was he doing?

Suddenly, he wanted to hurry this game up. Then slink back into the simple life he'd had before participating in this charade.

"What's taking the two of you so long?" Chip asked, and the other couple looked in his direction. Gabby's cheeks were flushed.

The thought that it was Nathan who put that smile on her face renewed Chip's competitive spirit.

"Done!" Nathan said. "You're up first, Chip."

The game charged forward, and Chip had one goal and one goal only: to beat Nathan. He ignored the historical fact that he'd never come close to Nathan's scores. With every turn Chip took, he focused on his steps, the strength of his throw. The spin. A regular at bowling he was not, but he remained determined and unflappable.

Miraculously, at the start of the tenth frame, he was up by two points. Nathan was second; Gabby was third, and Regan was barely on the scoreboard.

"You've got this." Regan offered her fists for him to bump, adding a couple of snaps—something they'd made up in the third frame.

He nodded, then stepped up to the bowling-ball rack and wiggled his fingers over the fan.

"Someone's superserious." Gabby strolled past him.

"I know what you're doing." He kept his eyes on the pin-setter at the end of the lane.

"I don't know what you're talking about."

"You're trying to distract me."

"You're right. Except…"

He turned to look at her and their gazes locked. Something else was in her eyes. Was she flirting with him? "Except what?"

"I don't have to try."

She was right, of course. He was fully distracted well before this moment, but not for the reason she believed. It was her proximity, and the soothing tenor of her voice. Even the way she bowled—she had this quirky throw that, if done improperly, could launch the ball backward toward the spectators.

Clapping from behind him filled his thoughts. "C'mon, Chip. Bring it home."

Right. Regan.

Regan, *his date*.

Chip took two deep breaths, wound up, and let go of the ball.

Only two pins fell. With the next throw, only one fell.

"Argh!" Chip spluttered. "That mother—"

"Mr. Lowry, don't you dare!"

Chip froze at the sound of his name, and turned to the left, to see Daria, along with a few more folks from the senior center. They were dressed in their finest bowling outfits and looked to have just arrived. "Sorry, ma'am."

"It's just a game, son."

"Yes, ma'am."

Mollified, Chip walked back to the bench and sat next to a giggling Regan.

"You're right about small towns," she said.

"I'm lucky I didn't get an ear twist in the process." He eyed Nathan as he stood and took his turn. "As long as he doesn't get more than four, I'll be good."

She mused. "I'm happy I got a fifty."

"I don't care what my score is, so long as it's higher than his."

As soon as the words left his mouth, Chip regretted it. Whether or not Regan noticed, he was acting out of character, and inappropriate, because he and Gabby were just friends.

Especially since he'd had a hand in bringing Nathan and Gabby together.

What was he doing taking a part in this shenanigan? Was he so much of a glutton for punishment?

While his mother had taught him that he should try to help others when he can, he didn't think she meant for him to do so at his detriment.

Because all of this was starting to mess with his head.

So, Chip shut his eyes as Nathan wound up for his next throw.

Afterward, at the shoe-return counter, Nathan caught up to Chip. Regan and Gabby had gone ahead to get their names on the list at Crest Pizza.

"That was a good game, man," Nathan said.

Chip inwardly bristled at the loss that would haunt his thoughts forever. Nathan had usurped them all with a turkey: three strikes in a row.

"Yeah, back at you." Chip led the way to the register to pay for him and Regan's games. "So how are things going tonight?"

"Way better than expected. It looks like she's opening up too."

Chip frowned. "Yeah?"

"Yeah. Especially when I apologized for the times we didn't hang out enough with our friends." He half laughed. "Thanks for that tidbit by the way. Makes me wanna cringe for how I acted with her before."

"We all make mistakes." Chip reluctantly said. While he was glad that Nathan had learned from his, he could feel himself losing any chance he might have Gabby.

Even if she wasn't Chip's to begin with.

"It makes me appreciate what we've got now. I don't know the last time I had this much fun." After accepting his receipt, Nathan asked, "I do have a question."

"Sure." Chip pushed the glass doors open, unsettled by Nathan's use of "what we've got now." As if to say that he *had* Gabby after two short dates.

Chip stepped aside as pedestrians walked past on the cobblestone sidewalk.

"Serious question. Between you and me, and I promise that it won't piss me off."

He heaved a cool breath into his lungs and looked back at the bowling alley's front windows, lit bright from the inside. The moon was out, though there was a little bit of light left in the sky. It was the season of change, and as he and Nathan headed toward the parking lot, Chip was sure he knew what was coming next.

"You and her, were you ever something…after she and I split up?" Nathan's voice trailed off.

Yes, Chip wanted to say. Absolutely yes, they were together, so it was best Nathan give up his dream of getting her back. But that was a lie.

Still, Chip was curious why Nathan suspected a relationship. Was Chip that transparent? "Nope. Just friends. Why?"

He heaved out a relieved smile as he peeled off toward his car. "You know what? Forget what I said. It's my imagination, clearly. With the way the two of you are so close, and with how you were so protective and not wanting to put in a good word for me at first." He pressed his lips together in thought. "I've been doing some work lately with my therapist. Have I mentioned?"

Chip stopped at his car. "A therapist, huh? No, you didn't say. That's great, man."

Chip was still speaking the truth, but his heart cracked a smidge. A self-aware Nathan was what Gabby had wanted.

"Like I told Gab. I'm trying." He opened his car door. "Anyway, see you in, like, thirty seconds."

"See you there." He ducked into his car and followed Nathan the short distance to Crest Pizza, which had a line out the door.

And though Chip would put on a smile the rest of the night, he knew it wouldn't be sincere. Nathan's intuition, that Gabby was opening up, and that there was something between Chip and Gabby, albeit one-sided, was spot on, and that was the problem.

Chapter Nine

Eight days until the wedding

"I have never seen this many people in here." Liza popped off a couple of beer caps. "What the hell is going on?"

Chip filled two tumblers with ice, noting the laughter around him. It was a Friday night, Mountain Rush's busiest day of the week, but the crowd was especially thick. The line was four deep for each bartender, and little space existed between people. And since Friday nights were also karaoke night, there was a brave soul singing their heart out, while the audience joined in the chaos.

All good things, in Chip's mind. "They're here for the Sotheby-Matthews wedding."

"But it's not for another week."

"Remember that big wedding last year, with Maggie Thurmond? Wait. You weren't here yet."

"Nope, but I heard." She accepted a credit card from a guest. "She hosted a wedding here, right? I grew up with stacks of her magazines. My mother was obsessed with her."

"Yep. That wedding made it to all the magazines. This year the Thurmonds did a huge shout-out on their socials telling everyone to visit Peak, and this is the result."

"I still don't understand that sorcery. Social media. I

suck at it. Though, I need to learn it. Apparently we don't do enough of it," Liza said.

"Who said?"

"The big boss. He thinks we could do better, and somehow I'm supposed to fix it."

He handed drinks across the counter and accepted cash from the customer. "How've you been settling in?"

"Good. Getting used to things." She twisted her hair onto the top of her head and stuck a clip in it. To a woman leaning across the counter, she said, "Sweetheart, I promise I'll get to you next, okay?"

She mouthed an "oh, my God" at Chip.

He laughed. "For what it's worth, I'm no good at social media, either." He took another order, returning to his previous thought. "Eight days. It's eight days until the wedding."

She finished up pouring something on the rocks and handed it to its recipient, then snorted. "You know it down to the day?" She gestured to another guest waiting.

"I'm with Gabby all the time. She's got it down to the hours."

Liza's eyebrows rose as she turned to pull from the keg. At the same time, a screech from the microphone rippled through the bar, and a collective groan sounded through the space. "Oh, my God, I hate it when that happens."

"Same." He gestured to a guy who'd been waiting too long, touching his ear because he couldn't hear him above the noise.

"Shenandoah Pale Ale!"

Chip nodded at him.

"You guys aren't together, are you?" Liza asked.

He shook his head. "Nah."

"I don't get it. She's here all the time, or you're out with her. She looks at you with doe eyes and you're like a puppy trotting after her…"

He was grateful that no one was listening to their conversation among the madness, and thankful that he had an excuse to look away, so that she couldn't see him wince.

Because while her description of him had been said in jest, it painted a pathetic picture of how he was acting.

Did he really trot after her? Was he that desperate for her attention?

But wait…did Gabby actually look at him with doe eyes?

"Not sure what you're talking about," he said.

"Look, I know I'm new here. I know I'm not a part of this web of Peak drama." She winked. "But… I've worked in bars in all my life. I can read people, even back when all I could do was sit and do homework while I waited for my mom to finish work. The both of you?" She nudged past him with a finished cocktail in her hand, and paused, leaning in. "Are sitting on a tree. L.O.N.G.I.N.G."

He snorted, "I think that whatever lens you're reading through needs some Windex and a good shine, my friend."

Though, inside, he wished.

Then again, what exactly did he wish for? That Nathan wasn't his best friend so he wouldn't have to consider the bro code? That Chip wasn't such good friends with Gabby so that he wouldn't have to risk her friendship if he'd had the bravado to bare his feelings? That Nathan hadn't worked on himself so that he could be a better man for Gabby?

This wasn't just a simple falling-for-your-best-friend situation. Other people were involved. Two important people he didn't want to lose.

Liza continued, "Okay, that's fair. I'm assuming there are feelings based on what I see. But are you seriously telling me there's nothing there from you?"

"We're just good friends."

"Nope, that's not an answer." She swiped a credit card

through the terminal. "You went out the other night. I saw you all at Crest Pizza. That so-called 'double date.' You were sitting next to one another."

"We were sitting across from our dates."

"Who does that in a booth?" She threw her head back and laughed. "C'mon Lowry. I can see it on your face."

"Look, let's say I did…you know…say something to her." He topped off the pint of Pale Ale and handed it to a guest, who passed him his credit card.

"That would be brave, with the other guy and all." Liza wiped down a spot where someone spilled their drink.

"Right? There's no way she feels the same way."

"She says she loves you all the time."

"She says that to everyone."

"Respectfully, for a guy who takes all kinds of business risks, you're a fraidy cat when it comes to this." Liza grinned, then took another order and brushed passed him. She gestured toward the front door. "And, oh, my goodness, speaking of the devil herself. Or maybe an angel for you."

Chip spotted Gabby's bright smile in the crowd. She unwound her scarf and her hair fluffed up around her. She raised a hand up as if to say something, but was pulled aside by a group of women.

"Whiskey sour!" a customer barked at him.

"What's that?" He touched his ear. "I'm missing the magic word."

The man huffed. "Please."

"That's more like it." Chip went to the opposite side of the bar and as he finished making the cocktail, Gabby came around. "Roller skating!"

"What's that?" He passed Liza, who winked at him knowingly.

Gabby followed him, parallel to the bar. "Tomorrow night. Are you busy? With Regan and Nathan. And me, of course."

"Roller skating?" A whine escaped his lips as he settled the guest's bill. Bowling was one thing, but he hadn't roller-skated in years. "Is the rink even open?"

"They close at midnight. Doesn't it sound like fun?"

The noise was getting to him. He couldn't think *and* listen to a guest. Was he happy to see Gabby? Absolutely. But the idea of another date didn't sound appealing at all.

The other night he'd left Crest Pizza with heavy feelings of guilt, and something else he couldn't describe.

Like a puppy trotting after her...

"Hold on a sec..." He raised a hand toward the back room to signal for reinforcements. A minute later, another bartender, Jay, entered the bar.

"I need a break. Ten minutes?" Chip said.

Jay nodded. "Got you."

To Gabby, Chip said, "Meet me in the hallway in a couple of minutes."

She gave him the thumbs-up and made her way to the back.

Once Jay was settled, Chip stepped down from the bar area. On the way toward the hallway, he found Gabby cornered by a couple of women. He caught her eye and offered his hand, to extricate her from the situation.

She took it, grabbing it firmly.

Her warm hand in his, he led her to where it was infinitely quieter.

"Thank you so much. They wouldn't stop talking." Gabby was flushed, cheeks visibly pink, even in the dim light.

"Who were they?"

"I don't even know. They were talking about Maggie Thurmond, though. The power of her promo is amazing."

"So they recognized you?"

"Apparently. Whew. It's wild out there."

It took another second for Chip to realize that they were still holding hands, not until her gaze landed on where they were linked.

He gently let go and stuffed his hands in his pockets. "Now, what's this about roller skating?"

"Before we go into that… I have great news." She was positively bursting and he couldn't keep from grinning himself.

"What is it?'

"Speaking of the power of promo, we've got some interest in the puppies."

Gabby had uploaded the photos the other day, and admittedly, Chip hadn't kept up with it. From work to dates, and actually taking care of the puppies, he had forgotten about it.

"Really?"

"Yes. They look like legitimate inquiries. Locals." Her smile was bright. "I've started to make a chart on how we should pick the new parents." She counted the tasks on their fingers. "When it's time, we can include them when Doc comes to make his well puppy visits. The hopeful parents can bring their family members, so that the transition is easy for everyone."

"So much information." Still, his heart squeezed that she'd been doing her own research.

"Exactly, we can't give these puppies to any old stranger."

"We? When did this become a *we*?" Though, in saying it, Chip liked the sound of it.

Her cheeks reddened. "I'm involved now. I want to make sure our babies go to the right place."

Our babies.

Chip knew she didn't mean anything by the term. That's who Gabby was—a woman who was willing to jump into any major task the same way he did, with gusto.

Still. The thought of *their* babies.

Would they have dark hair like hers, or streaks of blond like his? Would they have her brown eyes or his gray? How tall would they be? A good eight inches separated him from Gabby.

A nudge on his foot refocused him. "Hey, are you listening?"

He pressed his fingers against the bridge of his nose. Where was his brain? Apparently gone into fairy tale land where they were life partners.

It was because his emotions were pulled thin. "Tired, sorry."

"Okay then, no more talk of charts. How about I come by before roller skating tomorrow and sit down with George to figure things out? Or the next day, before our study session."

He peered at her. "Then it would be the second time that you don't study during our 'study session.' Scratch that, our fourth. We're not really doing your schooling any justice here."

"Other things sometimes take priority." Her gaze moved away from his.

Interesting. She was shirking. Something was up. It was his turn to nudge her foot. "You *are* studying more than the hours that we've been together, right?"

"When I can."

"Gabby."

"Okay. Not really." Her face crumpled. "I'm not feeling it. With this wedding and now the puppies."

"Nuh-uh. Don't you blame the puppies." He stepped closer so he could get her attention. He tenderly held her by the forearms. "Listen. This is for real. I'm your accountability buddy and I'm holding you to it and…" Except the rest of his words dissolved as he looked down at her.

At her parted lips, as if in anticipation of a kiss.

And, oh, did he want to.

He wanted to press his lips against hers, wanted to taste her. He wanted to breathe in her same breath.

"And what?" she whispered.

Oh, God, what was he doing?

Chip came to his senses and backed up a millimeter. "And… I want to make sure I hold up my side of the bargain. You asked me to help you and I am. Unless…"

She swallowed, and for a beat she didn't speak. "Unless what?"

Chip inhaled to reset himself, then took a full step back. He was warm all over.

A walk, he needed a walk and a cold bucket of water to the face.

"Chip?"

He cleared his throat, thinking back to a previous conversation. "Unless…you really don't want to retake the test."

She frowned. "Not retake the test? That's not even an option. Why would you say that?"

"You mentioned it that day at the senior center. After cha-cha. Maybe you're right—you're so busy. Some space from all these big things could…"

She shook her head vehemently. "I wasn't serious. You finish school, then you take the tests. That's the plan."

He held up his hands. "All right then. Test, it is. But you're going to need to study."

"I know." Her expression was stern, the opposite to how she was earlier.

"So then…" He used a light tone, to somehow salvage this conversation. "What is this about us roller skating?"

"Roller skating?" She blinked.

"Yeah. You said something about another date."

"Right, sorry. I was thinking about…" She half laughed. "So, um, I think I'm going to ask Nathan to the wedding. He's already going, so it'll be as easy to switch his seat next to mine."

"Oh." Chip swallowed this bitter pill. A pill he had put right into her hand. "Bowling must have gone well for you."

"It did. And he dropped me off at home and…" Her voice trailed and it was almost wistful.

He raised a hand in objection, if anything, to distract himself from the pain. "No need to kiss and tell."

"I'm not saying a thing!" Her expression was mock shock. "But I think I'm comfortable enough for him to be my plus one. My family already knows him. The aunties think he's really cute—"

"Then why wait? Why not ask him now?" He interrupted. *And there would be an end to these dates.*

"Because he said something that night, when he dropped me off. I had complimented him on how things feel so easy between us, and he said, 'Well I'm on my best behavior.'"

"Is…that bad?"

She stuffed her hands in her pockets. "Logically, I understand that we're in the beginning of our reunion and that things unfold over time. But when he said that, he reminded me of the times when he wasn't on his best behavior."

"You're asking Nathan to a wedding. You're not proposing."

"You're right. As usual. But another date will help me feel better about it." Then, she pressed her hands together in prayer. "So will you come to roller skating?"

"I'll give Regan a text."

"Already done." She beamed. "We exchanged numbers. I love her, by the way."

"Well, I'm glad you approve." Chip looked down at the

floor—by the end of the night it was going to be sticky and disgusting.

"She says she's free, and since you are, too, I'll tell Nathan it's a go. Okay?"

"Yeah. Sure. Okay." He rested a hand behind his neck. It was clammy from all the thoughts running through his head. Relief that Nathan had been good to her. Dread that things were slipping from his fingers. The puppies. The senior center. All going according to plan, but it was going too fast, and he wasn't sure how to stop a train that'd clearly left the station.

Gabby started, waking from a nap with a gasp, and her eyes opened to a dark room. Next to her, her phone buzzed with a notification.

She'd planned to lay down for just a second, not fall asleep.

She pressed her fingers against her eyes, then reached across to her phone. The screen showed that two hours had passed, and it was almost nine at night.

Groaning, Gabby sat up on the couch and took in her messy living room, a train wreck of the incomplete and indecisive, and found no solace there. And how could she? It reflected exactly where her mind was.

In chaos.

While it was par for the course to let things go as she came upon deadlines, with four big things going on at once, she had lost control.

Three she could do. Four? Four was a beast.

Wedding.

Nathan.

Puppies.

Exam.

Gabby had had a full night of productivity planned after her quick trip to Mountain Rush to talk to Chip. She'd been ready to face these four things and somehow right her life. With her conversation with Chip cycling in her head—*you are studying more than the hours that we've been together, right?*—her motivation had been renewed to hit the books.

But how could she do that now, when things were happening? More emotional, confusing things, like Nathan.

And Chip.

Okay, fine. There were five things she was dealing with, with Chip taking the top spot. Two dates she'd been on with him, albeit double dates and not *with* him, per se, but still, she'd gotten to know another side to him. What he was like when he shaved and dressed and sat close to his date. What he was like engaged in quiet conversation, opening doors.

What he was like when he competed. That was hot.

Was it sinful to ogle someone else's date, especially while on her own? Absolutely.

And holding hands today...and the kiss, or what she thought was going to be a kiss in that darkened hallway. The intimate moment had lasted a couple of minutes, max, but it had stirred up the thing in her belly that she'd tamped down while on her date with Nathan. In truth, she'd been ready to initiate the kiss, knowing that Chip would have hesitated because of their friendship.

She had, for a beat, thought something unfolding between her and Chip, and that maybe the love of her life had been standing right in front of her all along.

But it was too late for all of that, wasn't it? Their friendship ran too deep, and she didn't want to be responsible for coming in between him and Nathan.

She must have been taking things out of context. The inquiries about the puppies and the recent Maggie Thurmond promo had been a boost to her day. For the first time in the last few weeks, Gabby felt triumphant. That what she was doing had impact.

Perhaps the chemistry she was feeling tonight was one-sided. Because she'd seen how he'd looked at Regan on their date, with this kind of awe. And she was jealous.

God, how embarrassing. He'd saved her from making a fool out of herself by stepping back. It wasn't just because Nathan was his best friend—but because it would have ruined them. And once more, she would have fulfilled what seemed to be her fate, which was to be alone.

Chip deserved someone who was steady and focused, like Regan. Not like Gabby, who overthought everything. Who, despite her supposed ability to organize, had a house that looked like it had been ransacked.

So, no…she wasn't studying now, even if she had a few minutes to herself.

A knock on her front door snapped her out of her thoughts. "Who is it?"

"It's Mom!" Eva had a key to her house, but thank goodness had the sense to maintain boundaries. Though, Gabby figured that it had everything to do with her mother walking in on Frankie and Reece, once upon a time.

Gabby grimaced.

She had misspoken. She had *five and half* things she had to manage. The half thing was a subsection of the exam, which was to admit to her mother that she hadn't passed her test.

She hadn't been alone with Eva in a few days, and at their last meeting, they'd talked weddings.

Gabby had forgotten all about not telling her.

Denial was a sweet thing, until it came time to face the truth.

Here it goes.

"Come in!" Gabby made to stand.

The door opened, and Eva blew in, waving around a fistful of magazines. "I saw your porch light on so I thought I would stop in with a couple more ideas for color schemes, and I wanted to get your take—"

Her mother eyed the myriad of shoes at the door, Gabby's coats draped over her couch, the piles of purses and receipts and take-out bags. Without fanfare, Eva bent down and picked up said take-out bags, then brought them straight to the garbage. "What the heck?"

"I know, I know." Gabby held up a hand. "It's been a wild season."

"Honey, you're a busy woman. If you need help, we can get housekeeping to head here, too. There's no shame in it."

"No, that's not it. It's just…" She wiggled her fingers like jazz hands. "When my brain's a mess, it all comes out here, too. It's a process."

"Did you have dinner? Are you hangry?"

"I don't know. But before you go mama bear on me, I have to tell you something." Now that she thought about it, she didn't remember the last time she'd had a good meal. Maybe at Crest Pizza, the other night, when instead of sitting next to Nathan, she had chosen to sit next to Chip. Because she was most comfortable with him.

Because she trusted him a hundred percent.

"Yes, yes. There's time for that later. Let's put some food in you first. Hmm." Eva peeked inside the cupboards and pulled the refrigerator door open. "Sweetheart! No wonder you can't tell up from down. You have nothing in this house. When was the last time you went grocery shopping?"

The more Eva talked about Gabby's lack of sustenance, the more Gabby felt out of sorts. She went to her couch, grabbed an armful of clothes and trudged to her laundry room. She tossed the clothes into the laundry basket, stopping to absorb the state of that room, too. "I don't know. Last week? The week before? I forget. I've been going to Frankie's for dinner when I haven't gone out."

"We'll need to fix that," she said.

Gabby heard the refrigerator shut and her mother's footsteps. Then, beyond, the sound of her front door opening. "I'll be back."

"Wait!" She peeked out of the laundry room, noting the living room was empty, and whispered, "Mom, I didn't pass my test."

Did that count?

Gabby groaned.

Laundry it was then, so she started a load. She threw in the outfit she wore for bowling and then came upon the shirt she wore when she photographed the puppies.

Six.

The puppy's eyes came to the forefront of her memory, followed swiftly by Chip's hand on hers, and then glimpses of him during their dates, when the familiar swirling started in her belly.

"I'm back," Eva said, after the door clicked shut. "With leftovers. I'm heating them up."

Gabby woke from her thoughts and started a wash load.

When she walked back into the kitchen, it was filled with the delicious scent of vinegar and garlic.

Eva took a glass storage container out of the microwave. Then heaped a helping into a bowl, and handed it to her with a spoon and fork.

Sinigang. The ultimate comfort food. Made with fish, in a sour tomato broth, and served over rice, it filled her chest with warmth...and she hadn't yet taken a bite.

Gabby hopped onto a stool, with guilt coursing through

her. Her mother was so intuitive and kind, and now Gabby was going to upset her. "Thank you."

"I made a big pot of it yesterday." She reached over and tucked a strand of Gabby's hair behind her ear. She lifted her chin. "You look tired."

"I am."

She frowned. "Is work too much? Should we get you another assistant? What if I took Frankie off some of her other work and have her *really* be your right-hand person. You know she'd love it."

Gabby guffawed, breaking the seriousness of the moment, and sat up. "She'd love it a little too much."

Gabby mixed the broth with the rice, broke up the fish, and mixed that in, too. The act calmed her down. Maybe it was as simple as eating a good meal that could straighten her out.

She moaned at the first bite.

Eva took a seat across from her with a self-satisfied look. "It makes me so happy to feed you. I know you're grown, but it's such a simple pleasure." She linked her fingers together. "So tell me. Are you worried about your test results?"

Gabby stilled, eyes on her food. "About that. Mom, the test really sucked."

"I don't have any doubt you'll pass. You're so smart. You understand numbers. I remember when you were a kid, you memorized the first twenty numbers of pi."

"Thirty-two, actually. But that's memorization." She looked up with a twinge in her chest. "Nothing like this test."

"I know. I'm just putting it into some context. Some of your classmates didn't even know what pi was, even if you had been studying it. All that to say, that you have an affinity for numbers, a gift. So you mustn't doubt."

It was too much, this confidence in her.

"I failed." She took another bite and breathed in, enhancing the flavors of the food, hoping to fill the hole in her chest.

It didn't work.

Eva gasped. "Failed? You think you failed?"

"I know I did. It was right there on the screen. Fail."

Her expression changed, from shock to sadness. "But…"

"I've known for a couple of weeks."

She frowned. "You're only telling me now?"

"I was…scared to tell you."

"But why?"

"Why? Because of this, of how you look. Upset. I don't want you to be upset."

"Upset? Oh, sweetheart. Yes, I'm upset, but for *you*, not for me." She pressed a hand against Gabby's forearm. "Maybe I didn't emphasize it enough when you were growing up, but failure isn't always a bad thing. Especially in business."

Not when it came to tests, though, she wanted to say. Her mother always said things in a way that made everything seem so simple, even when things got complicated. There was only one way to answer, and that was with optimism. "I guess, yeah. I'm retaking it, though."

"That's the spirit. A lot of studying, good food, and good sleep, and I don't have any doubt you'll get there. You'll see."

"Right." Though, despite an attempt at a smile, all Gabby felt was doubt.

"Now, is there anything else? I heard William's out of the picture and that you and Nathan are hanging out. Does that have anything to do with your confusion?"

"Who told you?"

"Who *hasn't* told me?" She sighed. "And history has shown that whenever Nathan shows back up, you get flustered, and not in a good way."

"He's changed."

"Is he though?"

"It seems." She thought back to all her interactions with Nathan thus far, and the effort he was putting to show how he's been working on himself, was evident. "I'm asking him to the wedding."

"Oh. Wow. Already. So it's serious."

"No, it's not but I can't show up alone."

"Ay nako, Gabby."

There it went, the little Tagalog saying that was a sure sign of an incoming lecture. She had to save the moment. "It's fine, though. We're taking it slow, and he's already going to the wedding. That part isn't a big deal."

She pressed a hand against her chest. "So what's going on then? If it's not the wedding, or Nathan, and you've just talked about your test… I know there are puppies—"

"The puppies are great. The puppies are perfect."

"Alright, so?"

"I don't know."

And yet, she knew it had everything to do with Chip. Things were confusing because of her best friend and his involvement with every other part of her life.

Gabby relied on everyone doing their jobs. Just as everyone knew that Gabby could be depended on to plan an event, she required the same of her vendors.

Just as she relied on her mother to know exactly when she needed to eat, and depended on Frankie to lay on the tough love, on Jared to bring the good vibes into every moment, Gabby leaned on Chip as one of her best friends.

Someone she could turn to. To commiserate with. To celebrate with.

Not to hold her hand, right? Not to almost kiss her. Not for her to wish that she was the one he was dating.

If she were being honest with herself, there had always

existed a sliver of attraction. Didn't one admire and have a general attraction for their closest friends?

But that sliver was now a chasm that she could no longer ignore. And it was wrong, with how he was with Regan.

"How did you know that Dad was it? Or that Cruz was it?"

Eva sat straight in her seat, and her cheeks darkened. "Oh, wow. That's an interesting question."

Eva was a strong woman, and Gabby had put her on a pedestal for a long time. She'd admired how her mother held herself with pride. But she'd learned that as much as her mother was a professional, she had a softness to her. And last year, Gabby saw for the first time how her mother was human.

Gabby now knew that Eva had her misgivings; she didn't always talk about her emotions. Her mother was a stellar advisor, but kept her deepest thoughts hidden.

"I suppose..." She cleared her throat. "It was about whether I would want to live life without them. With your dad...it was such an easy decision. From the moment we met, I was smitten.

"After he died, though, I learned to live without him. I figured out that I *could* be alone for a long time. I suppose that's why it was tougher for Cruz to get under my skin. He had to make a good case for being someone I couldn't live without." A shy smile graced her lips. A second later, she blinked, as if remembering that she wasn't alone. "I knew when I knew. It came with time and struggle. But as soon as I figured it out, I didn't want either one out of my sight."

I want that.

Those words echoed in Gabby's head.

"Is Nathan, this time—" Eva began.

"No." Gabby shook her head. "It's funny, you know? Every other time I got back together with Nathan, my imagination ran right to the altar, and now...no. I think *that's* what's throwing me off the most. He's saying all the right things. He's become the person I had wished for way back then."

Her mother smiled. "Business or personal, you know that it's always okay to change your mind, right?"

Gabby shook her head. "But what if changing my mind means blowing things up around me."

"Then you blow things up. Matilda and Jared did so—you were there when he revealed his secret. And Cruz and I did, too, though for each of us, it was more of an internal change." She examined Gabby's face, and Gabby's warmed with vulnerability. "I can't speak for Jared and Matilda, but for me and Cruz, we took solace in our friends and family while we worked things through. So whatever you're deliberating, sweetheart, I'm here for you."

Gabby nodded, though she wasn't reassured. When blowing things up involved your best friend, it risked their friendship.

And she couldn't be the person to ruin it.

Chapter Ten

Seven days until the wedding

The threat of a lonely, solitary life pushed Gabby onto Chip's front porch the next day. She pressed the doorbell with force.

"C'mon, answer." She bounced on the balls of her feet, clutching her phone with the most recent message up and ready.

The inner door opened to Chip's confused expression as he popped the storm door open. "Hey. Did I miss a text? I thought we were meeting later at the rink."

Gabby's vision skewed and her head tilted right. Her jaw dropped. "O.M.G. You got a haircut."

Chip's shaggy hair was gone. Now, the sides had a natural fade, with the top a smidge longer than the rest.

His cheeks reddened, and he rested a hand behind his head. "It wasn't supposed to be this short. I asked Krista for a trim, then she suckered me into trusting her, and voilà."

Voilà, indeed. The floppy hair had been Chip's signature look. It perfectly reflected his easygoing nature. And now, he looked…grown. Gabby had always thought him handsome, but this was next level.

"Do you not like it?"

"No, I do. It's hot." The word was out of her mouth before she could hold it back. She bit her cheek.

"Yeah, whatever." He grinned. "So what's up?"

Gabby recalibrated, relieved that he didn't catch her ogling. "Sorry. Is this a good time? I hope it is, because I have something to show you and—" She held up the phone, and took a deep breath. The emotions were rising up out of her and she didn't know what else to do.

"Yeah, of course." He gestured her in. "Breathe, Gab. What's going on?"

"Okay, so we really need to discuss some things." Gabby had been talking to herself on the way to Chip's house, even turning back a couple of times in doubt. She had been up all night after her conversation with her mother, ruminating about the ways in which she'd gotten off track from her usually organized life, and admittedly, she wasn't of rested and sound mind. But time was of the essence.

She stepped past him, and attempted to ignore how good he smelled and that his current outfit—stonewashed jeans and a neutral sweater—was new, too, and continued in.

Chip frowned. "This sounds serious."

"It is. Because it's going to change everything."

George Lowry was just beyond the threshold, holding two puppies, though neither was Six. "Oh hi, Mr. Lowry. Hi, puppies."

She would allow herself to be distracted for a second. She scooped a puppy into her arms and breathed her in, to fortify herself for what she was about to admit. *Give me strength.* "Is new puppy smell a thing? If so, I want to bottle it."

George smiled, a rare event. "A puppy looks good in your arms."

"They feel good, too." She peeked up at Chip, and then askance at George.

"I should leave the two of you to it." George scooped the

puppy back into his arms. "You sound like you're champing at the bit."

"I am, sorry. But would you mind grabbing Six?" She was grateful to George for reading the room, because this was something she had to run by Chip first. Nothing stayed secret for long, and this was something she needed his thoughts on.

"Will do."

"Thank you, Mr. Lowry."

Gabby watched as George walked away, and only when he was around the corner did she turn back to Chip.

"So," he said. He had his arms crossed in front of him.

"I had this whole big talk with my mom, about the ability to change our minds. I don't know if you could tell, but I've been kind of a mess lately."

"I've noticed that you've had a lot on your plate."

"I have. But I think it's because everything feels like it's up in the air. That test threw me for a loop, and all this dating stuff, with Nathan and previously with William.

"I'm always so worried about everyone else and their expectations of me, and what others want. And I have such tight control of what I think should be happening. But I never really considered that I can change what I want, or *who* I want. And I want someone who will be able to give me unconditional love, to be with all the time, to accept me for who I am."

"Oh?" He stepped closer, with interest in his eyes. Gorgeous gray eyes that were usually hidden behind his hair.

She refocused.

This was it. She was going to say it. "And then I got a ping on our socials."

Chip blinked, confused. "Socials."

"For the puppies."

"Ah." He stood straighter. "The puppies."

"Yes, there's a couple who is interested in Six. And I don't want her to go to them. *I* want her."

"So you want to adopt Six?" he asked, deadpan.

"Yes." Smiling, she willed a happy tone. She had hoped for more enthusiasm from him. "When it's time, of course. Is that okay?"

Beats of silence passed. Was her decision rash? Did he not approve?

Chip crossed his arms and he peered at her. "Didn't you say the other day that you were too busy to raise a puppy? That, quote, 'with my luck, I'll forget to feed it'?"

She cackled, feeling the tension break. "I hate that you remember everything."

"How do we know you're not going to give her up later on?"

She gasped. "Chip! I would never."

"Hey. I'm just doing my due diligence. How do I know the reason you want Six isn't because you saw that someone else wanted her?"

Stunned at the implication, she quieted.

A smile crept onto his lips. "I'm just giving you a hard time, Gabby."

It took another half second for her to realize what he'd said. She shoved him gently. "Ugh. You."

"I couldn't resist. Seriously, though, you're going to make a good mama."

"You think so? I know I've got a lot to learn. I'll need to make sure my house is puppy-proofed. Good thing it's one level, and I have a massive backyard. Though for sure, I'll still keep her on a leash when she's little, because apparently eagles are notorious for—"

"You just made my point…you're going to be great. And

besides, the puppies need to stick around another few weeks. Lucky's got a lot to teach them."

A bark sounded from somewhere in the living room, followed by paw steps on the hardwood floor. Lucky came from around the corner and planted herself next to Gabby. She patted her on the head. "How did she—"

"Dad taught her her name. And to bark whenever she hears it." Chip rolled his eyes. "It's ridiculous. Last night, I caught her lounging on my bed."

Lucky's tongue lolled out, and though appreciative of Gabby's petting, she was looking right at Chip.

Gabby tried to contain her glee. It was obvious that Chip was falling in love with Lucky. It was all in his faint denial. "So what did you do?"

"I pushed her off. I can't have all that dog hair on me." He gestured toward the living room. "Lucky, go see George."

And sure enough, Lucky barked and took off. "That was… impressive. She knows her name, knows your dad's name, and already staked a claim on your bed."

"It doesn't mean anything."

"My opinion? You're just delaying the inevitable."

"And that is?"

"That Lucky already considers this place home."

He shrugged. "I get the final say."

There was bite to his tone, so Gabby held back. It was so unlike Chip to object this strongly. Then again, if the last time he'd had a dog was when his mother had been alive…

She bumped him gently. "I'm just giving you a hard time, too. You've gotta take what you dish out."

"I know. The hardest part of this decision is the idea of telling Dad she can't stay. Anyway." He ran a hand through his hair. "If you can make a note on Six's online photo to say she's taken, that would be great. We're having the vet come out examine all of them next week. You're more than wel-come to be here for that. He'll be available if you have any questions about her health."

"Great." She was doing it. "I'm going to be a fur mama. Thank you." She linked an arm around Chip's waist and hugged him.

He wrapped an arm around her. "I'm glad she's going home with you. Maybe I'll even come over and play."

She tilted up her face at him and said, "I hope you will."

He rested his chin against her temple, the moment com-forting.

So comforting that she didn't want to let go of him.

So comforting that she didn't, and instead leaned into him.

He tucked her in even closer and covered her with a warmth that she hadn't felt in so long. In too long.

She wanted to be held like this forever. By him.

"I thought…" he began, voice rumbling. "I thought you came over to say…"

Hearing the seriousness in his voice, she looked up. "Say what?"

"That you…" he whispered, looking away.

She heard the rest of it in her head. *You wanted me.*

She knew the words because it was what she felt for him.

"Look at me." Gabby wanted to gauge how he felt about her. All this time, he'd encouraged her to date Nathan. He seemed to like Regan.

This close, she could swear that something was there.

Their gazes locked. His eyes conveyed a message she couldn't read. But he didn't let go of her; they were centime-ters apart and no part of her wanted to step away, either. His hands were resting on her shoulders, and hers were on his hips. How they got there, she didn't know, though none of it felt awkward. None of it felt forced.

Then again, with Chip, she'd never had to think twice about who she was, never had to doubt her motives.

With Chip, she was herself.

Chip knew her intimately.

Though now, Gabby considered intimacy in other ways.

A zing of need made its way all the way to her belly—an urge to feel every part of him sparked within her. She spread her fingers across the soft fabric of his shirt, against his broad back. She sensed the warmth underneath, and the image of them, skin on skin, flashed in her imagination.

For a beat she considered stopping, until she felt a hand creep up to the back of her neck.

Her imagination turned to reality when he cupped her cheeks with his hands.

Gabby quietly gasped, overcome with tingles and heat, as if tiny fireworks had ignited in her body.

She raised herself on her tiptoes in longing, shut her eyes, and anticipated a kiss.

"Gabby." Chip's voice was a rumble. "Is this what you want? Because I've wanted this. I've wanted *you*."

She opened her eyes and was met with a mirror of her emotions, his expression almost lost in a mist of attraction. Of need.

There were thoughts about the repercussions of the line they were about to cross… Yes, she was having them, but they were muted, smothered by the swirl of emotions that had been surfacing in bits the last few weeks.

So she went with the most prominent thought, and that was… "Yes, I want this."

Uncoiling herself from him, she pressed her hands against his chest. His heart pounded against her right palm. It raced, like hers. Still, she couldn't tear her eyes off his face, his eyes, his lips, which were parted. All of him was too far away, so Gabby pulled him down by his sweater collar.

Planner Gabby blew things up.

His lips were soft, searching, and she allowed for exploration. She was eager herself, and seconds later, she wanted more. Wanted to be closer. Wanted that same warmth except in a fully horizontal way. His fingers were in her hair, hers tore at his shirt.

"Ahem."

The voice came from somewhere, and at first, it was a nuisance, like a buzzing fly.

"Lucky," the voice said again.

Then, a bark.

Chip stilled.

Gabby's eyes flew open and met his. Once more, they were mirrors, and right then, what was clear was their shock.

Simultaneously, they turned toward the voice and the bark. To George Lowry, looking askance and holding Six, Lucky by his side, head cocked in curiosity.

"Dad," Chip said, after a breath.

Gabby's chest heaved belatedly. *Oh, my God.*

She'd kissed her best friend.

He wanted her just as much as she wanted him.

Someone had witnessed their kiss. Three pairs of eyes had no doubt bore witness.

Which meant it was real, and she and Chip would have to deal with this. Along with Nathan and Regan.

Her first instinct was to sweep it under the rug. This kiss couldn't go further. It shouldn't have happened to begin with.

George passed Chip a phone, then unloaded Six into Gabby's arms. "I was grabbing Six, and your phone...kept buzzing over and over. Nathan."

"Thanks, um..." Chip couldn't meet Gabby's eyes.

"I've got to get back to the puppies. They're everywhere these days." George hesitated and rushed out with Lucky at his heels.

Silence settled between them, while Gabby scoured her brain on how to escape. She had to get out of there. She couldn't believe that she'd allowed the kiss to happen, that she'd risked this awkwardness, her friendship with Chip, and Chip's friendship with Nathan, for a moment of lust.

She pecked Six on the nose, feeling the guilt well inside of her. "I should go."

"Hold on a sec," Chip said, just as his phone buzzed. Looking down at the screen, the caller ID was of Chip and Nathan, a photo Gabby had taken a couple of years ago, of the two leaning against Nathan's precious BMW.

It was another sign. A reminder that what they had done was wrong. "No, it's okay." She smiled. "Look, that was… We don't have to talk about it."

"But we should." He frowned.

"It was…a kiss." She infused levity into her tone, straightening. She couldn't find the words to explain. Instead, she was flooded with thoughts about what could happen if she couldn't fix this. "And you're one of my best friends," she said definitively. That part was a hundred percent true. And from that, the rest of the words seemed to have a road to follow. "We don't have to talk about it."

"Got it." His eyes dropped to the floor for a beat and then rose to meet hers. They were dark—bothered, if she was being honest, but she chose not to think about it.

She couldn't.

"Take care of my baby, okay." She handed him Six. "I'll see you later. Love ya." With a final, casual hug, she backed out of the house and scurried to her car.

The next thought came down like lightning.

Later meant in a couple of hours. For their double date.

* * *

Was a kiss really just a kiss?

From his personal romantic history, the kisses that Chip had shared with people hadn't been. From his first kiss, when he was eleven—her name was Josephine, and it happened one day after school, when he'd walked her home from the bus stop—he remembered all of them.

He didn't know what that said about him, that all of the kisses he'd tendered were on purpose. He'd meant for them to happen, and the people he'd kissed had welcomed and meant their kisses, too.

He'd waited so long for his first kiss with Gabby. He could barely keep the tremble from his voice when he'd asked her if she wanted it, too.

So what the hell happened?

Chip was in his bedroom rifling through his clothes. He was undecided on what to wear roller skating, even if what he had now was basically a capsule wardrobe. The last week had brought about an overhaul in his outward appearance. With the previous two dates, he'd opted for simple outfits in variations of blue, black, and brown, and a couple of items that were white and gray. And his hair—what had started as a mistake, he admitted, looked pretty damn good on him.

But his insides were topsy-turvy.

Twenty minutes had passed since Gabby left. Twenty minutes since she'd told him it was just a kiss to her, and he'd let her walk away without talking about it.

That was the hardest part: the fact that he didn't have the wherewithal to demand that they discuss it. He let her go without protest, and she'd all but run out of the house.

Didn't he deserve an explanation? A moment to discuss?

Chip felt heat coming from his left, and he knew its source before it spoke. "Where are you going?"

"Out." Chip attempted to maintain his poker face, though the thought of a roller-skating double date sounded about as painful as Gabby walking out on him. How was he going to put on a happy face for Regan, who didn't deserve any less than his best?

And how was he supposed to pretend nothing happened in front of Gabby and Nathan.

"This another double date?"

"Let me guess how you know." He glanced at his dad, who hovered by the doorway. As usual, Lucky was by his side. The dog sat, mouth slightly agape, eyes bouncing between them, probably passing judgment.

Sighing, he whispered, "Damn small towns." Chip turned back to his clothes. Nothing looked suitable to wear.

"That's right. Damn this small town that has looked out for you all your life. I had enough people tell me what you've been up to. And all I have to say is make it make sense to me."

"Make what make sense?" Black Henley. Blue jeans. That would have to do. Chip pulled out the hanger and placed the clothes out on the bed.

"That you're alright with Gabby dating another guy. That you're going on a date with another woman. You're not fooling anyone. It's not just friendship with the both of you."

Chip fiddled with the clothes on the bed, unwilling to look at him. "Dad. Not now. I've got to change."

"No."

Anger rose from the pit of his belly and he turned. He wasn't the type to lash out at anyone, at his father most especially, but the nagging and criticisms, though constant most of his life, gnawed at him. Couldn't a guy get a moment to himself without having to be chastised? He was an adult. "Are you still here?"

Lucky whined and jumped on Chip's bed. She lied down

and rested her chin on her front paws. The sight took Chip's mood down a notch. And against his better judgment, he scratched the top of Lucky's head.

He felt minutely better.

Just a smidge. And to his credit, the dog let him without fuss, unlike the man in front of him, who was succeeding at getting under his skin.

"Son. This...isn't you. You're the most straightforward person I know. You give to people who ask for help. When you say you're going to be somewhere, everyone knows you'll be there. When you receive, you return the favor, sometimes tenfold. What you're doing right now isn't straightforward."

Chip half laughed. How could he explain or change something that took two to fix? "Right, sort of like Lucky."

The dog barked, though Chip kept going. "Was that straightforward of me, too? Last I remember, I said there would be no dogs on the bed."

"You're changing the subject, yet again."

"Dad. It was an accidental kiss between friends." Though Chip said it with a steady voice, inside, he knew it was a lie.

What *had* he expected from that kiss? What had been his end goal?

While it was happening, his brain had envisioned them together. In a tried-and-true relationship. For those seconds, he was damn near grateful that they were taking steps toward forever.

That was the problem, he realized. That he had romanticized this whole thing with Gabby. He'd put her too much on a pedestal.

This was his fault.

George was still talking, "An accidental kiss would have stopped the moment you touched one another. But I kept time. It was at least seven seconds."

"Dad, for real?"

"I cleared my throat at least twice." His cheeks reddened. "It was a real kiss."

He was right, as he usually was. The start of the kiss might have been accidental, but the letting go, or the *not* letting go, was not.

Not a single part of him wanted to pull away.

"It's complicated."

At that moment, his phone, sitting face up on his bed, buzzed. The damn thing lit up with his and Nathan's picture.

"I know exactly what that complication is." His father wagged a knowing finger at him and left his room. "Lucky!"

The dog barked, and at his father's exit, the dog leapt off the bed to follow him, knocking one of Chip's pillows loose, which fell against a framed photo on his bedside table.

Chip reached out in time to catch it before it fell on the floor.

The photo was of him, his parents, and Goose. He was young, about thirteen. He hadn't hit his growth spurt, still wore braces that glimmered in the sun, and he'd had one friend to his name: Nathan.

Small towns had their pros and cons. Pros were that everyone was connected somehow. Friends became family. Support, if one wanted, was everywhere. But the cons… There were an equal amount, and one was that when a person was categorized a certain way, they were considered that way for a long time.

Chip had not been the popular one, was slightly awkward-looking at the turn of elementary school, not quite athletic, despite his long arms and legs, and that came with some teasing.

But Nathan always stood up for him, stuck by him. Still did to this day. That sometimes made it easy for Chip to excuse his friend's antics, his previous penchant for arrogance and entitlement.

They all had their roles, and Chip had been perfectly fine as the sidekick. It was what he was used to.

So, yes, Chip had been avoiding calling Nathan back. He'd wanted to process what had happened without hearing his best friend's voice in his ear. But with the way Nathan was blowing up his phone, it meant something was going down.

While Chip didn't have the wherewithal to deal with the additional guilt of knowing he'd kissed his best friend's ex, he couldn't avoid him much longer.

Chip snatched the phone up. "Hey, Nate."

"Bro, what are you doing?"

"I'm home, taking care of puppies." He shook out his shoulders. The way Nathan spoke to him sometimes, in this demanding way, and the fact that the guy couldn't greet him properly—it sometimes hit wrong.

"No. That's not what I mean."

There was true anger in his voice and Chip frowned. "What's going on?"

"What do you think is going on? What have you forgotten to tell me?"

"Um." Chip internally scrambled for purchase, eyes wandering to the clock beside his bed. Thirty minutes since Gabby had left. Had she called him and told him? How did he find out? Chip's voice cracked. "I don't know what you mean?"

He leaned on his elbows and looked down at his stockinged feet, at the multicolor gray-and-white fibers of the plush carpet below.

The overwhelming, sickening feeling lodged itself in the top part of his belly. It was familiar, though something he hadn't felt since high school. As he'd grown to be more successful, more involved with the community, when people forgot about his awkward years, followed by his sad, grieving years, that feeling had fallen away. He'd become more confident.

Or so he'd thought.

"When I got the email, I couldn't believe it. How do you expect for me to take this without talking it over with me first?"

Chip was silent, not really knowing what to say. He shut his eyes and waited for the onslaught, for the accusation.

"Why'd you do it?" Nathan urged. "Why did you move up construction—"

"I swear I…" Chip didn't finish the sentence, caught on the word *construction.*

"You can't plead the Fifth. The contract just pinged through, and what the hell, Chip?"

Chip bit his lip, to keep from groaning in relief. Contract. Construction. The senior center. "Justin sent over the changes."

"Yes, and holy shit, the cost. I know it will be done faster, but now I have to come up with the financing much earlier than I expected. I'm not like you, man. I plan everything to a *T.*"

Chip didn't like the insinuation. His money was inherited, sure, but he'd worked to grow it, and to help people with it. "What do you mean, not like me?"

"Seriously?" he scoffed. "That's all you're getting from our conversation? Not the fact that you made a decision for the both of us? That's not how this is supposed to work."

The disappointment was clear in his voice; Chip steeled himself, reminded himself of all the decisions he'd made in the last week. This, at least, was something he could fix.

It brought on a new wave of guilt.

"I'm sorry," Chip said, for all the reasons that Nathan didn't know about.

Nathan exhaled. "It's fine. It's just… I don't know if I can sign this today. Have you agreed for the work to start?"

Chip shook his head at himself this time. That he hadn't thought about this. "I have. But you can take your time. I'll take care of it. We can work out the details."

"Fine. Thank you. But Chip?"

"Yeah?"

"Next time, just talk to me, okay? A text, a call. I mean, we double dated and everything. Did you just forget?"

"I…did. My bad."

He sighed. "It's okay. Sorry I yelled. I was just shocked. I felt blindsided."

Guilt rocketed through Chip and he rested his hand against the back of his neck. "It's fine," Chip said, though with effort.

But it was all far from fine.

George was right. Chip was way off the track.

Chapter Eleven

As the saying went, things happened in threes. In this case, it was how many times Chip had fallen on his ass.

The only positive thing was that Great Oak Skating Rink was far enough away from Peak that very few people had seen him stumble.

Except, of course, for the members of their double date.

Regan stuck a hand in front of his face. She was laughing, her hair wild from their loop around the busy rink. Her cheeks were red, matching the gloss of her lips. She was beautiful in every way, but Chip's focus was elsewhere. On Gabby, who was urging Nathan off the wall across from them.

He took Regan's hand, though, glad for the help, and she lifted him to his feet. Still unsteady, he felt the brush of bodies as they skated past, heard the range of volumes of conversation around him, and braced himself for another impact.

It was chaos, inside and out.

Groaning, he palmed his behind as he inched over to the wall. Then, "Push It" began playing overhead, and cheers erupted, bringing a bigger crowd onto the floor.

"Are you okay?" Regan asked. She head-bopped to the beat, not a bit fazed.

Then again, she had been skating backward just moments before he fell. For this activity, Chip's only consolation was that he wasn't the worst of the bunch.

"Me? Yes. My pride, not so much."

"Aw, you aren't so bad." She nodded over to a couple of trick skaters in the middle of the rink who were breakdancing. "In comparison to those folks, though…"

"I am definitely out of practice."

"Are you sure you knew how to skate to begin with?" She raised an eyebrow.

"Okay, fine. I always sucked."

"Trust that you're not as bad as Nathan over there. I don't think they've gotten out to skate at all." Giggling, Regan slid her gaze to the right. At that moment, Nathan stumbled, arms flailing. Gabby reached for him and they fell into deep throes of laughter, as if completely unaware that the rest of the world existed. The joy was palpable in both their faces, and combined with the way Gabby was looking into Nathan's eyes, it made every part of Chip wince.

"Though, it doesn't look like they care much as all," Regan continued.

"No, it doesn't."

He thought back to the moment Gabby wrapped her arms around him. At his decision to kiss her, which now seemed fuzzy, except for her clear consent. He could have sworn that she had met him halfway, that she'd pulled him down by the shirt.

Look at me, she had said.

Since he'd arrived for this date, Gabby hadn't looked at him once. She'd been cordial, but was quick to skate off with Nathan. And despite being around all these people, the noise and Regan, all Chip felt was alone. Alone in his feelings. Alone in his worry for the moment when he'd have to tell Nathan about the kiss.

If Nathan had been upset about the contract, something

that was easily solved, how would he react if he found out about Chip and Gabby? *When* he found out.

"Is there...something wrong?"

Chip refocused on the face in front of him. "What's that?"

"You look upset." The crease in between Regan's eyebrows deepened. "Was it something I said?"

His breath left his body. What had she been talking about? "What? No... No...of course not."

What was he doing? How could he be so rude? He was ignoring this kind person because he couldn't get his mind off of his own drama. "It's not you."

"Those sound like famous last words."

"No. Not at all." He rested his hand on her wrist and a realization descended. This public display of affection was as far as they had gone. A handshake when they first met. Brief hugs for greetings and departures. The occasional hand-holding, but nothing more.

"I've been having fun on our dates." Her eyes dropped to the floor for a beat before meeting his. They flared with something, as if demanding a response.

She deserved a response.

He said the first thing that came to mind. "Me, too. You're really great."

When the words left his lips, he grimaced. It was unfeeling, and not worthy of someone he was on a third date with.

By Regan's fading smile, she agreed with this. "Great... Is that it? The ice cream, the bowling, this whole endeavor of risking our lives and limbs?" She gestured to the madness around them.

He could kick himself.

This was not going well.

The music changed to a pop song and the crowd began to sing. The noise was stifling, but it afforded Chip time to think. Regan was unhappy, and to have a third person displeased with him in one day didn't sit well.

She pressed her lips into a thin smile, and gestured with her head toward the booths that lined the perimeter of the rink. "Wanna sit?"

"Sure!" he yelled above the noise and followed her out of the rink on unsteady feet. He slid into the cracked leather seat across from Regan. The rink had a server that took drink orders, and they placed theirs.

After a few seconds, Regan placed a hand at the center of the table, to get his attention. "Do you and Gabby have something going on?"

Stunned, Chip opened his mouth, though nothing left it. Had she asked this question yesterday he would have vehemently said no.

But now, what could he say? That yes, he'd thought for those seven seconds—as his father had timed—that they did have something, but she'd rejected him? That he was brokenhearted at the moment. And that he was a jerk to have gone through with this date with Regan, even though his mind had been on Gabby.

But hard conversations about himself, about his own misgivings, weren't something he did. "Why do you say that?"

"Something's amiss. I hate to sound clingy, since this is just our third date, but usually by now there would be more. Hell, by now we would have at least kissed. And I have to know—is it me?"

Right then, Chip should have been trying to save this. Ragan was perfect—he had been saying it this whole time. Even now, with the way she wanted to communicate so openly, that alone was special.

His basis for his attraction to, and affection for, Gabby was friendship. Regan could be that person, too, couldn't she?

Yet, as he looked across to her, he knew he couldn't lie. Regan was a good person. And someone who deserved the truth.

This isn't like you.

His father's words returned to him.

Her expression softened, despite his lack of an answer. The corners of her lips lifted into a small smile. "I knew it."

Chip could feel himself relax. To have someone else know his secret, someone else besides his father, was a burden he hadn't realized he needed to surrender. Still, he wanted to clarify. "It's really not like that."

"Why don't I take a shot at it. You're good friends and have been for some time. But you caught feelings, though you don't want to make a move because you think it will compromise this love triangle going on between you, her and Nathan. So here you are, watching her date him while trying to date someone new, too."

Said out loud, he felt the wrongness of what he'd been doing. "I am definitely a dick."

"That all depends."

"On?"

"If you've been just wasting my time, or if you were actually trying to get to know me, but finding that no one can replace her."

He blew out a laugh, though the truth was bitter in the back of his throat. "Damn. You're observant."

"It's what I do. I suppose you can take a counselor out of the session, but not the session out of the counselor." She sighed. "Did I call it?"

"Regan, to be honest, in the beginning I swiped right because I needed a date."

She frowned. "That's why one usually swipes right."

He took a breath. "It was a favor to Nathan. He needed a wingman to help him with Gabby, and I agreed."

Her lips parted. "Oh."

He peeked up at her, anticipating her anger, though none showed through. So he kept on. "But you are...pretty damn amazing. And we got along so well—I wanted to get to know you. I still do. But everything got twisted. Gabby asked me to join them for the second and third date, and as much I've loved hanging out, it killed me to watch her dating, too. And then today happened."

"What happened today?"

Chip told her about the kiss, and the potential consequence to his friendship with Nathan. Finally looking up from his hands, which he had been wringing, he said, "Am I still the asshole?"

"No. You're not." Then she smiled.

"You're not mad at me?"

"No, not even a little bit. I don't like the fact that you swiped right for me to fill in as a date. Then again, what are those apps for but to do just that? I swiped right back because I was super bored being home. I was feeling lonely and took a chance. Lucky for me, it was you on the other end of that screen. You're a good person. So who am I to judge your reasons? No one is perfect."

"I don't know. You're pretty damn close to it."

"Listen, I'm still single for a reason. While you might be a people pleaser—"

"Whew, am I ever." The lessons had been swift the last week.

"My superpower is that I can find something wrong with anyone. And why I overthought our dates and concluded that things weren't right between us. So, no, I'm not perfect."

The server returned with their sodas, and they both took a sip.

She continued. "But I'll take the compliment. Now, I wonder what we should do?"

Her straightforwardness was refreshing.

"If you're open to being friends…"

"I'd like that. To be honest, the lack of romantic pressure is a breath of fresh air. It's not that I don't find you attractive, but just as you knew right away that I wasn't the one, it was the same for me." She sipped on her drink. "And what are you going to do about her?"

They both turned toward where Gabby and Nathan were gingerly skating along the perimeter of the wall. Nathan's face was set into a grimace.

"What can I do?" he said. "She made it clear that it was a mistake and something we both needed to forget."

"And you're going to accept that?"

"Not sure I have a choice. I don't want to force myself on her."

"It's not *forcing* to ask for clarification. You're friends, right? Friends converse. Friends are honest with one another. Both parties."

He thought back to the main reason why he couldn't be with Gabby at all. "There's Nathan, too, and he's a business partner for one of my projects. It's so complicated that I wonder if it's better that I don't do or say anything at all."

She sighed. "Really?"

"If I let it go, life will move on. I've been doing it this way for years."

"And how has that worked out for you?"

"Touché. But there's not much else I can do, can I? Or else I risk adding more drama to everyone's life."

"You're a business guy, right? You can't run a business

without facing the drama head-on." She shrugged. "Suit your-self, though. I don't think I would be able to keep quiet." She tapped her glass against his. "You ready to go another loop around the rink? They're playing my song."

"Bizarre Love Triangle" by New Order blared through the speakers.

"Yeah, let's do another round." Though as he stood and made his way to the rink, he hoped that that he wouldn't get hurt.

Gabby was in pain. As she hobbled toward her car with a sore ankle, she attempted to keep a smile on her face.

Roller skating allowed her and Nathan to bond in a way that hadn't happened in the past. It was as if being the worst skater between them had unlocked his vulnerability. He'd carried the conversation throughout the night, about work, his future goals, his regrets. He hadn't stopped talking, and was still chattering next to her, this time talking about trav-eling to Vermont to be mentored by another orchard owner since Cloud Orchard wanted to expand.

Gabby was grateful for this one-way conversation, since she was trying to nurse a greater pain located in her heart. From the moment she'd left Chip's house, she couldn't ban-ish the memory of how their kiss ended. Of Chip's expression when she'd told him that what they'd shared was just a kiss.

She only wished she had ibuprofen in her purse to at least aid with her physical pain. Nathan had been so bad at roller skating that he could barely keep upright. And when he'd fallen, he'd threatened to take her down with him, and suc-ceeded several times. Her thighs were going to be black and blue in the morning.

The pain in her heart, though, was all her fault, and there was no medicine for it.

They made it to her car. Nathan's was parked across the lot. He opened the door for her after she unlocked it. "This was more fun than I ever thought I'd have, even with how much I sucked."

"I had a good time, too." So long as she hadn't glimpsed Chip and Regan together, that was.

What was worse than walking away from her best friend after their first kiss? Seeing him with another woman.

At one point during the date, Chip and Regan had disappeared somewhere, and her mind meandered down the rabbit hole of concocting stories as to where they'd gone, and what they were doing.

Had they gotten serious?

Were they intimate?

And was it her business, seeing that she'd walked away from him?

"I'd love to see you again, if you're up to it. Maybe alone this time? Like a hike? The weather's warming up." Nathan's smile was sweet and expectant, as if he knew that a fourth date was inevitable. And before her kiss with Chip, she would have been all for it, too.

But the kiss.

Oh, my goodness.

Heat clambered up her neck at the thought of Chip's lips on hers, at the touch of his fingers against her neck, and she inhaled a deep breath to center herself. *Stop it.* The point of this date was to solidify that she was going to ask Nathan to the wedding. Her plan had nothing to do with kissing Chip.

A kiss that came with a whole host of consequences, some she didn't want to think about.

"Speaking of the warm weather." She thought back to her meeting with Matilda and Jared, when she'd assured them that the weather would turn. See, it was fate! What she was about to do was the right thing.

She cleared her throat; her voice box was closing up. Like the warm air had constricted it somehow. "Jared's wedding. Where I need a plus-one."

He beamed. "Oh?"

"Yep. Would you like to go with me? I understand if you already have a plus one—"

"Nope, I was planning on going solo. But I'd love to go with you. Remind me of the dress code?"

"Semiformal."

"Ah, no worries. I'm covered. And the wedding registry?"

"It's online." She smiled for good measure. This was exactly what she'd wanted. Her problem was solved. She was going to the wedding with a plus-one who was sure to be fun. Someone who knew what questions to ask, knew what to wear. Someone who was employed, who had hobbies, who was down for anything, even roller skating. Most of all: everyone knew him already. Maybe her aunties would finally quit asking about her relationship status.

He was the perfect wedding date.

Still, it felt so wrong.

"Great," he said. "I can get them a separate gift, or if you'd like, we can go in together. Whichever you prefer is fine."

"That's so thoughtful." The guy even thought of the present. "I've already gone in with my sister so..."

"I'll make sure to snag something for them, then."

What more can I want?

The better question would be, what should *I want,* her conscience countered.

"I'll text you a photo of my outfit. Maybe we can match?"

"Easy peasy. And maybe we can get lunch sometime before then?"

"Yes, that sounds good." Gabby's mind was still on *should* and after a brief hug, she slipped into the driver's seat. Nathan shut the door and stood back as she started the car and drove out of the parking lot.

On the long road back to the B & B, Gabby's mind continued to cycle on the words *should* and *could*. As the youngest, as the child of a mother who had done it all, with a sister who continued to defy social norms, *can't* wasn't in her vocabulary.

Saying that she couldn't do something meant that she simply hadn't tried hard enough. So Gabby did whatever she had to do. She gave *can't* the middle finger by finishing the thing, even if it wasn't always perfect.

But did that apply to relationships? Just because she and Chip had kissed, just because there was something she felt in that kiss, didn't mean that she *should* take the next step that could destroy the friendships around her.

Okay, so maybe that was a little bit dramatic. But she was sure of one thing: if she acted on her attraction and affection toward Chip, she would come between him and Nathan.

"I'm doing the right thing," she said to the open road in front of her.

Then why did it feel so wrong?

Ringing sounded throughout the car. Frankie.

Damn. In all her drama, she'd forgotten that she'd agreed to sit with Liam tonight.

See? This was why she couldn't be with Chip. Drama and Gabby did not mix.

Gabby pressed Accept on the Bluetooth and answered without preamble. "Hi, Ate Frankie, I'm on my way home now."

"Okay. I hope I didn't take you too early from your date."

She swallowed her relief that she got the timing just right.

"No, it's all done. What are your plans for your date? And who are you going with?"

"Just a late-night coffee. But I don't want to talk about that. I want to talk about you. How did this one go?"

"Why won't you tell me who he is?"

"Because it's no big deal. Now, tell me about roller skating."

"It was good. I asked Nathan to the wedding." Seconds of silence passed. "Hello? Still there?"

"Yep. Still here. So you asked Nathan to the wedding."

"Yeah. Who else?"

Again, more silence. "I don't know."

Gabby groaned.

"What? What did I say?"

"It's what you didn't say," Gabby said.

"I have no idea what you're talking about. What's wrong? Better yet, get here faster. How far away are you?"

"About five minutes."

"Love you." Frankie hung up, and minutes later, Gabby pulled into the gravel drive of Spirit of the Shenandoah B & B. She followed it to the rear of the home, where her family's personal vehicles were parked. The first house down a small path, next to a sign marked Private, was Frankie's cabin. It was brightly lit, a beacon against the dark mountain backdrop. With her phone flashlight on, Gabby followed the path to the house, up the two steps under the wide porch, and entered the cabin without knocking.

Her big sister's cabin was cozy, with monochrome decor and without a stitch of clutter. Over the hardwood floor were wide rugs, the washable kind, and potted plants lined the floor-to-ceiling windows in the living room.

It was impressive, really, how Frankie could keep the place so clean with a rambunctious nine-year-old. Then again, Liam had many similar traits to his mother. Like how he immediately put away his toys after playing. How he rinsed his own dishes before putting them in the dishwasher.

Frankie and Liam cleaned up their messes.

Unlike Gabby, at the moment.

"Hello?" Gabby kicked off her shoes at the door and called up the stairs.

"Tita Gabby!" Sounding like a herd of galloping giraffes, Liam bounded down the stairs. He was already in his flannel pajamas.

Gabby opened her arms to him, and he wrapped his around her waist. "Dang. Did you grow in the last day?"

"Soon I'll be taller than you."

"Don't say that. That makes me sad. I want you to stay a baby."

"I'm not a baby."

"Okay, bud. Time for bed." Frankie padded down the steps, dressed in flare leggings and an oversize sweater.

But it wasn't those things that made Gabby gasp.

It was the fact that Frankie's hair was straight.

Frankie was a curly girl, and had been for the last couple of years. Growing up, though, she had always flat-ironed her hair. She'd spent hours on end in front of the bathroom mirror making sure her hair had not a stitch of frizz in it. Then, on the day of her divorce, she embraced her curly hair, including switching out all of her hair-care products.

With the big hair came the even more bombastic attitude.

Maybe that was unfair.

Maybe Frankie had kept a part of herself under wraps while married, and after her divorce, the curly girl emerged like a phoenix from the flames.

What did this mean, though?

"Mo-o-om…" Liam hung his head. "It's the weekend."

"Ahem, but who wanted to be on travel soccer and has a game tomorrow at eight a.m.?"

"Me." He stuck out his bottom lip.

"Exactly. Your dad's going to be here at seven."

"Fine."

"I'll be up in a little bit, okay?" Gabby winked at him. It was their sign that they would have a late-night dessert.

"Okay. 'Bye, Mom."

"I'll be home soon." Frankie kissed her son on top of his head, her hair cascading like a curtain.

Once Liam made it up the stairs, Frankie glared at Gabby. "Why are you looking at me like that?"

Gabby pointed at her hair. "Because of that."

"Is it messed up?"

"No. It's…"

A smile appeared on her face. "Oh, you like? I thought it was time for a change."

"Who's this date with again?"

"Just…someone."

For a beat, Gabby swore she saw it, the rise of color on her sister's cheeks. Every part of her wanted to call it out. Heaven knows that Frankie would have done so if their roles were switched.

But Gabby didn't want her sister to be defensive. "I hope you at least told *someone* the details."

"Don't worry, I told Viv," she said of her best friend, while checking her watch. "But before I leave, tell me what's up with you. Mom said you were upset yesterday."

Gabby sighed. "Of course, she said something."

"Just as I'm sure she would tell you if there was something up with me, or that you and I would talk if there was something up with Mom. We're all we have." She peeked at a mirror hanging in her hallway and pursed her lips. "I do love this lip color. Anyway. Spill. What's up?"

There was no use resisting. Gabby was on the verge of exploding with her spiraling thoughts. "I kissed Chip."

"What the—"

She plopped down on the leather sofa and groaned. "I mean, I'm not really sure who kissed who first, but he kissed me, and I kissed him, too."

"Ah, no wonder you were being cagey in the car." Frankie's lips wiggled into a grin; Gabby detected Cupid in that expression. "Define this kiss. Was it a peck? A couple of seconds? A full-on make-out session?"

Gabby faltered. "Door number three."

She covered her mouth. "When?"

"Earlier today."

"But you asked Nathan to the wedding?"

Gabby winced. "I did."

"That must mean that you didn't like the kiss." Frankie grabbed her purse from her closet.

"That's the thing... I *did* like the kiss."

"I'm so confused."

"Me, too."

How was she going to fix this? Or should she even try?

Frankie's phone buzzed. "Argh. Should I cancel this date? I should stay here with you."

Gabby shook herself awake. "Are you kidding? You shouldn't."

"But you need me right now."

"I'm fine. I swear." She walked her sister to the front door and opened it. "I've got studying to do. And this might be your last chance to get away, since the festivities start tomorrow."

The aunties had arrived one by one in the last couple of days, and the first reunion activity was hiking in the morning.

Oh, God, was Chip going to be there, too?

"Let the games begin," Frankie said, eyebrows raised.

Gabby breathed against the pressure in her chest. "Right? So enjoy."

With one foot out the door, Frankie added, "Promise me we'll talk about things later. I'll be back in a couple of hours. Don't do anything more complicated than what you've done so far."

"I promise. Believe me, my goal is to have the quietest night."

Chapter Twelve

Gabby jinxed herself; she'd spoken too soon. Because the night was as quiet as a coyote emitting a mating call.

Her phone hadn't stopped buzzing. She'd answered a couple of inquiries from folks interested in the puppies. After her promised dessert time with Liam, the DJ emailed: he'd come down with mono and Gabby had had to send out SOS signals to local leads.

Yet it didn't hold a candle to the crisis that she was currently facing: Matilda on Frankie's front porch, crying.

"Mat, are you okay?" Gabby ushered her inside. Matilda wore a hoodie and leggings. Her hair was coiled in a bun, and her face was streaked with mascara.

Her expression crumpled further. "I can't stop crying."

"Oh, dear." Gabby led her to the kitchen. "Can I get you something? Tea? Coffee? Chocolate?" She dug into the cupboards. Surely, Frankie had sweets lying around, but all Gabby could come up with were fruit snacks and granola bars.

They would have to do. She snagged one of each and pressed them into Matilda's hands. Then, her eyes locked on Frankie's minibar.

"Or will vodka be better?"

"As much as that sounds tempting, I'd better not."

Gabby pulled out a kitchen chair for her. "Please sit."

"Thank you, and also for texting me back. Honestly, I wasn't sure if you'd be awake, and then I saw you drive up."

"What's going on?"

"Do you think…? Are we going too fast?"

"We?"

"Me and Jared. We only really met a year ago, and here we are, about to tie the knot. A knot that I thought I would never tie again."

Oh, no. Her bride was having cold feet. While it wasn't unusual, Gabby hadn't thought it would happen with this wedding. Matilda and Jared had been steady and calm throughout the process.

"Are you sure you don't want wine?" Gabby wasn't the type to push alcohol, but she might need it herself.

"Actually, a little glass sounds good. White, if Frankie has it?"

"Oh, believe me, she has it." Gabby went to the bar, and just as with the rest of the house, all the bottles were dust-free. "Prosecco?"

"Sure."

Gabby plucked a bottle out.

"Are you sure it'll be alright with Frankie?"

"Abso-freaking-lutely. If she was here, she would have poured us a round the moment you stepped inside."

Gabby popped the cork and poured Prosecco into two glasses, handing one over to Matilda. After watching her take a sip and then taking her own, she sat. "So what happened today?"

Matilda stared into the sparkling wine. "We were talking about combining our households, you know? I still have my house down the hill, full of my things, and his cabin up here is full of his. It's a beautiful cabin, big enough for the both of us. We decided that it made sense for me to move into his cabin, since we'd both be closer to work. We could rent out my place, and start building equity together."

Matilda's voice seemed to settle, and her shoulders lowered. Gabby smiled to encourage her to keep going, though inside she braced herself to discover something terrible about Jared.

Gabby had heard it all: secret addictions, a partner's faults, gripes, and complaints. Clients confessed their own sins to her, as if she'd had the power to absolve them.

In general, though, most of her clients' gripes were the result of triggers, stemming from the past. The stress of wedding planning had a way of digging up deep issues they hadn't yet reconciled.

She wasn't sure if she wanted to hear any of Jared's faults. He was her brother, after all. Some things were too close for comfort.

"We were moving my books today," Matilda said now. "I have a lot of books."

"I remember."

A lot was an understatement. Matilda had bookshelves lining one entire wall in her living room, and had piles of unread books on every surface.

"He was shocked, seeing the boxes in the car. As if he hadn't seen them before. As if he hadn't looked through my bookshelves a million times before. As if he hadn't been to a bookstore with me." She heaved a breath. "Then he said, 'Are we keeping all of them? I'm not sure we'll have room.' Can you believe that?"

"Did he bring them into the house?"

"I mean, he did, and then as I opened the boxes he suggested donating books I hadn't read or liked. As if I can split them up. Gabby, he wants me to give away my babies."

Gabby exhaled, and took a sip of her wine, relieved that

this was far from a scandal, though admittedly, something Jared shouldn't have said. "That must have upset you, Mat."

"I'm still upset. It's like me telling him that he can't travel with his knives. Do you know that he takes those knives everywhere? Those overnights we made to the beach? He brought those damn knives with him. Not one or two…but all seven. And a can opener and a Microplane. Once, he packed his cast-iron pan in his luggage. And did I question it?"

"Of course, you didn't."

"That's right. I did not. Because he's a chef, and I know that they're attached to their knives and tools and whatnot. My poor basic coffeepot has taken a back seat to his French press, because he loves that thing so much. When he moved all his things from Louisville, it included this hideous leather chair that doesn't match any of my things, but did I think twice about keeping it? Nope.

"And now he wants me to declutter my books? It made me think—does he really know me? Everyone knows that my books are important to me. That they keep me company. That they're part of me."

She continued on—Gabby could tell that so much of what she was sharing stemmed from wedding angst. There wasn't an ounce of real malice or fear in her voice. And once Matilda slowed and took another sip of wine, Gabby spotted an opening and leapt into it with what she hoped was helpful advice.

"If I was in your shoes, I would have felt the same way, too. It doesn't help that things are super-stressful right now, with just a week before the wedding. With B and B stuff gearing up, you both are so busy with work and planning. It has been a lot, in addition to the moving that you're doing. And I also think it's valid to ask all of these hard questions…"

Gabby paused. "Can you tell Jared how you feel? Speaking as his sister, and as someone who witnessed your relationship from the very beginning, I can guarantee that if he knew you were feeling this way, he would think about what he said. Jared loves you so much, Matilda. More than that—he really likes you and respects you, and wants you to be happy."

She sniffed. "But shouldn't he just know? Just as I know about the big things he loves?"

"I suppose ideally they should be able to read our minds. But sometimes, though we might know someone really well, it's hard to discern how they're feeling. Or sometimes, you can take for granted how the other feels, because you know them so well."

As she said the words, Gabby felt the sentiment in her own heart. At that moment, she wished she knew what Chip was feeling. All this time, she had been consumed with the fact they *had* kissed, but not much more than that.

Chip had said that he'd wanted her, but did he have feelings for her, too? Were they two separate things? Chip had supported her dating Nathan. Surely that had to mean he thought the kiss was a mistake, too.

Matilda drained the last of her wine and looked down at her empty glass. She swirled it awhile in thought. "I'm scared, Gabby."

There it was, a truth that Gabby felt, too. She could only nod.

"I've done this before, you know," Matilda croaked. "I've walked down the aisle. I've given someone my forever commitment, only to end up divorced."

"Matilda, your ex—" Gabby shook her head. Matilda's ex, Noah, had remarried last year at the B & B. Working with him had been a bear. Looking back, the fee, while beneficial for the B & B, hadn't been worth it to Gabby. If he had been the same kind of man toward Matilda, there was no question why she'd left him.

Matilda had never discussed the reason they'd divorced, but Gabby suspected it wasn't amicable.

"Yes, I know Jared isn't Noah. But I'm still me. What if I make the same mistakes? What if my judgment is still off and…" She looked up at Gabby. Though her tears were gone, her expression was serious.

Most of the time, Gabby's kept her advice to her clients light, though insightful enough to give them some reassurance and send them out the door. But this was different. Matilda was family.

Gabby needed to say the next words with care. "I didn't know you when you were with Noah, so I can't speak to that, but I can speak about what I know of you now. What *I* love about you, I suspect, is very much what everyone loves about you. You're honest and kind, straightforward and loyal. But no one is perfect, and everyone is allowed to make mistakes. That includes you.

"And I can't let you blow off the importance of the other person, your partner. How the both of you interact, how the both of you choose to compromise, and what you bring out in one another. The relationship is as much Jared's as it is yours, so for you to hold the full responsibility for it isn't fair, is it?"

Gabby's voice cracked at the very end of that sentence. Chip had given her the same advice. And her messy insides, her inability to organize, all of it was due to Chip.

Correction, it was their togetherness that was doing this to her. She'd felt the first tremors long ago, and the double dates had been mini-earthquakes. And the kiss. The kiss was a meteor that blew everything up.

Because she *had* wanted him to kiss her.

Gabby *liked* Chip. She might even love him in all the ways that made their friendship so special. But she was scared, too.

"What did I do?" Gabby whispered.

"What?" Matilda asked, frowning.

"I'm sorry." Gabby pressed her fingers against her temple. "Matilda, you and Jared... There are no guarantees to anything. You knew that when he first came onto the property and you fell in love. I think you should go home and tell Jared exactly how you feel, no holds barred. I think you'll feel better."

Eyes glassy, she said, "You don't think he'll be mad? Or regret that he married an emotional person? That I'm so... high-maintenance or—"

"I bet he's going to feel so bad about what he said. I bet if you told him you wanted to move every single thing into his cabin, to replace everything he has, he would absolutely say yes. He loves you that much. He loves you more than anything."

Matilda began to tear up again. "He does. I know he does." Gabby leaned in for a hug. "Thanks, Gabby. I'm sorry for barging in like this."

"No such thing. We're sisters."

Gabby walked Matilda to the door. As Matilda stepped over the threshold, Gabby waved goodbye.

After checking on Liam, Gabby tore open a package of fruit snacks and gobbled them up. Then she took her phone and stared at it.

She had to take her own advice.

Gabby video-called Chip. Heart thundering in her chest, she planned what to say. That the kiss meant something to her, and she wanted to know how he felt about her. That it was time to talk about them.

She was going to apologize for asking him to forget about the kiss.

The phone picked up on the first ring. The image on the screen was blurry, shifting as if trying to right itself. Noises and voices commingled. There was giggling. "Hello? Hello?" Chip said, laughing.

The giggling sounded like it came from Regan.

They were still on their date.

Of course, they were still on their date. They'd been having an amazing time, the last she saw.

"Hey—" Gabby said.

"Gabby? S-something wrong?"

"No, everything's fine." She hedged on what to say. "How's everything?"

He sighed. The screen showed only half his face, but he rolled his eyes. "Gab, did you need something?"

His tone was harsh. "Um…no, I'm sorry to bother you."

"Yeah, it's always like that. You're sorry… I'm s-sorry… is time to stop being sorry. Maybe it's just time…to accept."

His words were slurred and nonsensical, though she recoiled from the tone.

It had been a mistake to call.

"I'm gonna go. We can talk in the morning," she said.

He snorted; he was grinning. "Yeah, maybe?"

"Maybe?"

"Yeah. Maybe I won't be ready to talk. Maybe I won't be in the mood. Maybe it's better to go find another *friend* to talk to."

Then phone went dark—Chip had hung up.

All Gabby could do was look back at the screen, in shock.

Six days until the wedding

"No-o-o." Chip turned away from the bright sunlight, groaned and slung his arm across his face. Who the hell had pulled back his black-out curtains? "Give me a minute, will you?" he groaned.

Boundaries. Chip needed to set boundaries. He'd been encroached upon from all sides. He didn't have space for himself, room to breathe.

The fact that his dad could enter his room, as if Chip was still a teenager and living under his roof?

Then his brain backtracked. When had he returned under his roof?

Chip's eyes flew open. A white dresser came into view. A plush gray area rug. A vanity with a myriad of tiny bottles on the tabletop.

His brain scrounged for memories from last night, which didn't help the vise squeezing his head.

He rolled onto his back. Up above him was a vintage chandelier, not his standard dome light.

What the hell?

He ran a hand against the sheets he was lying on what were too soft and plush to be his. He turned his head to the right, and spotted a woman asleep next to him.

Not a woman—Regan. Facing away from him, she was under the covers, with her dark hair splayed across her pillow.

"Oh, shit." Chip's heart rocketed to his throat. His consciousness broke through the last of his haze and memories from last night came rushing back.

Walking a mile from the rink to Mountain Rush for more drinks.

A ride share to her house.

A movie and a nightcap and a stumble toward the bed.

And nothing else. Not even a kiss.

Chip heaved a breath and braced himself before pulling the covers off his body. He was fully dressed. Sweater, jeans, socks.

"Oh, thank God," he said, and laughed with abandon.

With it, the rest of the night unlocked and his body loosened. Snippets flew past. Of he and Regan recounting their entire relationship histories. Raiding her refrigerator and finding it emptier than his. Ordering food delivery at midnight because they got the munchies.

It had been a fun night, even without Gabby.

It's possible, his brain teased.

"You're thinking of her again, aren't you?" Regan said.

Chip turned to her; she'd pushed the covers down. She was wearing a T-shirt and propped herself up on her elbow. "You can admit it, Chip."

"I am. Thinking of her."

"I'm not surprised. You talked about her. All…night… long." She sighed, though she was grinning.

"Oh, God, was I that pathetic?"

"Did you think that I was pathetic talking about the ups and downs of my love life?"

"Not at all. Or I don't remember feeling that way."

"Well, same. Sometimes a good venting session is necessary." She covered her mouth with a hand. "Oh, my God, do you remember the phone calls?"

He inhaled and sorted through his memories. A couple broke through, of watching Regan on the phone while he dug into the beef and broccoli.

His tummy grumbled, but not in a good way.

"Sort of?"

"Devon was shocked. I don't think he expected that on a Saturday night. But he deserved it. I didn't realize how much I held inside me for this long. But you inspired me. The way you went off when she called you."

He frowned. "Who called me?"

"You don't remember?" Her eyes rounded. "A certain woman called you and well, you said on video chat, and I quote, *'now* you want to talk? Go find another *friend* to talk to.'"

Chip searched his memories, but all he could find was a haze of chatter, and the phone ringing and… "Oh, my God. I said that? Where's my phone?" He slid out of bed and scanned the table and the dresser. Then, crouching, he spotted it under the bed.

Sitting with his back leaning against the bed, he thumbed straight to his recent calls. Sure enough, an incoming video call was logged from Gabby.

He exhaled a foreboding breath.

"I asked if you wanted to call her back, and you refused." Regan sat up.

"I have to fix this," he said belatedly, not knowing if this was his issue to fix. Or maybe his subconscious had expressed the frustration he was too cowardly to show. He *was* angry at the heart of it. He *was* disappointed in her. He'd put so much stock in their friendship, in their ability to communicate. "Then again…it's always me fixing things."

"You're friends. You just need to sit down and talk about this. Sure, it'll be awkward—"

Chip was half-listening, he was scrolling through texts that had come in from the night before. Then, one from this morning, from Cruz: I need your help today.

"You should call her. Right now," Regan said.

Chip wasn't convinced. "Maybe. But it looks like something's going on at work."

"Oh, no. Are you missing a shift?"

"I'm supposed to be off today." Chip guessed that he was being asked to cover for someone. He was tempted to ignore the text—had Cruz contacted him first because he knew Chip would move mountains to grant anyone's favor?

But this was Cruz, who didn't know about any of his internal conundrums. "Do you mind if I make a call?" he asked.

"Not at all. I'm going to change out of my clothes and

brush my teeth. Freshen up." She jumped out of bed, and as she padded to the bathroom, Chip dialed Cruz.

"Hey, Chip," Cruz said. "Thanks for getting back to me even though it's your day off."

The sound of Cruz's obvious gratitude eased Chip's soul. It was good to be needed. It was also good to be thanked.

"Yeah, sorry. I didn't see your text until now." He stood and looked out the window. The sun was out and high, the sky blue and without a cloud in sight. Perfect day for a hike.

"River called in sick," Cruz said of another trail guide. "And we've got a huge group today. It's the Espiritu reunion."

"That's today?" It had slipped his mind.

"Yes, and there are about ten novice hikers, and now there's only me. It's a short one, on Spirit Trail, then coming back through town. With this group it'll be about two to three hours. I know you probably have a ton of things planned, but I was wondering, if you had time—"

The idea of being out in the cool air sounded like a perfect way to clear his head, just until he could figure out what to do with Gabby. Speaking of. "Is Gabby coming?"

"Not sure, but I expect her to be there."

Would Chip be able to avoid her, at least until he could form his thoughts?

"I reached out to the other trail guides, so no pressure. But in all honesty I'm considering canceling or turning away some of the group. I don't know if I can safely take all these people out without help."

"No, don't do that." Chip couldn't ruin the reunion because of drama between him and Gabby. "I can come in. What time?"

"In a couple of hours. That good for you?"

That gave him enough time to check in with his dad and

the puppies, shower, and put some food in his belly. "Yep. I'll be there."

Chip hung up and he sat back on the bed. He leaned his elbows on his knees and shut his eyes. His head was pounding, belly twisted up, heart turned upside down.

Regan walked in. She'd changed into joggers and a hoodie. "Everything okay?"

"They need me at Cross Trails to assist with a hike. And Gabby might be there."

"Ah, she mentioned going." A smile grew on her face. "Sounds like the perfect time to talk things through."

"Maybe." Chip gazed at Regan with another level of appreciation. He reached out and offered his hand.

She took it, and shook his arm playfully. "Last night was fun."

"Right? I *am* fun."

She plopped down next to him, sighing. "Yes, you are. You were the center of attention at Mountain Rush. Do you remember?"

He chuckled. "That might have been a result of a little too much beer."

"No matter, it still came through. After last night I can confidently say that you are not the asshole. A little too willing to fade into the background, maybe, but my first impression of you was right—you're a good guy."

He hefted himself to his feet and Ragan walked him to the front door. "Regan…"

"Don't say sorry that we didn't work out, because we're past that."

"I wasn't going to say that, though I appreciate that you did. What I wanted to say was, thank you, for being so understanding and great all around. There's a lucky person out there for you."

"Back at you, but in your case, we know exactly who that is. So don't give up that chance."

A pit formed in his belly. Because he wished it could be as easy as that. He nodded.

"We should go out again, maybe on another double date, with other dates next time." She winked. "And if you need anything, I'm here for you."

She leaned in and kissed him on the cheek.

And though Chip felt light-years better about their friendship, it was his relationship with Gabby that he had yet to contend with.

Chapter Thirteen

"This will not be a peaceful hike, but an entertaining one," Cruz snickered under his breath, just loud enough for Chip to hear. He handed him several walking sticks. "Our goal is to get everyone there and back safely. Every single person here is a beginner."

"Got it."

They were adjacent to Cross Trails, at the mouth of a minor path that would lead to Spirit Trail. Turning around, Chip faced the gaggle of hikers. They were all women of varying ages; the only one familiar to him was Eva Espiritu. Gabby was nowhere in sight.

"They look very prepared, though," Chip noted. Each person wore a hat, and all were currently spraying on bug repellant or sunscreen.

"Always a plus." Cruz waved at Eva, who gave him a thumbs-up. "It's time." He frowned at him. "You look worse for wear, man. Will you be able to hang?"

"I have electrolytes in my water bottle," he admitted, but with the reminder of his physical state, the pounding in his head returned.

"I've got ibuprofen if you need it." He slapped him playfully on the back, then marched to the front of the crowd. He raised a walking stick. To everyone, he said. "Do we have everyone in your group? Eva, I thought Gabby and Frankie were coming?"

"Liam didn't feel well this morning, so Frankie's staying home. And Gabby…" She grabbed her phone from her back pocket and glanced at the screen. "Should be here soon."

"Filipino time!" one of the women said. Chatter followed.

"We can hang for a few more minutes." Cruz said. "Until then, I'm going to have Chip pass out the walking sticks, and we can discuss some of our trail rules."

Chip offered sticks to the hikers, and all but Eva took one. He also checked for untied shoelaces and proper footwear, and assessed what everyone had brought with them.

You could never be too careful, especially with beginners.

Cruz took the floor once more and provided safety instructions: he discussed the difficulty of the trail, how it was important that all hikers stay together, how often they would stop and eat.

Hands shot up with questions.

Where can we go to the bathroom?

How fast are we going?

What happens if someone gets lost?

There were more, which Cruz answered by rote. All the while, Chip looked out for any sign of Gabby.

"Finally!" Eva exclaimed.

"Sorry. I got in late last night."

Chip looked toward the sound of that voice, and watched Gabby approach in full hiking getup, complete with hiking boots and a bucket hat.

One thought struck him.

How late had she gotten in?

Stop it. It's not any of your business. You had your own sleepover.

Gabby reached her mother's side in time to catch the last of the safety briefing.

Cruz clapped. "Is everyone ready?"

The crowd cheered.

"Alright. I'll be in the front, and picking up the rear will be Chip. Chip, raise your hand."

Chip did what he was told, eyes grazing the crowd until he locked in on Gabby.

She had an unreadable expression.

"No one should get ahead of me, and should you trail behind, then Chip will stay with you. We promise that we won't leave anyone. Let's go."

The crowd shuffled forward, and Chip waited until the last person entered the trail before he joined them. From afar, he tracked Gabby as she walked next to Eva.

As the hike began, so did the chatter.

The conversation meandered, from the wedding to the next activity in the reunion, to food. There was criticism and gossip and laughter, which Chip allowed to bypass him.

Instead, he looked ahead to the horizon.

He couldn't remember the last relaxing hike he'd had, for some time to himself, and time to think. So he focused on the sound of his steps, and the wind against his skin.

"So Chip's your name?" One of the women had lagged behind. She was petite, and appeared to be in her fifties. A visor covered more than its share of required real estate.

"Yes, ma'am."

"Please. Don't call me *ma'am*. Call me Tita Darlene. *Ma'am* is...too old. Too formal."

"Alright then... Tita Darlene. Chip's my nickname. My given name is Charles."

"Ah, Charles. I like that. How old are you?"

"I'm thirty."

"Interesting." After a pause, she asked, "And is this your only job? Do you have real employment?"

"Mom!" another voice called, and another body drifted back. This woman was younger, Chip's age this time, with long dark hair coiled into a bun. She rolled her eyes for Chip's benefit. "Please excuse Tita Cupid." She took her mother's side.

"What? There's nothing wrong with making small talk. Is there, Chip?"

"Um, no?" Chip wasn't sure how to answer, though he appreciated the comic relief.

"I'm Kaitlin," the younger woman said after she gestured for her mother to move on; Darlene did so with a huff. "One of the cousins. Gabby and Frankie's first cousin. We're here from Oregon."

"How's your trip so far?"

"Good. It's beautiful here." She peered off in the distance. "Okay, now that my mother isn't within earshot, I apologize for her line of questioning and the future questions from the other aunties. They are notorious for being nosy and for matchmaking, especially since there are a couple of us in the group who are single."

He laughed, remembering what Gabby had said about her aunts. "Gabby mentioned it."

"Oh, so you know my cousin?"

"Yep."

"Hold on a sec." She shut one eye in thought. "She told me about you. One of her BFFs...the entrepreneur."

"Yeah, that's me. The BFF." Though when he said it, the feeling that coursed through him was bittersweet. He adjusted his pack.

"It's nice to meet you then. A friend of my cousin is a

friend of mine." She looked up toward someone calling her name. "Gotta go."

"I'll be here," he said, as he watched her jog up to the group.

A mile passed without issue, though slowly. And while Chip normally would enjoy the pace, would take the time to enjoy every step of this trail that he knew so well, he couldn't help but watch Gabby through the crowd.

She was still in conversation. In fact, she hadn't stopped talking since the hike began, her attention drawn by her family. She continued to smile, her laughter sincere.

As if she was unbothered.

Chip was feeling hot under the collar, but not in a good way. He was irritated and *decidedly* bothered. How could she be so happy, so social after last night, or after yesterday? Did she simply not care? Did he not stand out at all in her eyes?

A screech from the front of the pack pulled Chip from his thoughts, and he immediately jogged into the crowd. He heard gasps and chatter as he weaved by, until he came upon Cruz on one knee, next to an older woman who wore a pink visor.

She was holding her ankle.

"Everything okay?" Chip asked.

Cruz tenderly touched the woman's ankle. "Does it hurt there, Leanne?"

"A little." Then she hissed. "Oh, more. That hurts more."

"Do you think you can walk?"

Cross Trails had procedures in place to help with injured hikers, all the way up to rolling in a stretcher to remove them from the trail.

"I think so." She rotated her foot, though gingerly.

Chip knelt. "Let me wrap that ankle for you, and let's go from there. Is that okay?"

Leanne nodded.

"This is a good time for a break." Cruz smiled. "Everyone, let's find a spot somewhere in this area. Please don't wander off without telling me." Then with a final nod to Chip, he ushered the group off the trail.

Chip shrugged off his backpack and pulled out his first-aid kit as Leanne took off her right shoe and sock.

He unrolled the gauze. "I'm going to wrap it so it's snug. You'll feel more stable on your feet."

"Thank you."

"You're welcome."

"If I can't make it through the whole hike, what's going to happen with the group?"

"Depending on how you feel, I can walk you back. That's why there's two of us, so there's always someone who's free to help out." He began wrapping the gauze from the middle of her foot, and made his way up her ankle. "This good?"

"Yes. It's just fine. It feels better already. You're good at this."

"Oh, thank you."

"And you're so handsome, too. Not for me, of course. My husband, Alfaro, was a model in his twenties. So I know what handsome is."

Chip had no idea how to respond, so he just said, "Thanks." He felt the heat of her gaze, though didn't bite. It was time to scurry out of the spotlight. Standing, he held out his hand. "Ready?"

"I think so." She grabbed on to it. As she got on to her feet, the rest of the group clapped.

Still, her face crumpled. "Ow."

Cruz walked over. "How does it feel?"

"It hurts a little. I'm not sure I can do the rest of the hike."

"I can take her back," Chip offered.

"That might be a good idea." Cruz said. "It would be good

to send you with someone else, too, in case your ankle gets worse."

"Good idea."

"I want Gabby to come with me." Leanne gazed up at them, the disappointment now replaced with eagerness. "What if I need to go to urgent care? She has a car."

"I was just about to suggest something to that effect." Cruz frowned. He looked out to the rest of the crowd getting their things together. "Gabby?"

Gabby walked over with concern on her face. "Is everything okay?"

"Leanne was hoping you could take her back to Cross Trails with Chip."

"Iha, I'm injured." Leanne said. "You can come with me and my new friend, Chip."

"Of course," Gabby said, briefly glancing at Chip, with humor in her eyes.

Tita Cupid. There was more than one in this group.

"Of course," he echoed back. And as if reading his mind, Gabby laughed.

It took a few minutes to coordinate the rest of the group, but finally, Chip, Gabby, and Leanne headed back down the trail.

They walked three across, until Leanne said, "You two go ahead. Your steps are bigger than mine. I'll go slow and listen to my audiobook." With a shove, she brought the two of them together.

Chip laughed under his breath, and after looking over his shoulder, noted that Leanne had lagged a few feet behind them. "That was subtle."

"Tita Leanne is the queen of subtle. Not."

"When you talked about the pressure of bringing a date

to the wedding, to be honest I didn't really understand what you meant by it."

"And now?"

"Now, I know better."

At the mention of the wedding, Chip felt the awkwardness between them grow. He inhaled a deep breath and tried to gather fortitude. "Gabby, I think we need to talk about us."

At the same time, Gabby said, "I'm sorry about what I said."

He turned to meet her eyes. "Really?"

"Really. Running out of there like that. It was so…middle school." She gazed out in front of them. "I'm embarrassed with my behavior. You deserve better than that."

"It was jarring."

"You made that clear from our phone call last night."

He winced. "Yeah, honestly, I don't even remember it."

"Ah, you had that much fun?"

"Actually, it was…fun. Regan's great."

"I'm sure."

Silence built between them, and Chip wasn't sure where the conversation was going. Now that she wasn't jumping in to share her feelings, he hesitated in showing his cards. In that one kiss, he'd exposed his full deck. And part of him was tired of it.

Still, he spoke one truth. "This sucks."

"I know." Her body seemed to hunch. "It's only been twenty-four hours."

"Less than that, actually."

"Right, less. I was just so sad."

"Me, too."

"I don't want us to fight," she said.

"Well, technically, we weren't fighting. It was just a kiss."

Again, the awkwardness. So much weighed in the balance

here, of what Chip could lose, and how important Gabby was to him. And then there was his pride. His own acceptance of who he was to Gabby.

In the past, he could pretend that he adored her just as a friend, and now—now they couldn't talk about it in a straightforward manner.

How was that fair?

Still, there was silence on her end.

"Chip? I liked the kiss, too. That's why I had to take off."

"Really?" Surprised, his heart kicked up a notch, and he couldn't help smiling.

"Yeah." She slowed, facing him.

He frowned. "Then why do you look upset?"

"Because. We've made a mess, haven't we?" She lowered her voice and gave Leanne the side-eye. She was a good ten feet away and had placed earbuds in her ears. Gabby snickered. "Do you think she's been listening in on us?"

"The bigger question is, is she even hurt? I don't think she's limping," Chip said.

"We're going to have to watch her closely." Her gaze was back on him.

He nodded, looking down. He understood where this sudden levity was coming from. The rejection was about as clear as the path through the trees.

"But this doesn't mean that I didn't like the kiss. Or that I didn't want it," she said.

This was a surprise. "So it *did* matter."

"Oh, my God, yes, it did." Her face softened. "Did you think it didn't?"

He nodded, and the admission allowed for the pain to flow through him.

"Chip." She shook her head, clasped his hand, and squeezed firmly. "I'm sorry I said that. It wasn't just a kiss, and that's what makes it so hard. With you, I can see it being way more than that."

Chip had rarely allowed his thoughts to meander beyond friendship. And after their kiss, his thoughts hadn't gone past having this conversation with her.

But more? Did she mean it?

"Ow!" A yelp from Leanne halted their conversation.

"Tita!" Gabby shot forward to her aunt, who was crouched on the ground.

Chip ran over and lifted Leanne to standing.

"I twisted it again." She hissed against the pain, putting her weight on one foot.

"We should take you to the clinic," Gabby said.

"Agreed," Chip said. Remorse washed through him. They'd assumed that Leanne had been faking it when she had been in pain all this time. "We only have about a half mile left. Tita Leanne, why don't you lean on the both of us and we can help you the rest of the way."

"Okay." Leanne hobbled. "Thank you both."

"It's no problem," Chip said, meeting Gabby's eyes.

The rest of their conversation would have to wait.

Out of breath, Gabby slipped into her car and drove to the trailhead. She'd jogged ahead, per instructions from Chip, and through a back driveway brought the car closer for her aunt. Their plan was to bring Tita Leanne to the urgent care clinic straight away.

But that wasn't the only reason her heart was pounding.

With you, I can see it being way more than that.

She couldn't believe that she'd admitted her innermost feelings. With how Chip's face lit up, he felt the same way, too.

And yet, why didn't she feel the same hope?

Instead, what she felt was pressure. Pressure that she wouldn't be able to do it right. That she was going to ruin this, too. That in the end, she would be exactly as she was now—alone.

After she parked, Gabby called the urgent-care clinic to check on their wait time. Twenty minutes. Perfect. Had to love Peak UC. Jumping out, Gabby once more entered the trail, relieved to find Chip and Leanne nearer than anticipated.

"Hey, you two." She smiled to ease the moment and hopefully the worry on Leanne's face.

"Hey, stranger." Chip played along. "Have trouble parking?"

"Nope. And the clinic's wide open for you, Tita." She scooped her aunt up by the waist on her open side, and with their help, Leanne barely had to walk.

"Whoa!" Leanne laughed.

"Just a few more steps!" Gabby giggled, and to her relief, they exited the trail. She popped the passenger door open and assisted in lowering Leanne in. "There you go."

She closed the door, exhaling a breath. She turned around to Chip. "Thank you. What an ordeal."

"It's not over yet. Cruz will want an update, for sure."

"I'll follow up. What are you going to do now?"

"I'll jog the other way and meet up with the group."

"Good idea." She wasn't sure how to move forward after their interruption; then again, what else was there to say? "Are we…okay?"

Confusion passed across his face. "Is our conversation over?"

She looked around, as if the words were plastered on signs around her. "I'm not sure what else to say. Despite how I feel for you, I don't know what we can do. That kiss meant so much to me. *You* mean so much to me. This last day had been horrible. But there's Nathan. Regan."

"Right, Regan." He half laughed.

She wasn't sure what that meant, but she went on. Now that she was processing her thoughts, things were starting to flow. "Yeah. You have something good with her. I have something good with Nathan now..."

"Regan and I are just friends. And you and I..."

She looked down, anticipating his question.

"You didn't say," he whispered, lifting her chin. "You didn't really say how you felt about me."

Guilt swirled around her. Guilt, because what she was feeling was wrong, and the wrong timing. Guilt, because she couldn't lie to him, not when she was looking into his eyes.

"Do you really need for me to tell you?"

"I told *you*. Do you remember what I said?" His voice was husky and low, a little dangerous, and so different from his usual self. Her belly churned with need.

Is this what you want? Because I've wanted this. I've wanted you.

She swallowed against the memory. "I do."

"I meant it."

"I know." She felt it in the kiss, in the intensity that ran through her body. In the way she was so consumed by it at the moment, and would be for days after.

But what Chip wanted now was her feelings.

The problem was that she couldn't be sure if she was making a mistake by feeling them, by even thinking about sharing them.

"And then what?" she asked him.

"What do you mean?"

"If I tell you how I feel, what happens next? You and I ride off into the sunset?"

"Damn, make it sound worse, will you?"

She hung her head. This conversation was running away from them. "That's not what I mean."

"Then explain. Because honestly, Gab, I'm tired of being on the sidelines. The last twenty-four hours was an eye-opening lesson that I have put myself last in everything." He shut his eyes. "Especially with Nathan."

"I… I don't get it."

He shook his head, as if remorseful. "The double date was rigged. He asked me to come on the date to help him along, and I agreed."

She was hearing things. "What the hell?"

"He wanted another chance, and even if I had these feelings for you, I agreed to be a neutral presence, so that you'd be willing to get to know him again."

Ripples of shock zipped through her. "So wait. You tricked me into dating Nathan?"

"I didn't trick you."

"So there was no tricking involved?"

"No, I helped him. Like with buying the chocolates, and encouraging him to talk more, to show you the ways he was different."

"You still lied. And now I'm supposed to open myself up to you, when it could hurt other people, including the best friend you were tricking me into dating? I don't understand."

"Look, I didn't plan the kiss. I tried to keep my feelings for you locked away. But the more we spent time together on our dates…well, it happened, and here we are. The one thing that hasn't changed from the beginning is that I have always wanted to be with you, Gabby. Everything has been about me wanting to make you happy, to look out for you, to keep you safe."

She snorted. "Yeah, and how did that turn out?"

Hurt flashed across his features. "Exactly. I tried. I failed. And I'm done trying to please everyone and then hoping that you'll finally see me."

She let the silence draw out between them, her thoughts frozen on the consequences of their actions, on what had transpired behind her back. On the fact that all she wanted was for things to go on as they used to.

"I need to go," she said. "Lov—"

"No. Don't say it." Chip stepped back and hooked his thumbs underneath his pack.

"Oh…okay." Gabby's heart hurt, but she cleared her throat against it. It was fair, what he was asking. "I'll text you updates."

"Sounds good." He was already walking away, and he raised a hand for a goodbye. Without anything else to do, she rounded the car and entered the driver's seat.

"Iha, that was intense."

She shook herself back to the present and started the car. "Yes, but we'll get you to the doc soon."

"No, I mean the both of you." Leanne tsked.

Backing out, Gabby maneuvered the car out of the lot and headed south toward the clinic, not answering.

"Your mom said that he's one of your friends," Leanne said.

"He is." *And hopefully will still be*, she thought belatedly. Just the idea of losing him created a ball in the middle of her chest, but that was the risk, wasn't it? Better than everything else falling apart around her.

Gabby turned on the radio to tamp down her thoughts, and thank goodness, Leanne said nothing else as they drove to the urgent-care center. The lot was empty, a miracle, and check-in was an easy process.

They were taken back within the half hour.

Dr. Kuang was the provider on duty, and he examined Leanne's foot. "Mrs. Espiritu, tell me when it hurts, okay?" He rotated her foot clockwise and counterclockwise.

Gabby, sitting in the corner of the room, zoned out. Leanne had insisted that she chaperone, though she would rather have splashed water on her face. Had that conversation really happened?

Her phone buzzed in her pocket. A text from Nathan: Wearing black for the wedding. That ok with you

Gabby didn't know how to respond. She had kissed his best friend who'd admitted to setting her up with him.

"Hmm, your symptoms seem a little inconsistent with a break or a bad sprain," Dr. Kuang said.

"How can that be when I can't walk, right, Gabby?" Tita Leanne said.

At the sound of her name, Gabby swam out of her thoughts. "Yep, we practically carried her back down the trail."

"Let's do an X-ray, just in case." Doc typed into the clinic computer. "Hang tight in here. After the X-ray's done and read by the radiologist, I'll come in and follow up."

"Thank you, Doctor," Leanne said, and after the door closed, added, "Did you see? He didn't have a wedding ring, iha."

She gave her aunt the side-eye. Always with her matchmaking. "He doesn't have a ring, but he does have a partner."

"Oh, darn." She snapped her fingers.

"As soon as I saw the name, I about freaked," a voice said from the door.

The person was her perpetual missing bestie.

"Bailey!" Gabby stood and they did their customary handshake, followed by a hug. It was rare to see him at work, and he wore the light blue scrubs of the clinic. "Oh, my God, what are you doing awake? I miss your face."

"I'm covering a shift for someone. And it sounds like we need a catch-up, but first..." He turned to Leanne. "Hi, I'm your radiology tech. Ready for your X-ray?"

"Ready whenever you are."

He rolled in the behemoth of a machine and asked Gabby to step outside into a secondary waiting area.

Gabby did what she was told and plopped down on the couch. She took the time to answer some emails, read through her notifications, and check her calendar. All of it mundane. Not enough to keep her mind off Chip.

The couch cushion next to her dipped. Bailey groaned. "Oh, my dogs are barking."

At the thought of dogs, she thought of Six, and then of the kiss. She buried her face in her hands.

"Oh, God, what's wrong?" He leaned closer to her and wrapped an arm around her shoulder.

"I don't even know how to start." She looked at her friend. "And you're in the middle of work, and my aunt's in a room."

"I have five minutes. Do you know how much good health care people can do in five minutes? You can legit save a live in five minutes."

Gabby realized that the kiss would affect Bailey, too. It would affect everyone in their four-pack friend group. The responsibility of it made her tummy turn.

"It would help if you opened your mouth and spoke," Bailey said sweetly.

So Gabby did just that. She explained what she could in one breath, and watched the train of Bailey's thoughts play out on his face.

"Damn. I knew that you all had been double dating, but this is complicated."

"Very."

"Does Willa know?"

"No. I haven't been able to tell her. Most of this happened within the last day, and with the reunion and wedding planning... I've lost track of everything."

"I'm sorry this is happening. How do you feel?"

"How else but pissed? He set me up with Nathan, as if I wouldn't be able to make that decision for myself."

Bailey grimaced.

"What?"

"I would have done the same to be honest. He was trying to do right by Nathan, and by you."

"Seriously?" She rolled her eyes.

"Hey, how many times did you complain about being single, or about that chump William? Friends do what they gotta do."

"But the worst part of it all," Gabby continued, to keep the ball on her side, to prove her point of her anger, "is that after we kissed, he expected something."

"What did he want?"

She shook her head at the convoluted conversation they'd just had. "He wanted me to choose him. He said he was tired of taking the back seat. And yet, moving forward would have hurt everyone, including Nathan."

"So what did you do?"

"Nothing. It's the best thing to do, for everyone involved."

Beats of silence passed in which all Bailey did was stare at her. "For everyone involved. Who is everyone?"

"Regan, Nathan. You and Willa."

"Hold on a sec. Keep me and Willa out of your mouth. We don't need to be in this equation, because this is about you and Chip. And Regan and Nathan—who the hell cares about them?"

Gabby was completely confused. "What are you talking about?"

"Babe. Every person you mentioned just now are adults. People who have formed prefrontal cortexes that can make decisions and regulate their emotions. That's not your responsibility. What is, is dealing with what happened between you and Chip, and what the future looks like."

Gabby recoiled inwardly, the blow of Bailey's words swift and sharp.

He continued, "I love you, you know? And I'm not excusing his behavior at all. But the bottom line here is…who do you love? And who are you willing to lose?"

"Bailey?" someone called from the front room, and Bailey stood.

He waved at one of his coworkers. "One sec."

Gabby stood belatedly, numb from the toes up. "I'd better get back with my aunt."

"Yeah, speaking of…" He leaned in, eyes wide. "At the risk of violating HIPAA I don't think she has a sprained ankle. She hopped off that exam table without a hitch. Not even a grimace."

Gabby smiled through her muddled thoughts.

Bailey walked her to the open door of the exam room, where Leanne was sitting on the bed, scrolling through her phone. He kissed her on the forehead. "Sorry for the tough love."

"Who knew you were such a hard-ass?" Tears threatened to flow, though she blinked them away.

"Sometimes it's needed. But in the end, it's you who has to do the work. Love you."

"Love you."

And with one last hug, he departed for another room.

Gabby greeted Leanne when she entered and took the same seat in the corner.

"Glad you're back, iha. Did you see that Bailey? No ring."

Now, having had her fill of humble pie, all Gabby could do at this ridiculous moment was laugh.

Chapter Fourteen

Four days before the wedding

"I don't know if this is a good idea." Frankie inhaled as she looked out the windshield of the passenger's seat of Gabby's car.

"I need you." Gabby reached for her sister's hand. "Please. I can't go in there and be in the same room with him."

"You won't be alone. You'll have Mr. Lowry and the vet and all those puppies."

"But I know that *he's* there." He, meaning Chip.

He, meaning the man that she hadn't spoken to days.

"But the consequences of *this*." Frankie raised her eyes to the rearview window, with the reflection of Liam in the back seat twisting a Rubik's Cube. He wore headphones that had his favorite instrumental music playing through it—Frankie believed in multisensory learning. She lowered her voice. "What if he falls in love with one of these puppies? You know I can't have pets. I don't like mess."

"I'll reassure him that Six will basically be his, too. We all but live in a family compound. We're all going to be taking turns with Six."

Frankie reared back. "Hold up. I didn't know that. Does Mom understand you've signed us up for a pet?"

"No." Gabby was getting flustered. "We can talk about this

later. We have to go in. I need to make sure I'm there for Six's vet appointment. Just please come with me. You promised!"

Frankie raised both hands. "Okay, alright, it's fine. We're going in. But take deep breaths. You can't go in there stressed out like this."

As if a couple of deep breaths would take care of that. Stressed out was her middle name. They were in crunch time for Jared and Matilda's wedding, and the reunion had taken up more of her time than she'd anticipated. This afternoon, the group was headed to Luray Caverns, followed by a picnic under the stars, and guess who was roped into keeping track of everyone because she'd done such a good job last time?

Yes, that was right. Gabby.

She inhaled even deeper than that last breath, remembering her conversation with Chip. Was that how their friendship was going to end? And was she supposed to just move on?

In the last couple of days, what Bailey had said began to settle into her psyche. Her anger at being set up had turned down to a simmer, but she still felt deceived. And she didn't know what to do with that.

"You need to chill out. You sound like you're snoring while awake," Frankie said.

"I'm so glad I have such a sympathetic big sister."

Frankie shook her head. "It's going to be fine, Gabby."

"How do you know that?"

She leveled her with a glare. "Let me get this straight. You've asked your ex to be your plus one at our brother's wedding, but you don't think you'll end up forgiving Chip, who made one mistake? If you can't see that, then in my opinion, it's you that must get their mind straight."

Ouch. The statement was about as painful as what Bailey had told her. "What is it with this tough love?"

"It's not tough, Gab, it's *kind*, because it's the truth. Let's go and get this over with, okay? The tension is thick in this car, and I'm not even a part of this drama."

Frankie turned and tapped Liam on the knee. He raised his eyes and took off his headphones. "Are we going in?"

"Yep. But repeat after me. No puppies," Frankie prompted.

"No puppies," Liam echoed.

Gabby led the way to the Lowry front porch and rang the bell.

"Door's open!" said George from the inside. And after a deep breath, Gabby entered, and momentarily froze.

Her eyes scanned the living room. No Chip.

She let out a breath.

"It's me, Mr. Lowry. With Ate Frankie and Liam!"

"We're in the back, come on through."

It was strange to see how the house had remained exactly the same, though the last few days bore a marked change to her and Chip's relationship. When she led her sister and nephew around the corner, the gates she and Chip had purchased at the pet store were still there, holding strong. Inside the pen were George and the vet, who was examining one of the puppies on a folding table in the corner of the room.

"Just in time," George said, waving. "Six is next on the exam list."

Lucky came up to the gate and rested her chin on it. Gabby petted her nose. "Hey, sweet girl." Turning, she waved Liam over. "This is Lucky, she's the mama of all the puppies."

"Hi, Lucky." He stuck out a hand, and Lucky licked it, then nudged it with her nose. He giggled, only to gasp when he spotted the puppies in the middle of the penned area. "Mom, the puppies are so cute."

Frankie's grumbling could be heard well before she stood next to Gabby. But just as suddenly, she stopped. "Oh, my gosh. They are like little angels."

Gabby's head spun like a lazy Suzan, as she expected that her sister was being her usual, sarcastic self. What she faced, however, was a woman in love.

Love, because it resembled the same way Frankie had looked at Liam as a baby.

"You're serious?"

"Yes, um." Her hand shot out. "That one. The white one that Doc is looking over. Is he spoken for?"

"I thought you didn't like mess."

"I don't, but I never said it wouldn't be worth it for the right thing." She sighed unironically. "So is he taken?"

"There've been some inquiries, but no deposits yet. It's one of the things I have to sit down and discuss with Chip and George. But as you know..."

Frankie waved the notion away. "I know, because you can't allow yourself to trust."

"Dang, Ate."

"Anyway," she said, emphatically. "Put me on the list. High on the list, if you can make it happen, okay?" Her eyes didn't stray from the puppy.

Doc picked up Six and said, "Gabby, would you like to watch the physical?"

"Yes, please." She stepped into the pen and met him at the table. As she neared, Gabby could swear that Six detected her presence in the way she wiggled.

Doc walked her through the physical and what he was looking for in terms of the general health of the puppy. He gave her a few pointers about things to watch out for in boxers, such as joint issues and bloat. Gabby opened her notes app and logged all the doctor's concerns; she was going to educate herself on how to give Six the best life possible.

"Do you have any questions?" Doc asked.

Gabby shook her head. She had zero questions, but a chest full of worry.

Doc handed her Six. "What we just talked about was probably overwhelming. Just know that Six, at this very moment, is fine. Time will tell as she grows out of this nursery and then into your home. But I don't have any doubt that you'll do great as an owner. You have our clinic to come to if there are any questions." He rubbed Six on the top her head, then gestured for George to hand him the last puppy in the bunch to assess.

Gabby took her time in setting Six down. She savored holding her. While looking into her eyes, her heart melted. "I swear, I will do my absolute best. I might make mistakes sometimes, and you'll have to deal with me figuring things out, but I love you already."

"As I said last time, you look good with a puppy in your arms," George said, while holding the white puppy.

Between them, however, was a massive elephant. "Mr. Lowry, about what you saw the other day..."

"You don't have to say anything, sweetheart. I know how these things happen."

"There have definitely been a lot of things happening."

"Seems like they're the kind of things that are keeping the two of you apart."

Thank goodness for the puppy in her arms. Gabby had something else to look at besides George. "We're trying to figure things out."

"No need for details. But Gabriella, my boy...while I give him a hard time, more than I probably should, he's always had a soft spot for the people he loves. His friends, his family. He does for others, you know? All I want is for him to have good days. He had good days with you. I hope that whatever this is, that you'll make up, because I think it would put a smile on your face, too."

George brushed past her with a nod, and met Frankie at the gate. He handed her the white boxer puppy, which she and Liam cooed over.

Gabby scoured her memory for the last true good day she had—the day of the kiss.

Chip spied through the miniblinds in his bedroom and watched Gabby's car back out of their driveway and head south on their street.

A knock sounded on the door. "It's me."

Chip took a seat at his computer and woke the screen with the mouse. A spreadsheet appeared on the screen, which he hadn't made changes to for the last hour, but his father didn't need to know that. "Come in."

Dad opened the door. He was without Lucky, a rarity these days. "I was hoping you were going to come out."

"I was busy." He gestured at the screen.

"Right. It's too bad. You missed Gabriella."

"Oh, really?"

"She brought Frankie and her nephew. Looks like they might be going home with two puppies and not one."

"Oh, wow." If he hadn't been turned inside out, he would have been jumping for joy.

"Gabriella said that we need to sit down and talk about plans for the other puppies. Lot of folks inquiring, and the puppies are getting older by the day…"

"Yeah, we can do that." Chip could be professional, and he could count for Gabby to be so, also.

What he hadn't been able to count on was the beatdown she'd given him during her aunt's rescue. And that despite her anger, she'd all but admitted that she did have feelings for him.

He still didn't understand how their conversation ended with him walking away, with him broken hearted.

And then to not have spoken. For days.

"Look, you have been spending an awful lot of time here in your room. I haven't seen you leave for work in a couple of days."

Chip snorted. "Are you keeping track of my shifts now?"

"It's hard to miss when you haven't put on a pair of jeans."

"First of all, there is nothing wrong with wearing joggers. And second, I didn't realize that there was a dress code for taking care of the puppies." He heaved a breath, understanding that he had to give his father an excuse for not being out and about. Anything but the truth, which was that he'd called in sick.

Under the weather, he had said vaguely. It was accurate, though, since a cloud had been over him, even following him into the house.

To his father, though, he said, "It just worked out that I don't have any shifts, so I thought I'd catch up on some paperwork. You know how these things go—once you're in the flow, it's better to stay in it. I've got things to figure out about the senior-center project."

About Nathan, he continued in his head. About *telling* Nathan.

He and Nathan had scheduled time to talk over the project. And he knew he wouldn't be able to sit there without telling him the truth. The guy was in sales. He could read people. He would know that Chip was hiding something.

"I'm meeting up with Nate in a bit." Chip shifted in his seat, in anticipation of what was to transpire.

"So you're gonna tell him?"

He shrugged. He and Nathan have never had any conflicts. For the most part, there was nothing for them to argue about. Nor had they competed, not seriously anyway.

He was going to deliver a low blow.

He was at the point of no return. How Chip was going to bring Gabby up, he didn't know. But he could no longer lie.

Still, it didn't meant that he couldn't wallow, understanding that he hadn't just lost Gabby, but he was sure to lose Nathan, too.

It didn't mean that he couldn't mourn.

"Well, so long as you get out of this house and see the sun."

Chip snorted. "Yes, Dad. You understand that I'm a grown man now, right? That I actually grew up, left for college, came home, and bought this house. I can keep track of my own schedule"

"Ay, don't give me any of that bluster. You can't blame a man for worrying about his son." He walked in and sat on the bed. Now, they were only feet apart.

Chip couldn't avoid his father's eyes. They commanded attention, even as a septuagenarian. And though over the last decade, he appeared to become shorter and leaner, he still had the same paternal powers that didn't let Chip get away with anything. While his mother had been the nurturer, George had been the provider, and the giver of advice, as well.

Chip knew some was coming, whether or not he wanted it.

"I'm sorry, Chip."

Chip straightened. That was not what he was expecting.

"For putting too much pressure on you. Giving you a hard time about going out, bringing in Lucky and the puppies, and then making you think that you weren't acting like yourself after I saw you and Gabriella together here. It was wrong. If your mom were here, she would have slapped me upside the head. You never need pressure to do good, because you are already." He half laughed. "I told those same words to Gabriella today, that you're a good guy. And then I realized. I don't tell you any of this enough."

Stunned, Chip just replied, "Aw, Dad, it's okay."

"No, it's not, and I'll do better. I can't say I know all the details of what's going on with you and Gabriella and Nathan and whomever else, but I hope that above all the fixing you all have to do, that you remember that you're important. But if that's something you can't remember, just know that you're important to me. And your mother. And to the dogs out there. That you should be able to get what you want, too."

Chip felt the rise of emotions in his chest, in his face. He blinked repeatedly to clear his head, so that he had enough fortitude to speak. "Thank you. That means a lot."

His father stood and held out a fist.

Chip bumped his own against it.

"I've got to get back to Doc."

Chip looked at his watch. "I've gotta head out, too."

"Good luck, son."

"I'll need it."

A half hour later, after he changed into something decent, Chip drove into the parking lot of the senior center. There was only a smattering of cars, though Nathan's motorcycle was tucked behind their contractor's truck.

Chip's heart accelerated to double time.

He could do this, however this was going to unfold.

As he walked toward the side door, though, he didn't have long to think about it. It swung open to reveal Nathan. His face lit up. "Chippie!"

"Hey." Chip leaned in for their shoulder bump. "How's your body feeling from skating."

"I'm still black and blue man, but all worth it." He held him by the shoulders. "You?"

"My pride's worse off than my body."

Nathan laughed; he seemed to be in a good mood. Chip suspected it had everything to do with having Gabby back, thought he'd expected some tension from their last conversation about the center's signed contract.

Chip wanted to take care of actual business first and foremost, so he said, "You want to head back inside to do a quick walk-through?"

"Yep. Ready. But before we do so…" He looked down for a beat. "I'm sorry if I jumped down your throat about the contract. I was surprised and—"

"You had every right. I should have come to you first, before agreeing."

"Well, I'm over it. Things look great in there, and I appreciate you fronting the financing until I get all the books under me. Anyway, I shouldn't have talked to you the way I did. We're partners, and I know I can get ahead of myself."

Chip tucked his hands in his back pockets, to offset the anticipation that Nathan might later recant all he'd said.

It was then that their contactor, Justin, popped out of the center. "Hope you don't mind, but I have to head over to my other site."

"We don't want to keep you, so let's start the walk-through." Nathan nodded to Justin. To Chip he said. "I hope we're good, for real."

"Yeah of course," Chip said, throat thickening with remorse.

Good thing that Justin took the helm with the walkthrough so that Chip could recover. He answered all of Nathan's questions, and seemingly to his satisfaction. By the time Justin got into his truck to head out, Nathan was beyond cheerful.

"Well, I've gotta go. Gotta get my suit to the cleaners." Nathan looked at his watch.

Chip felt the pressure against his chest. Now was the time. "Listen, before you go, I've gotta talk to you about something."

"Course, what's up? But oh, before you do, I just want to say…thanks. For everything, you know, with Gab?"

"Oh, I don't know. All I did was show up."

"But that was everything. You being at these dates helped Gab feel more comfortable. And to tell you the truth, it helped me too. When you're in front of the girl you love and your best friend, you want to act even better than before."

Stop, please, was what Chip wanted to say. Because he didn't deserve his friend's appreciation.

"I count myself lucky, you know?" Nathan was still saying. "That you had enough faith in me."

Chip couldn't take much more, with guilt eating him up. "I appreciate you saying that, though you might not feel the same way after you hear what I'm about to say, Nate."

"What's up?" His smile faded. "You look like you're about to drop a bomb."

"You might feel that way."

"Well, out with it, bro. Is it the project?"

He shook his head.

"Is it George? Something happen? Or you?"

The fact that Nathan swerved to ask about his dad or him deepened his guilt. Chip had to spit it out.

Chip's chest was filled with dread. With fear. And yet, every part of him yearned to be free from it. He didn't want to carry this burden for much longer, and now that he'd told Gabby all he felt for her, there was nothing to lose, was there?

Except Nathan's friendship. He could lose that.

Chip started over. "It's about Gabby."

His eyebrows furrowed. "What about Gabby."

"Um." Chip opened his mouth, but nothing came out. In his mind, he stopped and started, though the words never quite made it to his voice box.

"Chip?"

He swallowed against the rock lodged in his throat. "I kissed her."

"Kissed who?"

"Gabby."

A beat of silence passed. "You—you what?"

"It just… I kissed her, and I didn't stop it from happening."

He stumbled backward as if Chip shoved him. "What the…? Are the two of you…"

"No, we're not together, but not for lack of me trying. But she turned me down, because of you. Because of you and me, and our friendship."

A maniacal laugh bubbled through him. "Well, at least *someone* had loyalty."

The words struck Chip right in the chest.

Then again, what Nathan had said was fair. "I'm sorry for not telling you sooner. For not being upfront with you. I thought that if I could keep my feelings for her under wraps, that they would go away. But then we kept going on all those group dates, and I couldn't deny that I wished that it was me she chose instead of you."

A sad smile appeared on Nathan's face. Chip had never seen it before, full of disappointment and hurt. "I can't even process this. I don't even know who you are. But…after this project, you and I? Are over."

Nathan brushed past Chip, shoulder-checking him. He grabbed the helmet from the back of his motorcycle and slipped it on his head. Then, he said, "It serves you right, losing her, too."

Nathan hopped on his bike and started it, the sound of the engine filling in the silence.

If only it could drown out Chip's regret.

Chapter Fifteen

Day of the wedding

"**D**ad, we're going to be late." Chip walked out of this bedroom, buttoning up his Oxford shirt. He had taken too long drowning his sorrows in the shower and then getting ready. In the last few days, it was as if he had been walking through a haze. His brain was goo, his limbs clumsy.

They only had an hour and a half until the ceremony, which should have been enough time to make it. But with how many people had been invited to the ceremony, it was best if they got there at least a half hour before.

Though he wished that there was a way for him to be incognito, or to somehow witness the wedding without actually attending and being noticed by Gabby or Nathan.

"Dad?" he once more called out, though clocked that there were extra voices in the house. Looking out the back windows, he saw an unfamiliar person with his father in the backyard. He checked the driveway, and sure enough, a car with out-of-state license plates was parked there.

Approaching the back doors, Chip noticed that both men were watching Lucky. The puppies were asleep in the pen, though alone. Their sitter, Sydney, was set to arrive in the next half hour.

"Morning," Chip announced himself, stepping out.

Both men turned.

"There he is. Son, meet Dean Harris," George said with a tight-lipped smile. "He's from up the street, from Five Star Boxers."

Five Star Boxers, the dog breeder they'd suspected Lucky escaped from. The dog breeder that was in truth a puppy mill.

Belatedly, Chip offered a hand and a smile. "Nice to meet you."

Dean nodded. "I'm sorry to stop by unannounced, but I just couldn't wait. We've been looking for Honey for months."

Chip frowned.

"Lucky," George said.

Lucky barked, right on cue.

Lucky was Honey. "Wow."

"Exactly what we said when we realized she was here all along," Dean said. "Someone clued us in on boxer puppies being adopted and we looked at the socials and lo and behold, there she was. We can't tell you how much we appreciate you all taking care of her and her puppies."

Lucky trotted up to Chip and pushed her nose against his thigh before zooming back to the other side of the yard. He was pretty sure that she'd smudged his slacks, but he didn't care.

Dean was here to take back his dog.

"She's been with us a while. Dad's been tracking her for months. And the puppies, we've made arrangements for placements. We took responsibility for the vet care."

"Like I said, we appreciate it." Dean's smile stiffened. "But I'm here to make arrangements to take her back."

Chip looked to George, and his father's face crumpled with worry.

"But she's not chipped. And when we checked with animal control, there was no report of a missing boxer. How do we know that she's yours?"

"Because she is. Watch this. Honey!"

Lucky stopped her play and perked up, then galloped over to Dean. She sat at his heels.

The evidence was damning.

Wasn't this what Chip wished for? To be relinquished of this great responsibility. He hadn't wanted a dog in the first place.

And yet, Lucky was the part of the family.

"Mr. Harris," Chip began.

"Dean, please."

"Mr. Harris," Chip repeated. "Lucky's not going back to you."

Dean's upper lip curled. "Is that right?"

"Yep. Not until we can get everything confirmed. Hell, I don't even know who you are. I'll contact animal control and the vet, and we can go from there. Until then, Lucky stays here, and so will her puppies. Now, we have an event to go to. Can I walk you out?"

Chip's heart pounded. He rarely had conflict with anyone, though in the last week he'd had more than he ever bargained for.

Then again, it was for things that were worth it.

With Lucky and the puppies, Chip hoped that he could still win.

Dean nodded and followed Chip around the yard to his car. "You'll be hearing from me." There was threat in his voice.

Chip was hit with a surge of protectiveness over Lucky, the puppies, and his father. "We'll be ready."

After Dean drove out, Chip entered his home and closed the front door. He locked it for good measure.

"What do we do?" George crossed his arms.

"I'm going to do exactly what I said. I'm going do my due diligence. And we're going to consult a lawyer."

"Lawyers are expensive."

"I know someone. A good one." One thing Nathan did well was translate all that bluster using his former life as an attorney.

George frowned. "But with how you ended? Has he talked to you since?"

"No, he hasn't." Nor had Chip expected him to. But they still had to work together with the senior-center project. "I'll text him and feel him out. If he says no, I'm sure we'll find someone to represent us. After all, are you prepared to say goodbye to the dogs?"

His father's face crumpled. "No."

"Me, either. But for now, we need to get ready for this wedding. We can't be late." He stepped out into the hall, but was pulled back by the arm.

"Son. Thank you."

"You don't need to thank me. I want Lucky here. This is her home."

A bark sounded from the living room, followed by Lucky's long stride and her body against his leg.

Dog hair be damned, Chip bent down and hugged Lucky by the neck. He was rewarded with a lick on his cheek.

For the moment, she made everything one hundred percent okay.

It was *the* day. The day that everyone had been waiting for. Everyone, meaning the entire town, and every single member of her family.

Wedding days were usually joyful ones for Gabby. While she fretted over the details up to the night before, she looked forward to the actual celebration.

Today, though, she was simply tired.

She tried not to show it. Powered by an energy drink and topped off by coffee and chocolate-covered espresso beans, she glided through the ceremony in a kind of haze. Thank goodness for her slew of assistants, a professional wedding crew who were as type-A about the plans she'd made as she was. Everything ran like clockwork and with the smoothness of greased gears. Everyone knew exactly what to do, and when.

And her bride and groom, well…they were flawless. When Matilda had walked down the aisle, the crowd seemed to hold a collective breath. Jared had burst into tears at the altar, and that had set off a waterfall of tears from everyone else in the congregation.

Which, unsurprisingly, was full. There wasn't an open seat to be seen—it was standing room only, with many folks opting to stand in the church's foyer to escape the concert-like crowd.

Now, at the B & B for the reception, the vibe was one of serenity.

Gabby's eyes scanned the crowd. A jazz trio welcomed in guests with a romantic tune. Her assistants were scattered in all the important places, ushering guests and ensuring all was running smoothly. Off in the distance, in Vista Point Two, one of the most beloved areas of the B & B to view the sunset, Jared and Matilda were taking photos.

At least the wedding was going well, and she'd been able to get up and do her job. And at least she had this job.

The lingering thought of her CPA exam flew in, and she promptly stomped it down. She couldn't even think of that. Not only did she need to get through this wedding, but also, as the days passed, she was no longer sure she wanted to take the test.

It also didn't help that she associated studying for her test with Chip.

Her current communication with Chip encompassed a few texts back and forth about Six, and nothing more. And since his texts were emoji-free, a sign that he was still upset, she didn't have the bravado to apologize.

But today, there would be zero excuses.

Her phone buzzed. It was Nathan: Just parked.

While he attended the wedding earlier, Gabby didn't get a chance to speak to him. She, however, saw him. Chip, too.

Curiously, Nathan and Chip didn't sit together.

Can't wait.

Another text, from Janine, a wedding assistant: the DJ is having technical issues.

I'll take care of it.

Gabby wound through the crowd, greeting guests along the way. She was given compliments, though none landed in her psyche. Despite it being the most anticipated wedding of the year, she couldn't access total pleasure, knowing that one of her most important relationships was falling apart.

She arrived at the dance floor, where DJ Drake was set up. He'd driven down from Northern Virginia for this event as her replacement DJ. For a guy who had a gig the night before, he still looked sharp. He wore dark shades, a newsboy cap, and all black. Though, his usual smile was replaced with a frown. "Gabby," he breathed out.

"What's up?"

"I'm missing a cable. I don't know where it could be. I had an assistant pack up for me last night, and… I'm sorry."

"No worries. Let me think." She ran through the resources in her head and looked across to the sea of faces. "Mik from the hardware store is here. I'm sure he can help. Just hang tight."

It was never a wedding without a hitch. Gabby readied a text to ask Janine to find Mik, when she rammed against a body.

"Umph." Jostled backward, she said, "I'm so sorry."

"No, it's fine." A pause. "Gab."

Chip. She inhaled a breath. He was handsome, in a navy suit. She detected a new scent on him, too.

So much had changed between them the last couple of weeks. What should have been an easy greeting, something that would have been punctuated with a hug and chatter, now teemed with unpleasantness.

It was written on the grimace on his face.

"Hi." She worked a smile on to hers, though it was difficult and painful. "You look nice."

"And you…you're gorgeous."

"This old thing." She looked down at herself, at the slacks and bolero she'd tried on weeks ago, though now felt like a lifetime. At that clothing shop, she'd resolve to shake things up. Now that she had, she had to put things back together. "Chip, I was hoping we could get a chance to talk. If…you could save me a dance."

"Yeah, of course."

Relief flooded her that he was willing to be in her proximity despite all that had happened. "Okay, um, I've got to find Mik, for the DJ." The information in her brain crisscrossed. "I'll find you, okay?"

"Sure, see you."

But she didn't get a step further. Gliding toward them was Regan. She wore a yellow dress; she almost looked ethereal. "Hi, Gabby. Congratulations on the event. It's fabulous."

"Thank you. I had a lot of help." Gabby contained her

surprise. Then again, plus-ones weren't labeled by name in the seating chart, and thinking back, Chip had RSVP'd so long ago.

And had she thought that he would come stag, when Nathan was her plus-one?

"But this was your masterful vision."

As much as Gabby wanted to delve into one of their friendly conversations, she didn't have the heart. Gabby had kissed Chip while knowing that he and Regan were seeing one another.

Gabby was that girl.

Inside, she grimaced.

"Well, well, well. The gang's all here." Nathan sauntered up to the group.

And though he was smiling, Gabby detected sarcasm in his tone.

Nathan pressed his cheek against Regan's. "You look great." Then, he bent down and kissed Gabby on the cheek. "And you are stunning."

Then he nodded at Chip. Chip responded with a "Hey."

A chill settled within the group. Gabby looked between the men.

What was happening here? Normally, the two would have shaken hands, hugged, or at the very least engaged in small talk.

Nathan grinned. "I love that we're here together, the four of us. Nicely paired together. Oh, and Chippie, got your text, and yeah...not sure if I'm available. Sorry, bro."

Chip's cheeks mottled and his jaw ticked.

She peered at the two men, standing side by side. Something was going on.

"Something up, fellas?" Regan asked.

"Nah," Chip answered back. "I should make my way to the bar, though. Wanna come Regan?"

Someone laughed, snapping Gabby from the moment.

What was she supposed to be doing?

Damn it. The DJ's cable.

"I don't have time for this. Not sure what's up between you both, but I've got a wedding to execute." Was she bothered? Yes, but this was the absolute wrong time for drama. From afar, she could see Matilda and Jared walking down from Vista Point Two. She reached out and squeezed Regan's wrist to send her solidarity, and said. "Catch you all later."

Then she walked away.

To her relief, no one stopped her. She found Mik and begged him for assistance, which he readily gave. He would take DJ Drake to his shop.

Her next task: to tend to her bride and groom.

Gabby ran toward her couple, who were seconds from being bombarded by guests. From the look on Matilda's face, a moment of rest was necessary.

"How about a few minutes to sit?" She pulled stray leaves from the hem of Matilda's dress, scooping the extra tulle into her arms.

"Yes, please," Matilda breathed.

She steered them to the couple's cabin, which had been specially remodeled over the last few months. The cabin was constructed with two separate entrances on opposite sides of the building, for some privacy between the couple as well as from other guests. There, Gabby had set up ice-cold water and a couple of mess-free snacks to tide them over until dinner.

The wedding party arrived and helped both bride and groom into their suites.

Matilda waved Gabby over. To her matron of honor, Krista, she asked, "Will you guys give us some time?"

Krista nodded and ushered everyone out. Once the door closed, Matilda melted in her seat. "Whew."

"You can say that twice, Mrs. Sotheby."

Her smile brightened. "I love how that sounds. So romantic, right?"

"Almost as romantic as your entire ceremony. So…how can I help you?"

"I wanted to get you alone, to tell you thanks for last week. Not only did we polish off that whole bottle of wine, but I took up all of your time whining."

"It's nothing. And it wasn't whining. It was…working out feelings, adjusting, you know?"

"Nope. It was whining." Her cheeks reddened.

"We'll agree to disagree. And it's what I do, for you as the bride, and for you as my sister." Gabby blew out a breath. "Sister…wow."

Sometimes, Gabby's was too busy to sit with how she felt. The last year had brought two new family members into her life.

"I feel very honored, Gabby, that I'm a part of your family."

Gabby blinked away the start of tears. "Nope. You can't do that right now. You can't make me cry. I am at work, dammit."

She laughed. Then, from the underside of her dress, she brought out a velvet satchel.

Gabby's eyes widened, and she extended a hand. The satchel was heavy against her palm. "I didn't know we were doing gifts."

"Silly, I have a living room full of them. Go ahead. Open it."

Gabby reached in and retrieved a silver bangle. It was solid and cool against her fingertips. "It's beautiful."

"I got Frankie something similar, and I have my own. Is

that cheesy, for us to have matching bracelets? I'm an only child, and I don't know, I always wanted siblings."

That was it—Gabby teared up. It was the accumulation of everything happy and sad and frustrating and confusing.

She pressed her cheeks to keep from her tears from flowing.

Matilda continued, "You gave me such wise words the other night."

"I assume you and Jared talked it through."

"We did, and I'm keeping every book." She heaved a breath and pressed a tissue against the corner of her eye. "I was so afraid of finding out something new and wrong about Jared that I was just looking for red flags, to get ahead of the disappointment I guess."

"No one can fault you for having a little bit of cold feet. You're not the first person to do so."

"I know, but it also showed me that I have more to work on. That I've got things to hash out. The good thing is that Jared's not afraid of it. It's like he sees right through the anxiety I have. He's patient like that."

"Don't sell yourself short. *You're* the catch: You have a way of reassuring him that he's exactly who he needs to be."

She half laughed. "I bet when it's your time to walk down the aisle, I mean, if you choose to, you're going to be such a whiz. You're going to know all the secrets and all the advice."

"Yeah, if I ever get there. At this rate, I'm going to be planning Liam's wedding and still scrambling for a date."

She frowned. "Why would you say something like that?"

"Because I can't seem to get this right."

"Wanna tell me more about it?"

"On your wedding day? No way."

"I have time."

"According to my watch, you only have another ten minutes before you have to make your entrance with your groom."

"Everyone can wait."

She grinned. "We can catch up another time. Maybe over coffee. Or a good bottle of beer. After your honeymoon. Okay?"

"Only if you really mean it. Sisters before misters, you know?"

"I love that you said that while wearing an A-line gown with three hundred people waiting for you out there."

"Though I would be happy taking off this dress and finding a good book to read with my husband by my side." She gasped. "Oh, my God. I have a *husband*."

"Yes, you do. And until it's time, I want you to sit and have something to eat. Okay?"

"Yes, ma'am."

As Gabby headed toward the door, Matilda called out, "Wait, one more thing. You were probably kidding around about being single when Liam gets married, and there's nothing wrong with that, if that's what you want. But a big part about falling in love, about letting love in, is just doing that. Letting love in. It's what I learned."

Gabby nodded, taking in her wise words, but wondered if that rule applied to her.

Chapter Sixteen

Gabby's problem wasn't that she was afraid of letting love in, it was that she continued to do so. As she watched Jared and Matilda take their first dance, with Chip in the background, it was a reminder that what her problem was discernment.

What does she do with the feelings she has for Chip? While the wedding kept her occupied, she yearned to be with him. As friends, as something more.

Would her conversation with Chip later on achieve anything but another fight? It was clear that there was strife between Chip and Nathan. Was it because of her? And what about Regan?

A tap on the shoulder brought her back to the present, and she turned.

Nathan. "Hey beautiful."

"Hey." This man, too, wasn't helping her indecision. Should she continue to date Nathan after today? Did she still feel anything for him?

What Nathan deserved was someone who would want him and him only, someone who hadn't kissed someone else and continued to think about that other person. No, she and Nathan didn't have an exclusive relationship, but in all the ways he was acting, he wasn't thinking of Gabby as a fleeting relationship.

Gabby couldn't wait until later to do something about

this. Every second that this facade went on was another inch deeper into the mess.

She was ready to be out of it. And in order to repair the present, in this case, Gabby had to address the past. She looked at her watch and noted where they were in the wedding timeline. "I have to take care a couple of things. But will you meet me over by the gazebo in about a half hour?"

He frowned. "Everything okay?"

"Yeah. But I think we're overdue a conversation. About us. Alone"

Nodding, a veil of worry descended on his expression. "I'll be there."

"You'll be okay?"

"Yes. Don't worry about me. I'm sure I can find a way to amuse myself."

As she walked away, Gabby looked for her assistant, Janine. After being stopped twice by guests and then posing for pictures with her cousins, she found her standing with one of the caterers.

"Janine," she said quietly, but vehemently.

"Yes."

"I'm going to check on the cake and make sure it's all set. But after, I need to take a break."

"Everything okay?"

Gabby didn't take breaks at weddings. It was against her work ethic, especially after months of preparation.

But there were exceptions to everything.

"Yes, I need to have a quick conversation, but without any interruptions. Do you have it from here?"

"Absolutely. We're past all the hard stuff."

"Great."

After double checking on the cake and stopping to chat with the caterers, Gabby made a beeline toward the man that had ruled her heart for much too long. She hiked to the gazebo, where string lights hung from above. As Nathan saw her coming, he stood from the gazebo bench and his eyes lit up with anticipation.

"Gab." He reached down to take her hand and she climbed the short two steps.

She felt her stomach give at the romantic setting, the music in the background, and this handsome man in front of her.

Gabby would need to be strong. She would need to say what she should have told Nathan long ago, but this time without any wiggle room.

She sat on the wooden bench and patted the space next to her.

"Are you having a good time?" Gabby rested both hands on her lap as he sat.

"Yeah, great. It's been a while since I've done a good cha-cha. Your aunties continue to be a hoot."

"At the very minimum." She laughed.

"How's everything going? Smooth sailing?"

"Yes. We're over the big obstacles. Though the staff doesn't rest until every last person is off property. You can't imagine the shenanigans people get into. I've seen a lot over the years."

Gabby was talking too much. Her fear was rising.

"All these little details," he said.

"We have to think of everything. Like a caterer dropping one of the cakes. Or someone from the bridal party breaking a heel. It's endless, though that's what contingencies are for. Which brings me to this conversation, which is well overdue."

His expression clouded over. "The fact that you equated us to contingencies…"

"Yeah." Her tummy seized. *Say something.* "We've been through a lot together."

"We have."

"Lots of ups and downs, and I hoped that you and I would always be okay. I was quick to say that we would remain friends. Small towns, right? Our families sometimes work together. We can't really escape Peak. But in doing so, I didn't allow myself to make a clean break, and you continued to think that you could come back to me whenever you got bored."

"Now, that's not true. Not this time."

Gabby shook her head. "You're right. Not this time. This time I do think you've changed. That whatever you needed to learn from our relationship, you have. But that's almost beside the point, because when I've waited for you, or when I keep going back to you, I don't get to see what's around me."

"With Chip." His eyes lowered. "He told me everything. That you two…" He shifted, visibly uncomfortable. "Did he tell you that I asked him to help with the double dates?"

She nodded. "I was mad, then I realized I didn't have the right. Because of the kiss. Are you…"

"Pissed? Yeah. I mean, that's crap for a friend to do that."

"He didn't just do it, you know. There were two of us. I wanted it, too."

"Then why aren't you together?"

She thought about it, finding the reason almost comical now. "Because of you." She raised a hand to keep him from interrupting. "I was worried about hurting your feelings. I was worried about getting in between your friendship. And I'm sorry I have." She reached out and held his hand. "I'm more sorry that I wasn't honest with myself to begin with. I should have just been paying attention to the way *I* felt, the way I have been feeling about Chip. I think that while we would have needed this heart to heart eventually, I wouldn't have hurt Chip."

"So you and me…"

She offered him a smile. "Can we still—"

"Oh, no, not the let's-still-be-friends speech."

"Is that awful?"

He bit his lip and looked away for a second. Then he half-laughed. "Yeah, but…no. It is what it is."

She squeezed his hand, and smiled. "These three dates have been so much fun. It helped me remember all the good times we had, and I'm thankful for that. But I need to move on. I hope you'll be happy for me." She inhaled. "And maybe one day, Chip will forgive me."

Gabby stood, ready to put space in between them. "I have to head back."

He let go of her hand, and linked his fingers together. "Not going to lie, I wish it were me you chose. But Chip—he's the best guy I know. He'll come around, Gab."

She took one step back. "Will you still stay for the rest of the reception?"

"That alright?"

"Of course it is." She looked off where from the dance floor area was aglow. "Weddings are magical nights. They're so hopeful. That maybe love will come for us too."

"Yeah…" his smile was pensive. "Hope so."

Gabby bid him farewell. She knew that in her case, that she would need to do more than hope.

She had to *do*.

Through Chip's point of view, the wedding and reception had passed in a slow-moving blur, aided by a couple of glasses of champagne and plates of food that were magically refilled whenever empty.

And despite the sheer amount of people present, he found

himself milling about alone, sitting at a six-person round table all by himself, nursing a Jack and Coke.

Thank goodness Regan—whom he'd asked at the last minute to be his plus-one—was an extrovert and an expert in social spaces. She had yet to sit since the dance party began. Currently, she was sitting with the some of the senior center members, laughing it up.

"Will you grant me the pleasure of a dance?"

Chip looked up to see Daria, wearing a sparkly, peach dress. Clipped into her hair was fascinator.

Chip jumped to his feet. "Look at you."

Her cheeks pinked, and she pushed him gently. "Now you, you don't have to say that."

"I mean it." He looked around. "Are you here with a date?"

"He's somewhere over there." She fanned her fingers toward the dance floor, and then fingered through the tips of her hair.

He peered among the guests. "Who's the lucky guy?"

"Someone." She giggled. "It's on the DL."

Chip coughed into his drink. "The DL?"

"That means it's a secret."

He bit against his cheek to keep from laughing. "That sounds…risqué."

"You have to keep things fresh at our age."

Chip debated sticking his fingers in his ears, in case she said anything else. "Well, are you…two…enjoying the reception?"

"I'm having the time of my life."

At least one of them was.

It wasn't all the way true. The wedding was one for the books: romantic, and despite the full church, felt intimate. And while he could count the weddings he'd attended with one hand, this one was lively and cheerful. The dance floor was swamped, the drinks were flowing, people were singing to the music, and the air was electric.

But with the puppies on his mind, with Nathan too pissed at him to consider providing legal consult, and with wondering what Gabby wanted to talk about, he had been content nursing his Jack and Coke.

"Everyone looks so good," she added, as if reading his mind, "but Gabby is especially beautiful, don't you think?"

They were going down this road again, and he had to put a stop to it. "Daria, me and Gabby? That's not going to happen. First of all, we both have other dates."

Shock appeared on her face. "You came here with someone else?"

"Yes, she's over there." He pointed out Regan. She was now dancing with a bunch of Jared's relatives whom she'd just met.

"She's pretty."

"She sure is."

"So why aren't you out there with her?"

"I'm not feeling the song. Later, though."

"Let's dance now."

"Oh, I don't know." Chip had planned to make it through the cake cutting and sneak away. He'd much rather spend time with the puppies.

"Charles Lowry, are you refusing me? I've known you since you were in diapers."

She didn't give him time to respond, grabbing him by the elbow and all but dragging him to the dance floor. She weaved him through bodies, the bass thumping under his feet.

"You sure you like this song?" Chip asked, moving to the beat. It was a recent hip-hop hit. To his surprise, Daria threw her back into it. And she had rhythm. From someone who didn't have any, it was more than impressive.

Chip might've had the best dancer with him. So he decided to let go, body and spirit, and tried to keep up with the beat and with Daria.

But his momentary peace flipped to awkwardness when they ended up right next to Gabby and his dad.

"Son! Finally on your feet." He gestured to Gabby. "Look who I convinced to take a break."

"That's great." He fought looking at Gabby, and focused on dancing with Daria, who, thank goodness, kept the attention on her. She brought out all the old-school dance moves, drawing cheers and applause from everyone around them. She was the perfect dance partner, the perfect distraction to his morose thoughts of his forthcoming conversation with Gabby.

What more could Gabby say to break his heart?

Soon, the dance song faded to a slow song.

"Alright, let's get these young kids together. Ready for me, Daria?" George said. "That is, Chip, if you don't mind."

"He's not the boss of me. You're mine, old man." Daria tugged his father away.

Leaving Chip and Gabby alone.

"People continue to be so subtle," Gabby said.

"Right…" He couldn't just stand there, and walking away would be rude. "Do you…want to dance?"

"Thought you'd never ask."

He took her into his arms, hands landing on her waist. Her hands were resting on his shoulders, and she leaned into him so that their upper bodies touched.

Did this mean that they were alright? Or was this a precursor to another rejection?

"Having fun?" She looked up at him.

"I am. Congratulations, by the way. Everything's perfect."

"Thank you, but you don't have to lie. Not all things are perfect. You and I, we're definitely not perfect."

"No." His chest was heavy. "I'm sorry that it's all messed up right now."

She shut her eyes, then opened them slowly. "*I* messed it up."

"We both did."

Her eyes glassed over with tears. "The thing is, I don't want for things to be messed up. And now, I'm afraid with the things that I said, with how long it took me to figure things out, that it's too late.

"I'm sorry I took you for granted, as a friend, as…more. I had these feelings for you, these moments when I felt more, but I wondered if it was just my imagination. The truth is, I didn't see you coming. I couldn't fathom that the person I liked most in the world could be the same person that I love."

Stunned, Chip leaned his forehead against hers. He could barely catch his breath. "You love me?"

"I love you. And not just in a friend way. I realized it once I cut the noise. Once I let go of meaningless ties. I don't know what it is about me that wants to hold on. I do it with everything, and when plans don't go as I anticipate, I try to push through it. I ignore my instincts and do what I think is expected of me. It's like that CPA exam."

"Are you…saying you don't want to take the exam?"

"That's the thing, I don't think I actually do. I started the course to learn more about how best to help with the B and B, but then I got caught up in what everyone else was doing." She shook her head. "Anyway, I'm totally digressing, probably because I've missed you so much. But I love you, Chip Lowry."

She wrapped her arms around his neck and pulled him in. He tightened his grip around her waist and breathed in the moment. His chest swelled with relief, with joy. "God, I love you, too, Gabby. And it's not just you who holds on. I do it too.

I think if I can just be a part of everything, if I can give people what they need and want, they'll always be a part of me.

"And now?" She settled back on her feet and looked up into his eyes. In them, he saw hope. He saw the future.

"That I can't make anyone stay. And I have to be okay with that."

"I'd like to stay…with you. For wherever this takes us. Even if it scares me, even if I don't know what's coming."

"Come what may, I'll be by your side. You'll never need to find a plus one." The words came unbidden, and Chip didn't hold back. He wouldn't anymore, not when it came to Gabby, to love. "Will you be my forever wedding date?"

She looked into his eyes, and he didn't detect a smidge of doubt in her expression. "Forever."

Around them, people clapped. The spell now broken, he found faces turned his way. Those around them had made room on the dance floor.

"Oh, God. Everyone just heard that," Gabby whispered.

"Yes, we did," George said from the perimeter of the dance floor.

The sound of Gabby's laughter soothed all of the hurt from the last few days. "Well, I meant it."

"Me, too." He leaned down and kissed Gabby. And knowing that he no longer had to worry, that this kiss was real, allowed him to melt into her.

And it was just the beginning.

"Do you know what would make this better?" she whispered after the kiss.

"What?"

"The Wobble."

And as if the DJ had been keyed in, the song began.

Chapter Seventeen

It might have not been Chip's wedding, but he bet he was as happy as the groom, because Gabby was going home with him.

Technically, after the last guest left.

Chip had just loaded the wedding gifts into Jared's car to help wrap up the evening, and was trudging through the gravel parking lot back to the B & B when the smell of cigarette smoke took his attention. To his right, he came upon Nathan's motorcycle.

Nathan stepped of the shadows, nodding as he exhaled smoke.

"Careful, that's stuff's gonna kill you." Chip slowed.

"I'll take my chances."

"Suit yourself." He walked past.

Normally, Chip initiated reconciliation, to fix any conflict. But he meant what he'd said to Gabby—he too needed to practice putting himself first.

And he'd already apologized to Nathan. Chip wasn't going to beg for his forgiveness.

"Look, I'm sorry too, okay," Nathan said.

Chip halted. He must have been hearing things. "Excuse me?"

"For putting you in the middle. And for not seeing it at all."

"It?"

"That you had feelings for her, too. Not going to lie. I still don't know how I feel about you and Gabby being together, but you were right. I had a million chances with her, and each and every time, I messed up. I know I have to move on." He took a drag.

"I'm sorry I didn't tell you," Chip said. "When something did happen."

"Yeah, I wish you did. Then again, I would have been pissed then, too. I'm not perfect, and I'm trying, slow but sure."

"I know."

He looked up and tossed the cigarette on the ground, stomping it to ashes. "Look, you're my oldest friend. I don't know my life without you."

Chip snorted.

"What?"

"I think that all the time, about you. You're my family, and that makes things harder, because there's no line between us. And my tendency is to give in, every time."

Nathan nodded. "I get I took that for granted. But I don't want to lose you. You mean a lot to me. I can't say I'll be able to talk about Gabby or be with you all for a while, but it doesn't mean that we're nothing. I care about you."

"Yeah, I guess I feel the same way."

Nathan grinned. So did Chip.

"Tell me you and I are good," Nathan said.

It didn't take Chip long to think about it. Things were going different between them. While Nathan would always be his friend, Chip would no longer be afraid to tell him how he felt. Good or bad.

With family, blood or otherwise, sometimes love with boundaries was the best outcome.

"We're good." Chip leaned in and hugged Nathan.

"Good, good," he said, then backed off. "And hey, the whole legal consult? Don't worry about it. We'll find a way to keep those dogs."

The breath left his lungs. "You will."

"I remember Goose. And it's been forever since you had a dog. Anyway, I'll call you in the morning and figure all that out."

"Thank you."

Nathan unhooked his helmet from his motorcycle. "Later, Chippie."

Chip stepped backward and waved one last time as Nathan started his bike, then continued his trek to the B & B.

Besides a few stragglers going home, his short walk was quiet through the dark lot. But he was drawn to another car with a familiar Top of the World Senior Center sticker on its bumper. His dad's. The dome lights were on, and music thumped from it.

"What is he still doing here?" His dad had left the party about a half our ago, claiming that he was ready for bed.

Two things Chip noticed as he walked up the driver's side: the windows were fogged up, and the person in the passenger seat was wearing something pink.

Or was it peach?

He knocked on the window. From inside, someone gasped.

The window lowered, though only halfway. His dad's eyes met his with a sheepish smile, with lips and cheeks smeared with red lipstick. In the passenger seat was Daria, biting her lip, on the verge of cracking up.

Chip cleared throat. "I, um…"

"Need something son?" George asked in his usual serious tone.

"No…no, just wanted to say, um…me and Gabby'll be.

I mean," Chip didn't know where to put his eyes, and he couldn't form words.

"You'll be staying the night with Gabby, dear?" Daria filled in.

"Yes, ma'am."

"Then I'll see you in the morning son. Night."

"Okay then. See y'all later." He tapped the car roof.

The window rolled up. Chip stumbled the rest of the way up the path.

Sometimes you couldn't make this stuff up.

And he couldn't wait to tell Gab.

Speaking of…

Gabby walked out of the B & B. She had since changed into a short, dark pink dress, and she was perfection. Chip sped up, magnetized by her, drawn in by her smile.

He hugged her. He wouldn't stop hugging her.

"Thank you, for helping out," she said.

"Anything to get you home faster."

"I need to get *you* home faster. Our babies need you."

There she went again with *our babies*. His heart couldn't take much more today, with how the night had turned out. He pulled her toward him and crushed his lips against hers. As she melted into him, he debated on begging her to ditch the rest of the night.

"What was that for?" She was breathless.

"A reminder for you to hurry up."

"There are only a handful of guests left. Once they're safely out the door and the cleanup crew's here, then I'll be on my way to you."

"I'll wait up for you."

"Your dad, though…"

"Heh," he half-laughed. "George Lowry is…busy at the moment."

Her lip quirked. "I detect a story in that tone."

"That can come later but," He peered at her playfully, his heart rate ticking up a notch. "More importantly, what were you planning to do with me tonight that we have to worry about my dad?"

She bit her bottom lip, and fixed his collar. "I dunno. Watch movies, have dessert. Work it off."

"And here I was thinking that we would sit and strategize on how to make sure we can keep the puppies and Lucky."

Determination settled in her expression. "We can do that, too. I already have ideas brewing." She tapped her temple. "But after the other stuff."

"In that case, I'll prep one of my rentals. It's unoccupied."

She fingered one of his lapels on his suit jacket. "Sounds like a fantastic idea. And also…"

Her tone had gotten serious, eyes glassy.

"What is it, Gab?"

"I want us to talk. About everything. I know not everything's fixed just because we made up. We have to talk about how I acted. How I can make it better. How I want you to know that you're everything and—"

"Oh, Gab," Her gently squeezed her upper arms, grateful that their friendship allowed for this understanding between them. "We'll talk. We won't stop talking. After all, I've got to convince you that I'll be different from the rest, and that I'll never fix you up with anyone again. And especially never to go roller skating."

She laughed. "Be serious!"

Gabby's phone buzzed, and without even looking, Chip knew their time was up.

"You've gotta go. I can't stand in the way of the wedding planner. I don't want the Espiritus mad at me. Text when you're on your way."

"Love you," she said, as per her usual, but she paused, smiling brightly. "For real."

Because this meant something different now.

He hugged her to him. "And I love you, for real. And for always."

* * * * *

Catch up with the previous books in
USA TODAY *bestselling author Tif Marcelo's*
new miniseries Spirits of the Shenandoah

Jared's story,
It Started with a Secret

And Eva's story
Love Letters from the Trail

Available now!

And don't miss Frankie's story,
Coming soon to Harlequin Special Edition!